ROUGHING THE PLAYER

CHICAGO OUTLAWS BOOK TWO

MAGDA ALEXANDER

HEARTS AFIRE PUBLISHING

ISBN-13: 9781943321070 for e-book

ISBN-13: 9781943321087 for print

Hearts Afire Publishing

First Edition: August 2018

❀ Created with Vellum

BOOKS BY MAGDA ALEXANDER

THE SHATTERED SERIES

Shattered Virtue

Shattered Trust

THE STORM DAMAGES SERIES

Storm Damages

Storm Ravaged

Storm Redemption

Storm Conquered

ITALIAN STALLIONS SERIES

A Christmas Kiss to Remember

My Smokin' Hot Valentine

CHICAGO OUTLAWS SERIES

Dirty Filthy Boy

Roughing the Player

ABOUT THIS BOOK

USA Today **Bestselling Author** Magda Alexander brings you the next **FULL LENGTH, STANDALONE** book in her red hot Chicago Outlaws series.

Most Valuable Party Boy

After a wild party brings the wrong kind of notoriety to quarterback Brock Parker, his team trades him to the Chicago Outlaws. As a backup. At this rate, he'll never make the hall of fame. Brock's one consolation is beautiful, hot Ellie Adams. His new sports agent. His high school tutor. The girl who got away.

Most Straitlaced Stick in the Mud

As a teenager, whip smart Eleanor Adams had fallen for Brock with disastrous consequences. But she'd picked herself up, dusted him off, and moved on. Now a sports agent, she won't risk her chance at success. Least of all to the playboy jock who almost ruined her life.

Most Notorious Scandal

But when another scandal threatens Brock's spot on his new team, Ellie moves in with him to save his career. Big mistake. Because she still has the hots for him. And the league's most notorious bad boy is quite gifted at giving her exactly what she needs.

A smokin' hot, STANDALONE, FULL-LENGTH novel with a guaranteed HEA.

CHAPTER 1

Brock
San Diego

"I'M GETTING TRADED?" I practically choke the life out of my cell phone, I'm clutching it so hard.

"To the Chicago Outlaws." My agent, Marty Chenovsky, jabbers on as if he hasn't dropped a major bomb on me.

"The fuck I am." Last season after San Diego's way overrated starting quarterback had gone down with a career-ending injury, I'd stepped in and taken San Diego all the way to the playoffs. Given my stellar performance, I'd expected to get the starting position. Instead, the bastards are trading me to Chicago?

"They need a backup quarterback."

"Why? The Outlaws have that kid, Pedro Santiago."

"Not anymore, they don't. They're trading him for you. He's coming to San Diego."

What???!!! "As their backup?"

"As their number one."

"What the hell?" My job's being handed to some wet-behind-the-ears kid barely a couple of years out of college? That's so not right. "He doesn't have my arm or experience."

"But he has God on his side."

"What's that supposed to mean?"

Marty clears his throat. "The new San Diego Missionaries owner has a Christian streak in him a mile wide, and Pedro? Well, he never misses church on Sundays, even when he plays out of town."

"And the last time I saw the inside of a sanctuary was when I was baptized." The only reason my parents had done that much was because their country club set expected it of them. Neither had given a damn about religion.

"It's more than that. Your lifestyle doesn't sit right with him."

My lifestyle. Chicks and wild parties, he means. "We almost made it to the Super Bowl."

"He thinks Pedro can get the team there as well."

"Yeah. Right. Good luck with that." Pedro Santiago may have a golden arm, but can he play hurt? When he subbed for Ty Matthews for a couple of games this season, the Chicago front line kept defenders off him. He could be a pansy for all the San Diego owner knows.

"I know it's short notice, but Chicago wants you there tomorrow. They already started training camp."

The Outlaws' rigorous camp is one of the reasons they won the Lombardi trophy last year. Still, I'm expected to jump-to just because they say so? The hell with that. I have things planned for this week.

Besides, I hate the fucking cold. My entire career I've played for warm weather teams. Clemson, the Florida Manatees. Three years into my NFL career, I'd been traded to San Diego. With its perfect weather and year-round mild temperatures, never mind all the bikini honeys on the beach, it had made this southern boy's heart happy. No way am I trading that for the frozen tundra of Chicago. "I'm not going."

"Well, guess you can always quit, or sit out a year."

He has me by the short hairs, and the bastard knows it. I've played football my whole life. Love it too much to give it up. "Not doing that."

"Well, then, you have no choice." He gives me a moment to let me come to terms with it. "I know this is not what you wanted. But they need a quality backup, and that's you."

This last season I'd loved the thrill of game day, the roar of the crowd. Hell, I hadn't even minded the aches and pains because I was their starting quarterback. I won't get that chance with Chicago. "Like I'd get to play."

"Actually, you will. For the entire season."

What's he talking about? I'm good, really good. But Chicago has one of the league's best quarterbacks in Ty Mathews. Last season, he took them all the way to the Super Bowl and won. Makes no sense they'd drop him for me. "How's that?"

"This hasn't been released to the press yet. They're waiting until you get to Chicago to make the announcement. But Ty Mathews needs shoulder surgery, and he'll be out for the entire season. That's why they want you. They know you can take them to the playoffs."

To give me time to think, I walk to the fridge, pop open a Corona, slug down a healthy gulp. "Keep talking."

"You have one more year left in your contract. You do well in Chicago, and the sky's the limit. You'll be able to name your own salary. Every team in dire need of a starting quarterback will want to snap you up."

Yeah, but in the meantime, I wouldn't have a starting position, would I? I'd only be a temporary replacement. Once Ty Mathews heals, he'll get his position back and I'll be back to being number two. Seven years into my NFL career, I should be a starter, not a damn backup. "I don't know, Marty."

"I know how you feel. You want to be number one. Well, this is your best shot. The Chicago Outlaws is the best team in the league. Lots of eyeballs will be on you. If you do a good job, other teams will come calling, and you'll get better endorsement deals."

With all the success I'd had this last year, I'd hoped some companies would ask me to hawk their products. But the only thing I'd endorsed this season had been a crappy, no-name razor. I want something bigger, something that will put plenty of zeros with double digits in front of them in my checking account. I also need that number one starting spot, because the way I'm going? No way will I make the Hall of Fame. This move would not be a guarantee I'd get there, but, Marty is right, it'd be a step in the right direction. I finish the brew, crumple up the can, toss it in the recycling bin. "Okay."

"Great." I can almost hear his sigh of relief. No surprise. If I don't agree to this, he doesn't get his agent's cut. "A word of advice, Brock. The Outlaws run a tight ship. So, you'll need to behave."

"What's that supposed to mean?"

"No excessive alcohol. No groupies. No orgies."

"Well, hell, what's the fun of playing football if I can't drink, screw, or party?"

"That's what got you into trouble in Florida, remember?"

Florida. Four years ago, I'd thrown a party to celebrate the Manatees getting into the playoffs. Security had been tight. They'd searched guests for drugs. But a player had sneaked in an illicit substance, and he'd died from an overdose. Though I had nothing to do with it, I'd been crucified by the social media. When the season ended, Florida couldn't get rid of me fast enough. They'd traded me to San Diego where I'd played backup quarterback for the last four years. Until this season, when I'd thrown more touchdowns and passing yards than the quarterback I'd replaced. And they pay me back by trading me because the new owner is a born-again Christian.

I wish I could tell them to go screw themselves. But I have no choice. It's either Chicago or sit out the season. And that's the kiss of death. Out of sight, out of mind in the league. No guarantee they'd even remember my name in a year's time. And I'm not ready to hang up my cleats just yet.

"When do I leave?"

"Tomorrow morning. I got you a ticket on the seven-thirty flight to O'Hare. I'll email you the details."

My pit bull nudges his big head against my knee, as if he's sensed my distress. I scratch his head. No idea if I'm trying to comfort him or me. "I can't fly out tomorrow. Butch hates flying, and I'm not going without him."

"We've made arrangements for your dog. Someone will come by later today to pick him up. They'll drive him cross-country to one of the best dog places in Chicago. Once you're ready for him, you can fetch him. Expect to get a call in an hour or so to arrange for his pick up."

A dog kennel. Butch won't like that. He hates to be penned up. I'll need to get him out of there as soon as I can. "What about my furniture, my things?" My memories.

"They'll be taken care of. We've arranged for movers to pack your belongings and ship them to Chicago."

"Where? I don't exactly have a place there."

"We've leased a two-bedroom condo for you."

He's thought of everything, hasn't he? But that's not going to work. At least not long term. "I have a four-bedroom house. Where am I supposed to put all my stuff?"

"The movers will handle it, Brock. Any extra furniture will be put in storage. It's only a short term-rental, so if you don't like it, we'll help you find another place. But you won't be there at first. You're reporting right to training camp."

I'll be staying in a condo, instead of a house. Butch will be penned up in a dog kennel, instead of running free. My stuff will be delivered and any extras will be put in storage. He makes it sound like everything will be peachy keen. Like hell, it will.

"I'm sending someone to meet you at the airport, one of our newer agents. She'll be waiting in the luggage claim area. Her name is Eleanor Adams."

Eleanor Adams? In an instant, the years roll back to the Eleanor Adams I once knew. The girl I never forgot. The one who got away. I rub the spot above my chest that always aches when I think of her. But Marty's junior agent can't be her. My Eleanor was headed for medical school someday.

5

"We don't want the public to know about your arrival, so she won't be holding a sign with your name."

"How will I know her?"

"Don't worry. She'll know you."

Makes sense. I'm pretty well known. But I've never heard of a chick sports agent, at least any that represent football players. A wild notion pops into my head. What if Marty's trying to get rid of me? "You're not pawning me off on her, are you, Marty?"

He barks out a laugh. "You'd be lucky to get her. She's hardworking, dedicated. A stellar junior agent. But no, I'll continue to represent you. You're my cross to bear."

Damn right I am. As much as I'm bitching, I wouldn't want to lose him. He's one of the best sports agents out there. "So why aren't you meeting me at the airport?"

"I have an appointment. One I can't break. Don't worry. She'll take good care of you. Feel free to ask her any questions about your contract with the Outlaws. Or anything else for that matter. She's thoroughly familiar with your situation."

My situation. Yeah, my well-and-truly-fucked-up 'situation.'

No sooner do I hang up with Marty than the phone rings. It's the dog service. Not taking Marty's word about its reputation, I pepper them with questions. They assure me they do this all the time and provide references, mostly military, for me to check out. After a few phone calls that reassure me Butch will be in good hands, I call back the dog service and ask them to come by in a couple of hours.

Butch glances at me, his big, brown peepers worried.

"Don't give me those sad puppy eyes. I can't help it, boy." I scratch the top of his head, right on the spot he loves to get rubbed. But his tail doesn't wag. Damn if he doesn't know something's up.

"Look I know Chicago is no San Diego. No sun. Cold enough to freeze your nuts off. Well, if you had any."

"Woof!"

"You're never going to forgive me for giving you the big snip, are you?"

"Rawr!"

"You'll love Chicago. You'll see." I don't know if I'm trying to reassure him or me. But I do know one thing that will make us both feel better. I grab his leash and head out with him. Gotta take my best boy for a run on the beach one last time.

CHAPTER 2

Eleanor

"ELEANOR? CAN YOU STEP INTO MY OFFICE?" Marty Chenovsky, my boss at Platinum Sports Agency, asks.

"Be right there." Not knowing how long it will be, I grab my coffee and iPad and head to his corner suite, wondering what assignment he has for me.

As soon as I step into his office, I shut the door. Marty's fanatical about keeping his discussions private. No need to have prying ears hear whatever he's got to say.

Over his half-moon glasses, he pins his gaze on me while I take a seat. "How long have you been here, Eleanor?"

Odd question. He hired me, after all. But I'll play along. "Just over a year." During that time, I've kept him informed about up and coming college jocks, worked on endorsement deals for his clients, and anything else he throws at me. So far I've come through with flying colors, but then, failure is not an option.

"You've done good work for me." He seems relaxed, but I can tell he's got something up his sleeve. His pleasant smile gives him away.

"Thank you."

"Which is why I believe you're the right person for this job."

I've witnessed his modus operandi loads of times before. So I know what comes next. Now that he's buttered me up, he's moving in for the kill.

"You've heard of Brock Parker."

My breath cuts short. My heart skips a beat. But I can't let Marty know how the mention of Brock's name affects me if I want to keep my job. So I dial back the panic and pin on a smile. "Yes, of course. San Diego Missionaries first-string quarterback."

"Not anymore, he isn't. He's been traded to the Outlaws."

"The Chicago Outlaws?"

He stares at me like I'm the prize idiot at the county fair. "Yes, of course. What other Outlaws are there in professional football?"

"None." Fighting to regain control of my breathing, I stare down at my iPad and hit a few keys to give the illusion I'm taking notes. "Is he coming here as backup?" I can't imagine him playing as the number one quarterback, not when the Outlaws have Ty Mathews who took them to the Super Bowl.

"Officially, yes. Unofficially, no."

I glance up. "What does that mean?"

"This is for your ears only. Do you understand, Eleanor?" His gaze drills into me.

"Yes, of course."

"Ty Mathews needs shoulder surgery. He'll be out of commission the entire season which means the Outlaws need a seasoned quarterback. That's why they traded for Brock."

"Who did they trade for him?"

"Pedro Santiago. He'll be San Diego's number one."

"Ouch." Brock's gotta be hurting from that decision.

"Yeah, exactly. Which is why he needs to be handled with kid gloves when he gets here."

And I'm the chump assigned to the job. But, hey, that's why they pay me the big bucks. "So what do you want me to do?"

"For starters, meet him at O'Hare tomorrow morning. I'll have my assistant email you the details. He'll need you to drive him to training camp."

"Okay." That doesn't seem so bad. Wait. "You said for starters. What else would you like me to do?"

"Caught that, did you?"

I nod while I wait for the other shoe to drop.

Leaning back in his chair, he temples his hands across his middle. "I want you to babysit Brock."

BABYSIT BROCK. Yeah. Sure. Piece of cake. Has he met him? For the last seven years, no one has been able to curb Brock's wild excesses. Not Marty, not his coaches. Not anyone I know. But now it's up to me to make sure he behaves? God help me.

At least I know some of his weaknesses which is why I'm waiting at O'Hare's baggage claim area, caramel macchiato and chocolate croissant in hand. The chock-full-of calories welcome wagon is not a wild guess on my part. He loves sweets. I've done my research on him. Not that I needed to do much. I've followed his career since high school.

True to his aspirations, Brock attended a southern college, Clemson University, where he'd earned glory for the most passing yards and touchdowns thrown in NCAA history. After graduation, he'd signed with Florida. Three years into his contract, he'd been traded to San Diego after things spun out of control at a house party. And just like that, he'd gone from a promising career to backup. I can only imagine how much that had to hurt.

I glance at my watch for the umpteenth time. His flight arrived ten minutes ago. So he should be here any second. I hope I'm ready for this.

As soon as he steps off the escalator, his gaze lands on me. To my surprise, his lips curl into that sensual smile I remember so well. If he was a gorgeous high school senior, he's downright stunning now. Six-foot-four of a well-muscled frame, honey blond hair and piercing green eyes would get any woman's motor running, including me. Most especially me.

He struts forward in his master-of-all-he-surveys sexy walk and the masses of humanity part. Some women stop and stare; others downright gawk. Can't blame them. It's not every day you get to witness a living, breathing sex god. But much as he did in high school, he ignores all the female adulation until he comes to a stop dab smack in front of me. "Well, well, well. Eleanor Adams. I thought the name sounded familiar."

"Hello, Brock. I got your favorites." Somehow, I keep breathing as I hand him the coffee and croissant.

"Thank you, darling." His southern twang gets my panties wet, the same as it did a million years ago.

I remind myself I'm older and wiser and not as vulnerable as I once was. Or at least I hope I'm not. Putting on my best professional front, I say, "Your bags should be coming out at carousel thirteen. This way." I point toward the idle conveyor belt, hoping his luggage doesn't take long to show up.

Rambling along in that easy, long-legged stride of his, he sips the brew, takes a bite of the pastry. "You were my Shakespeare tutor at Stonewall Jackson High."

And a fuck buddy one stormy night. But there's nothing to be gained from those memories, so I pin on the business smile I've perfected during the last few years and forge on. "That's right."

Done with the croissant, he tosses the wrapper into the nearest can. "So, what have you been up to?"

A strident, foghorn sound goes off at carousel thirteen, and the conveyor belt jerks into motion. "College followed by law school."

"Where?"

"Duke."

In a beauty of an arc, he lobs the coffee cup into the trash before pinning his gaze on me.

Knowing what's coming, I take a deep breath and brace for the hit.

"You left halfway through your senior year."

"Yes. My mom's fiancé got transferred out of town to a new position. She offered to stay so I could finish high school at Stonewall Jackson. But I didn't want to keep them apart. So we moved." I've practiced telling that story more times than I can count. It's the truth, just not the whole truth. When he doesn't question me further, I ease out a sigh. One giant hurdle leaped.

"And you're an agent now?"

"Yes. I'm in Marty's group." The sports agency pairs junior associates with senior partners. Since Marty recruited me, it was only natural to be assigned to him.

He comes to a dead stop in front of the carousel and stares at me. "Well, in that case, I want four million more."

My breath shorts. Didn't see that coming. Although in retrospect, I really should have. Regardless, I have to handle it. He's a client, after all. "They won't give it to you."

He taps his massive bicep. "This is certainly worth the money."

Unfortunately, that move gains us more attention. This is not good. Not good at all. If he's recognized, someone might start wondering what the San Diego quarterback is doing in Chicago. "Keep your voice down, Brock. Please."

He silently fumes while the bags roll by on the conveyor belt. "Any of these yours?" Please let one of them be. We need to get out of here. Fast.

With barely a glance, he grumbles, "No."

He's upset. I get it. Instead of giving him the starting spot, which he totally deserves, San Diego traded him. So, of course, his pride demands more money. Unfortunately, that's not how things work. I can't get into an in-depth discussion out here in the open. But given his level of anger, I have to give him some answer before he explodes. "You're right, Brock. You're totally worth more money. But you're under the same contract terms you had at San Diego."

"That's bullshit." His voice booms loud and clear over the myriad of conversations and heads turn.

If he got noticed before, it's nothing to what's happening now. If somebody snaps his photo and posts it on social media, the Outlaws' management is bound to get pissed. I have to manage him before he deep-sixes his career with the Outlaws before it even starts.

Last thing I want to do is touch him. I know what that will do to me. But from experience I know it will calm him down. I brush my hand across that massive bicep of his. "Brock. You don't want to start a scene in the middle of the airport. Wait until we get to the car. We'll discuss it then." The drive will give us enough time to talk.

His gaze lingers on my fingers, but he doesn't object to my suggestion nor my touch.

A minute later, his bags show up, and he grabs them. He remains silent on the way to my car while I struggle to keep up with his long strides. Once we make it out of the airport, I tell him what he doesn't want to know. "Chicago is only required to pay you the same amount of money San Diego did."

"Why?"

"You know why, Brock." He's been around long enough to know the NFL rules, but I'm not about to rub salt in his wounds. "Next year when you're a free agent, we can renegotiate if you wish to stay here. If you don't, we can shop around for a new team."

"We? I thought Marty was my agent."

"He is. But like I said—I'm part of his group. I perform background research, drum up endorsement deals, and meet with players when Marty's unable to do so, like I'm doing now."

The way he juts out his jaw reminds me of the tutoring session when I told him he needed to read the annotations to Macbeth, that reading the text was not enough. He'd resented it then, much as he's doing now.

"I want a new football team."

I briefly glance at him. "You know that already?"

"Chicago has Ty Mathews. They'll never give me the starting position as long as he's around."

"Okay. I'll pass on that information to Marty. We can't entertain any offers until next year, but in the meantime, we can keep our ear to the ground."

It takes him a while to stop grinding his teeth. "Guess that's the best I can hope for." He stretches his massive left arm over my backrest, pushes his long, powerful legs to the floor of the car, all in an attempt to get comfortable.

Darn it. My mid-size car's too small for him. I should have leased an SUV. "Sorry."

"For what?"

"The small car."

"I'll live." He squirms some more before turning to me. "I thought you would become a doctor. How did you end up a sports agent, Ellie?"

Ellie, I haven't been called that in forever. Prior to mom's marriage to Steve, she and I had moved in with my aunt who was also an Ellie. So to avoid confusion, I'd been rebranded with my Christian name, Eleanor. It'd stuck through high school, college, and law school as well. Although I'd initially resented it, now I'm glad it did. Eleanor is much more professional than Ellie.

"Medical school would have been too expensive. So I passed on that and focused on pre-law. Shortly before I graduated from college, I applied to Duke Law. They offered me a partial scholarship and off I went."

"Ellie, the brain. That's what they used to call you in high school," he says with a grin. "So what happened then?"

"I loved law school, but litigation did not appeal to me. So I explored other options. When I attended a sports agency seminar, everything seemed to click. I'd always loved sports."

"Yeah, I remember. You used to sit on the bleachers and watch us play."

"Yes." Can't very well tell him I was watching him and his mighty fine *gluteus maximus* more than anything else. "Anyway, after the seminar ended, the lecturer invited a few students to coffee at the school cafeteria. I dazzled him with my knowledge of sports, and he offered me an internship that summer. When I graduated from Duke Law, I went to work for him."

"But Duke's in North Carolina. How did you end up in Chicago?"

His questions unsettle me. I don't want things to get too personal between us. But he's a client, and we have thirty minutes to go before we get to training camp. Surely, I can deal with his curiosity that long.

"I met Marty at a meeting of sports agents. He saw something in me and made me an offer I couldn't refuse." Not only was it for a higher salary, but he promised me a junior partnership in three years' time. Even though I'd hated to leave the South, I snapped it up. My law school debt wasn't going to pay for itself. "So I pulled up roots and moved to Chicago."

"You never married?"

"No. Too busy with school and . . . other things."

When he wiggles his big body some more, I struggle to keep my eyes on the road and not where they'd love to stray.

"Marty said you guys leased me a place?"

A safe topic. Thank God. "Yes, a two-bedroom condo in a very nice building, close to the Outlaws' facility."

"Butch hates apartments. I'll need a house."

"Not a problem. Once you're done with training camp, we can find houses for you to look at. We didn't want to make that decision for you."

"I'll need a big backyard with a fence so Butch can run free." He stretches his arm and the scent of his woodsy cologne sets something loose within me. Some primal need dormant too long.

But giving in to that hunger is not an option. I have to do something fast. "Would you like me to stop so you can stretch your legs?"

"Nah, I'm good."

That makes one of us. Better focus on something else. Quick. "About Butch. Some jurisdictions prohibit pit bulls. North Chicago being one."

His head swivels toward me. "That's bullshit. Butch's perfectly well-behaved. He's never even thought about biting anyone."

"You're a responsible pet owner. Other pit bull owners are not. Some people breed them to be aggressive. But don't worry; lots of communities allow them. We'll help you find a place."

"I'll need a big house."

"For Butch?"

"For parties."

I glare at him. "No parties. No free-flowing fountains of alcohol. And definitely no photos of skimpily clad women in your bed." Last year, salacious images had hit the internet of a *ménage a quattre*— Brock and three sex partners—on a huge mattress fitted with red silk sheets. He'd laughed it off at the time. But more than likely, that had been the main reason he'd been traded away by the owner of the San Diego Missionaries.

He leans over to whisper in my ear. "Can I help it if the ladies want a piece of me?"

Every cell in my body comes to life, but I'll be damned if I let him know it, cocky bastard that he is. "Honestly, Brock. You're not seventeen anymore. You're thirty years old. You have maybe five good years left in your career. Do you really want to be remembered as a player who can't keep it in his pants? Or as NFL glory?"

He shifts to his side of the car, and the temperature inside the car plummets to a deep freeze.

God. Marty may have asked me to remind him of the rules, but do I have to act like such a bitch? "I'm sorry."

"Don't be." A muscle in his jaw ticks. "You're right."

"Then why—Never mind." Better quit while I'm ahead. Except I can't. He has to understand how easily he could lose it all. And this time, it might be for good. "Have you met Oliver Lyons?"

"The owner of the Outlaws? No. Not yet."

I need to be tactful and not lash out at him. So, I have to be careful of what I say. "He hates scandals. It's rooted in his personal history. Something happened that caused a lot of bad blood in his family. That's why he can't stand notoriety, especially the kind that shines a bad light on his team. Don't give him a reason to call you out. You might not like where you end up."

For a second, his jaw juts once more. But then it settles down. "Understood."

I take the off-ramp while he stares out the window in stone-cold silence. Well, at least it stopped his charm offensive. Last time he did that, it almost derailed my life.

The car's guidance system announces a turn into the Outlaws' training camp compound. Good. Last thing I want is to dwell on my past. Something I'm finding hard to avoid. Brock's nearness has awakened deep memories I'd thought long dead and buried.

Once we're through security, I park in a visitor's spot and pop open the trunk so he can retrieve his things.

Trying hard not to tremble, I hand him my business card. "My number. In case you need to reach me. Is there anything you want me to do while you're here?"

"Yeah." When he heaves his duffel bag over one shoulder and the bicep on his arm bulks, I forget to breathe. I knew he'd have this effect on me, and yet I agreed to drive him to camp anyway.

"Check on Butch. Let me know he's all right." Sadly, he's all business now.

I curse myself for missing his easy charm, his sexy smile. When will I learn? "Will do."

He walks away without saying another word. But then, there's really nothing more to say.

CHAPTER 3

Brock

THE CHICAGO OUTLAWS' training camp's not for pussies. San Diego's was a walk in the park compared to this team's bruising drills. After only one day, I feel like I want to curl up and die, but I gotta tough it out. Can't let anyone think the Outlaws' new quarterback is a wimp who can't handle his shit.

After the insanely early wake-up call at 6 a.m., I barely have enough time to wolf down oatmeal, eggs, and a gallon of juice before reporting to the training room for mandatory treatment of all my aches and pains. Even though I don't complain, the staff knows just what to treat. Obviously, not the first time they've been on this rodeo.

Strength training comes next—my least favorite part, but necessary as all get out. If you're not strong, you can get hurt, and that's the last thing I need. Next, we report to meetings—one with the entire team, followed by another with the quarterback coach. Then the real fun begins. We're sent to our lockers to suit up in twenty pounds of training gear for the first practice of the day. Even though I'm the quarterback, I'm still expected to participate in all the grueling maneuvers with the rest of the team. You ever done football drills with pads in eighty-five-degree heat? No? Well, it's a real treat. It feels like you're cooking from the inside out.

After an hour of torture, a whistle blows. "Fifteen-minute break."

Thank the fuck.

As I'm dipping my head in a bucket of ice-cold water, a voice rumbles over my shoulder. "You're doing fine."

I jerk up, shake off the water, spraying the starting quarterback of the Outlaws for the last two seasons, Ty Mathews. "Yeah?"

He doesn't bother to introduce himself. I'd be an idiot not to know who the fuck he is. "Yeah. Coach Grohowski is impressed."

I glance in the coach's direction whose expression has not changed since I walked on the field. He's still got that same scrunch to his mouth and beady-eyed gaze every time his glance lands on me. "How can you tell?"

"Trust me. I can tell." He bops me on the shoulder. "Just keep doing what you're doing."

"Will do." If I don't die from heat exhaustion first.

When the final whistle signals the end of practice, we head back to the locker room. After a quick shower, I'm ordered to the rehabilitation room where I'm given a full body massage by Sven, a Swedish masseur with ham-sized hands and the disposition of the Marquis de Sade. Before long, the massage table becomes a rack of pain.

After he's finished, I crawl back hunched over to my locker to get dressed.

"Hurting?" Trevor, my six foot seven center, asks. He's sitting on a bench slipping his size fourteen feet into a pair of designer loafers.

"A little." Pride drives me to straighten up and reach for my shirt, no matter how much it fucking hurts.

Trevor flashes a sympathetic grin. "Sven's a sadist, man. He loves to torture players."

"Now you tell me." I'd laugh if it wouldn't hurt so much.

He stands and slaps me on the back. "You'll be all right."

I scream silently. Bastard.

"You coming to the team dinner on Saturday, right?"

"Dinner?" We're being cut loose on Saturday afternoon and not expected to report back to camp until Sunday night. I'd planned to spend the time lying on a bed somewhere without moving a muscle. Or breathing.

"Yeah. At the Chicago Hilton. Seven o'clock. Nobody told you?"

"Nope." More than likely, they would have gotten around to it before the weekend. Probably after tomorrow's press conference announcing my presence in Chicago.

"All the players are expected to attend."

"Okay. I'll be there. Thanks for letting me know."

He pauses while giving me the once-over. Out of all the players, he's the one I've gotten to know best in the short time I've been here.

"If you need a date, I can hook you up."

"Nah. I got it." Can't very well show up at a team dinner without a chick on my arm. After all, I got a reputation to protect. Problem is, I only know one woman in Chicago, and I'm pretty sure she's going to turn me down.

Team dinners offer the usual locker room talk. Who got blown, who got screwed, what chick's willing to do what. Not only have I heard it all, but I've done most of it. Rather than join in, I focus on my food and keep my head down.

Done with the meal, I head back to my room, hoping to find oblivion. But first, I have to call Ellie. I dig in my wallet for her business card and punch her number into my cell.

She picks up on the second ring. "Brock?"

"Yeah, it's me. How did you know?"

"I programmed your number into my phone. Anything wrong?"

"You know that spot at the top of the head where my hair sticks up." I hope she remembers. A million years ago, she'd mentioned it a time or two.

"Yes." I can almost hear the smile in her voice.

"It's the only part that doesn't hurt."

"Ouch."

"Mom, do you know where—" A girl's voice. She sounds young.

The voice gets muffled as if Ellie has covered up the mouthpiece. A few seconds later, she returns to our call.

"Sorry about that," she says.

"You have a kid." Why I'm surprised is beyond me. She's certainly old enough.

She hesitates for a second before she says, "Yes."

When she doesn't volunteer more than that, I sense it's a touchy subject, So, other than a "That's good," I don't pry.

"Is there something you need?" Her tone's businesslike, yet not unkind.

"Yeah, ahh, have you heard about Butch?"

She laughs, a nice tinkling laugh that reminds me of that time long ago when we were young and she was innocent. So, so innocent.

"As a matter of fact, I have. They've reached Denver. Butch traveled well. He's probably enjoying a nice sleep right about now. They should make it to Chicago by tomorrow. The dog kennel's waiting for him."

"That's good." I miss the snuggle bunny. Even though Butch has his own doggie bed, he always climbed into mine.

"How long have you had him?"

"Six years. Since he was a puppy. A Florida teammate's dog gave birth to fourteen of them. Butch was the runt of the litter, but I fell in love with him. You have a dog?"

"No. Too busy with school and—"

"Your daughter."

"Yes." I'm curious as hell to find out about her kid. But it's none of my business, so I don't ask.

"Anything else?"

She's growing impatient, so I better get to the main reason I called. "Yeah. How would you like to attend a team dinner with me this Saturday?"

For a couple of heartbeats, she doesn't say a thing, and I hope like hell she's leaning toward yes. But then she says, "It would not be a good thing for us to cross the professional line, Brock."

Damn it. Should have known she'd come down on the other side. "You're not my agent."

"But I work for the agency that represents you. So, same thing."

"Have you met anyone from the Outlaws' team?"

"No."

"They don't know you then."

"Even if I don't know them now, I might meet them in the future if I represent one of their athletes."

Should have known she'd return a great come back. But I have one of my own. "Do you represent any football players now?"

"No. But give me a couple of years, and I will."

"Marty said you were good."

"I am. I do my homework, and I work very hard for our agency's clients."

"Do you have any of your own? Clients, I mean."

"Not yet. It takes time to learn the ropes. Get to know the athletes."

Marty might think the world of her, but she's got a long way to go. I've heard of a few women who represent athletes, but I don't know a single one who represents football players. "If you came to the dinner on Saturday, you'd get to know some. I can introduce you to the ones I know. In the meantime, I can keep my ears open to see if anyone is unhappy with his representation."

"You'd do that for me?"

"Of course, Ellie. What are friends for?"

"We're not friends."

Man, that's harsh. But I get it. She wants me to think of her as a professional. Thing is, I don't know if I can. Seeing her again stirred something in me, feelings I'd only felt when I'd been with her.

"We were friends once." And for one glorious evening, we were a hell of a lot more than that. I'd gotten a great grade on my Macbeth midterm, something I'd never expected to do. Wanting to celebrate, I'd driven through a hellacious thunderstorm to get to her. When the storm had knocked out the power in her house, she'd been terrified. I'd tried to comfort her, and before I knew it, we were doing the deed on her mother's kitchen table with me riding her bareback. Something I'd never done before. Or since.

"*That* was a long time ago." Clearly, it's something she'd rather forget. A shame. I never could.

But why would she want to remember? We were young and stupid. Well, she was young. I was stupid. But that's neither here nor there. Sensing I'm losing my window of opportunity, I change tack. "All right. Not friends. Business acquaintances, then. You scratch my back. I'll scratch yours."

"That's *not* happening." She thinks I'm putting the moves on her. Can't blame her. Not with my reputation.

But for some reason, I'm offended. "It's nothing dirty, Ellie."

"Then what is it?"

"Simple. You come as my plus one. I introduce you to some football players. At the end of the evening, you go home—alone—with the knowledge you've made some contacts in the team. Win-win all around."

"I don't know, Brock. It sounds skeevy not to identify myself as an agent."

"But you wouldn't be on the hunt for clients. You'd be my date. If anybody asks, which they won't. Please." What's wrong with me? I've never had to beg a woman to go out with me. They usually jump at the chance.

"When is it again?"

"Saturday at the Hilton Chicago. Dinner's at eight."

"Let me check my schedule." Something rustles in the background. A few seconds later, she's back. "That works. I can meet you there."

"Okay. Thanks." Can't very well say I'll pick her up. Although my SUV might be here by Saturday, it hasn't been delivered yet. I could rent a car, I suppose, but I don't know this city. And GPS gets you only so far.

"Anything else, Brock?"

I should let her go. She's got things to do with her kid. "No. That's it."

"All right."

But then the devil in me blurts out, "Wear something sexy."

She barks out a laugh. Usually not the sexiest sound on a woman, but somehow it works on her. "You're pushing your luck, Parker. You're lucky I said yes."

Parker. That's what she used to call me during our tutoring sessions whenever I did something she didn't approve. Somehow, it makes me happy to hear her call me that. "Yes, ma'am. Good night."

"Good night."

Well, well, well. So Ellie has a daughter. Who would have thunk? She's not married. Not that you need to be married to have a kid. But back then Ellie planned everything to the nth degree, so no way would she have a child without working it into her schedule. I rub my face and scoot deeper into the bed. Thank God I hadn't gotten her pregnant. We'd definitely dodged a bullet there. I'd been so embarrassed about not taking precautions, I'd stopped going to our tutoring sessions. The month and a half after we did the deed, I'd lived in fear of her telling me I'd knocked her up. After suffering the hell of the damned for six weeks, I'd manned up and asked her if everything was okay. When she'd said everything was fine, I was finally able to breathe. That kid would have been awesome, though. How could he not be with her brains and my abilities? But thank God Ellie hadn't been pregnant. Last thing I'd have needed in high school was a kid. But my carelessness taught me a lesson. After that night, I've never fucked a woman without suiting up.

I toss my cell on the night table and turn off the desk light. Lying in the dark, I wonder what Ellie's kid is like. Does she have her mother's smarts? Does she look like her daddy? Whoever he is, I hope he's treating Ellie and his kid right. Because if he doesn't, he's a total tool.

CHAPTER 4

Eleanor

*D*ARN IT. I whisper under my breath. The last thing I wanted was for Brock to know I have a daughter. Because once he learned I had a child, he might start asking questions. Who am I kidding? There's no might about it. He will ask questions—about her name, her age, her father. And that he must never, ever know. I'll need to skirt my way around the truth. No lies, though. If I even think about lying, he'll see right through me. He always could.

"Who were you talking to, Mom?" Kaylee interrupts, her face lit up with curiosity. That's when I realize, Brock's not the only one I need to keep in the dark.

"One of my firm's clients."

"Who?"

"No one you know." And no one she will ever know if I have anything to say about it. "Ready for your birthday party?"

To celebrate her twelfth birthday, she'd campaigned for a sleep-over with her closest friends. I'd been reluctant to say yes. Hosting a dozen pre-teens is not my idea of a good time. They talk too loud, giggle nonstop, and their main topic of conversation, at least among her crowd, seems to be boys. That last thing petrifies me.

Lips turned down, she shrugs. "I guess."

I guess? A week ago, she'd been so excited. What on earth has changed her mood? "What's wrong?"

"Meghan's brother."

Meghan. Her best friend whose older brother Mike is in high school. Last year Kaylee barely knew he existed. Seemingly, things have changed. "What about him?"

"I invited him, but he's not coming."

My mom alarm goes off. "Since when do you invite boys to a slumber party?"

"Mom." She scrunches her face at me. "Everyone does it. They don't spend the night. They just come for the party."

Okay. This is news to me. How do you even handle the logistics of such a thing? Kick them out at nine o'clock? That seems . . . odd.

She scuffs her toe into the rug. "But it doesn't matter. He can't make it."

My little girl's first heartbreak. With surely more to come. Boys, after all, will be boys, as well I know. "He's in high school, honey."

She tilts her head to the side. "What does that mean?"

"Well, high school boys tend to like high school girls."

"So I'm too young for him?"

"That's part of it. Yes."

"What's the other part?" She's nothing if not inquisitive.

"Well, high school boys like to date within their own school. Bringing a junior high student to a senior high dance is not cool."

"That sucks."

"You'll get there soon enough, sweetheart. The good thing is that you can attend school dances with boys your own age." She's growing up way too fast. Is it wrong of me to wish she'd stay a little girl just a little while longer? "Now how about we plan the party. What would your friends like to eat?"

"Well, Marcy's a vegan, Charlene won't eat anything that isn't gluten-free." She ticks them off on her fingers. "And Ki-Ki is a pesco-vegetarian."

Pesco what? "What on earth is that?"

"She only eats vegetables and fish."

Lord have mercy. "We'll need to plan the menu very carefully then." I retrieve a white legal pad from my briefcase, drop it on the table, and pat the chair next to me. "Sit."

An hour later, I have a list of food to buy and dishes to make. I'll need to recruit Mama for the event because I can't prepare all this food by myself. She'll love my asking her. After all, she and Steve moved to Chicago to be with us. After I told them about my job offer in the Windy City, he put the word out to the Chicago grocery store community that he was looking for a job. It didn't take long for a local chain to snap him up.

After years of him catering to a southern clientele, the Chicago population posed a brand new challenge for him. But he's excelled at it by bringing that famous southern hospitality to his supermarkets. He set up southern cooking demos at every one of the stores he managed, and Chicagoans took to southern fried chicken, fried catfish, with a side of greens, and cornbread pudding with a vengeance. Since he took over, sales at his grocery stores have soared.

The move hadn't been easy, though. After years of living in the mild temperatures of the south, we'd all found it difficult to deal with the cold and snowy landscape of Chicago. I'd worried about uprooting Kaylee from her nice, friendly school and dropping her into an environment filled with strangers. Turns out I had nothing to worry about. With the effortless charm she'd inherited from her father, she'd made friends easily. She had it all—brains, beauty, and charisma. Plus a good dose of street smarts. She can spot a lie a mile away. That's why I have to be so very careful around her.

There had been one more plus to living in Chicago. The move had given me the opportunity to become a homeowner. For the first time in my life, I own a house. Our home contains two bedrooms, one full and half-bath, and a decent kitchen. But the big plus is the huge backyard. When the weather allows, we gather back there to barbecue. Plus, Mama has started a vegetable and herb garden.

But the biggest advantage is to Kaylee. She's enrolled in the number one junior high school in Illinois. She's getting the very best education my tax dollars can buy.

With my future and Kaylee's education secured, I'd breathed easy for the first time in years. Until Marty called me into his office this week to tell me Brock Parker had been traded to the Chicago Outlaws. Just like that, the bottom had fallen out of my world.

"Earth to Mom." I blink back to find Kaylee waving her hand in front of my face.

"What?"

"I've asked you the same question three times."

"Sorry, honey."

Scrunching her brow, she studies me as if I were a puzzle to be solved. "You've been off the last few days. Since Saturday. The day you picked up Brock Parker at the airport."

My heart skips a beat. She has a sixth sense when it comes to me. She knows when I'm upset. But she can't find out what's bothering me.

But before I can point her scrutiny in another direction, she says, "He's a jerk."

That assessment surprises me. She's usually not that harsh. "Why do you say that?"

"Somebody overdosed at one of his parties."

"Honey, he didn't provide the drugs."

"How do you know?"

"The player who died brought it himself. They found drug paraphernalia on him." Why am I discussing Brock when that's the last thing I want?

"Doesn't matter. He should have been more careful about who he invited."

Eleven-year-olds about to turn twelve possess all the wisdom in the world. "He was a member of his team. It would have been weird if he hadn't invited him."

"Why are you defending him, Mom?"

"Because it's wrong to accuse an innocent man. Brock did not provide the drugs. He even hired a security firm to check his guests. But somehow, this player managed to sneak them in, and he paid for it with his death."

"How do you know all this?"

"Brock Parker is a client. It's my job to know his history—personal and professional."

She tosses her blond hair over her shoulder, its honey shade so close to her father's. "Still, he shouldn't have allowed it to happen."

"Kaylee, it's not like the player asked his permission."

"Besides, that's not the only reason I don't like Mr. Parker."

"Oh?"

"He has orgies, Mom."

"Kaylee! How do you even know that word?"

She scoffs. "I'm about to turn twelve. What do you think some boys talk about in school?"

Good God. "Sex?"

"Yep."

"You stay away from them, you hear me."

"I do, Mom. Don't worry." She twists her mouth, chews on her bottom lip. "Meghan's brother talks about him all the time."

"Brock Parker?"

"Yes." She huffs out a breath. "Mike wants to be just like Brock Parker. That's why I don't care for him."

"But I thought you liked Mike."

She lets out a dramatic sigh. "Brock Parker, Mom."

I'm getting whiplash from her zig-zagging. But I don't want her to think badly of Brock. Even if she doesn't know who he is. Even if I don't want to talk about him. I cover her hand with my own. "Honey, his career was ruined because of what happened that night."

Her glance cuts to me. "What are you talking about? He's a professional football player who makes oodles of money."

"Yes, but at the end of that season, he lost his starting quarterback position. He was traded to San Diego to play backup."

"Big woo. He still got to play football."

"Not as the number one. As a backup. And that's the kiss of death for a quarterback."

"How can that be? Last season he played the starting position for San Diego, didn't he? And he took the team to the playoffs."

Her breadth of knowledge about Brock alarms me. "How do you know that?"

She shrugs. "I looked him up."

Oh, God. If my heart stuttered before, it's downright thundering now. But I can't let her see through me. I have to stay calm. "Honey, it didn't matter how well he played. San Diego didn't want him as their starter. So they traded him to the Chicago Outlaws."

"As backup to Ty Mathews?"

"Yes. Honestly Kaylee, where does this sudden interest in football come from?"

Glancing down, she fidgets on the chair. "Well, Mike plays varsity football. I thought if I boned up on the subject, he might like me or something."

And we're back to her budding crush on her friend's brother. "Sweetheart."

She firms her lips as her chin comes up. "Don't worry. Now that you explained how things work, I'm over him."

I sincerely hope that's true.

Her cell phone rings, and she glances at it. "Meghan. She probably wants to talk about Brock Parker." She rolls her eyes.

What?!! "Why?"

"She saw him on the news. They showed that press conference when the Outlaws introduced him. Of course, Mike was watching. She flipped when she saw him. She thinks he's hot." Kaylee sticks a finger in her mouth and fake gags.

Meghan's skipping high school and college boys and going right for an older man? Hope her parents are keeping close tabs on her, because that girl is headed for trouble.

"Brock Parker might not be a jerk, but he's definitely a liar. When someone asked him how he felt about being traded to the Outlaws, he said he was thrilled to play for the best team in the league. He didn't look thrilled."

He'd need to say he was, even if he wasn't. It's all part of the game. I point to her phone. "Better take that call before it rolls over to voice mail."

She lets out a dramatic sigh. "Yeah." She pushes a button on the phone. "Hey, Meghan." And wanders out of the room, leaving me shell-shocked.

Meghan saw Brock Parker on TV but didn't realize how much Kaylee resembles him. Because if she had, she would have told Kaylee about it. I watched that conference. Brock wore a Chicago Outlaws cap throughout the interview. So she probably didn't get a good look at him. As boy crazy as Meghan is, she's probably going to do what every pre-teen girl has done since time immemorial. Pin Brock's picture to her bedroom wall. Kaylee's not stupid. Far from it. Sooner or later either she or Meghan will notice a resemblance. And then I'll be well and truly screwed. God. What am I going to do?

CHAPTER 5

Brock

ONCE THE PLAYERS ARE RELEASED after lunch on Saturday, they practically leave skid marks as they peel out of the Outlaws' parking lot. Not me, though. Since my furniture is still a no-show, I have nowhere to go. I'll just hang out until it's time to leave for the banquet.

The silence at camp is downright eerie. I miss the noise dozens of football players make—the grunts, the curses, the crunching of one body against another. But then football has been my whole life. Since I was eight in fact—the year my mother died.

My parents never had any use for me. They'd never intended to have children. But somehow my mother had gotten pregnant with me. After I was born, they'd hardly missed a beat. She'd continued with her hectic, country club social life, and he'd kept his nose to the grindstone, making millions from his pharmaceutical business. They never concerned themselves with me. That's what nannies were for.

After my mother passed away, there was even less of a reason for my father to notice me. All he cared about was his drug company so ignoring me was easy. A caretaker made sure I showered, ate and got to school on time. When I expressed an interest in football, he'd totally approved. Of course he had. I'd be spending more time away from home so he wouldn't be reminded of the one mistake he made. When he died from a massive heart attack during my last year of college, he didn't leave me a dime. My party lifestyle had been too much for him. But his pride prevented him from outright disinheriting me. After all, I was his only son. So he'd neatly tied up his millions in a trust fund which would reinvest his money and parcel out enough to cover my bare necessities.

I hadn't asked for a fucking dime. After I graduated from college, football had taken care of all my needs.

And it still does. Prime example is the limo the Director of Player Relations arranged for me. I'll be arriving at the Hilton in style. You gotta give the Outlaws credit. They do things right.

After grabbing my gear and the one nice suit I brought to camp, I head out. Rather than chance wrinkling my clothes, I plan to dress in the hotel room the team reserved for me. Sharp dressed man and all that. Tonight, I'll sleep on a luxury king mattress instead of the twin bed that almost took off my knees.

I really wanted to see Butch, but the dog kennel talked me out of it. They said it would be best if I didn't drop by until I picked him up for good. Makes sense. My buddy would probably get his hopes up. And then be devastated when he didn't come home with me.

On the way to the Hilton, I call Ellie to let her know when I'll be there. She should arrive a half hour after I do. After I change into my suit at the hotel, I park myself in the lobby to wait for her. Some of the women parading through the space are dolled up in shimmering, floor-length gowns. Hope Ellie's wearing something somewhat sexy. A bare shoulder, a hint of cleavage would do. But I'm not holding out much hope. She never was much for dolling up in high school. And now she's hell-bent on being a professional, so I'm guessing no peekaboo dress. Too bad, she has the most beautiful skin.

Antsy, I glance at my watch for the tenth time. Damn it. She should be here by now. Is she running late? No. She would have called. Still, it wouldn't hurt to check. As I'm about to dial her number, Ellie emerges from the elevator on the other side of the lobby. She's wearing one of those little black dresses that every woman owns. On most women, it's a utilitarian choice. But on her? It looks sexy as hell. As she glides across the room, I can't keep my eyes off her. It's only when she stops in front of me that I remember to breathe.

"Ellie. Good of you to come."

Her nervous gaze darts around the lobby. "I should have worn something fancier. Not that I have any such thing." She glances at me, her gaze filled with apprehension. "What do you think? It's not too plain, is it?"

Going by the tightening of my balls, hell, no. I smile, to put her at ease. "I'll let you know as soon as I put my tongue back in my mouth."

She appears adorably confused. As if she didn't expect that answer.

I leisurely take my fill of the wonder that is Ellie tonight. Her mahogany hair—half tossed back, half spilled forward across a v-neckline that hints at her sweet breasts. Fire-engine red mouth I want to taste, nibble, hell, downright devour. A rhinestone belt sharply shows off her tiny waist, and a flared skirt hides her treasures. I know what lies beneath that dress. Sugar and spice and everything nice, along with a hint of honey. I've never forgotten the flavor of her skin, the cinnamony taste of her breasts, and, most especially, the sweet intoxication of that spot between her legs. "You look lovely."

She breathes out a relieved sigh. "Thank you."

That's Ellie, polite to the end, even when she can't make heads or tails of me.

Rather than take her somewhere private and dark where I can do wicked things to her, I crook my arm. After all, I did promise to behave. "Cocktails are being served. Would you care for a drink?"

"A glass of white wine would be nice." She glances at the shimmery black wrap folded over her arm. "Should I check this?"

"If you wish. I can keep you warm if you get cold."

"Brock." An arched-brow reprimand. The first of the night, but, God willing, not the last.

With a smile, I beg for forgiveness. "Sorry."

Her "Umph," doesn't quite pardon, but it does give me a pass.

As we walk toward the cloakroom, I ask, "So, who's watching your daughter?"

For a moment, she tenses, but then her shoulders relax. "She's at a sleepover at a friend's house."

"Oh."

"I'd originally asked Mama, but—"

"Your mother's here?" I rarely saw Mrs. Adams during our tutoring sessions, but when I did, she was always nice to me.

"Yes. She followed us to Chicago."

Followed *us* which would mean her child was born before Ellie moved up north. That would make her daughter seven or eight? I can't imagine having a kid while in college, but Ellie must have. "That's great."

"Yes, it is." She doesn't volunteer more than that. Like before, I get the feeling she doesn't want to talk about her family life. Fine. I get it. I drop the subject, even though I'm curious as hell.

After checking her wrap, we stroll toward one of the bar stations outside the ballroom where the dinner will be held. She orders a glass of white wine. Needing something stronger, I request a neat whiskey for me. Since I'm staying at the hotel, I don't have to watch my alcohol consumption. That wouldn't be a problem anyway. I've never been one to get drunk. My vices have always been women and a great screw. The more, the merrier.

We enter the ballroom to find Trevor coming toward us, a gorgeous woman on his arm. With her chocolate skin, slender figure and majestic height, she could pass for a model. Hell, for all I know, she could be.

When they reach our side, I introduce him to Ellie. "Trevor Johnson, my center. Trevor, my date, Eleanor Adams."

"Pleased to meet you, Eleanor." He points to the lady next to him. "My fiancee, Bonita Martin."

"You're engaged. How lovely," Ellie says.

Bonita pats Trevor's bicep. "Yeah, I plan to make an honest man out of him."

I laugh. "Lucky him." I mean it. Even though I've never married, I understand the attraction of a wife and a family. It centers a man, roots him in something real. Don't know why I feel that way since I didn't have a happy home.

"We've been assigned seating," Trevor says. "You're in the front, next to Ty Mathews and his fiancée."

"Thanks for the heads up."

The lights flicker, and I turn to Ellie. "Looks like they're getting ready to start. Should we go grab our seats?"

She nods.

After a quick goodbye to Trevor and Bonita, I maneuver our way to the front of the room, holding Ellie's hand all the while. Our table is easy to spot through the sea of black and red. Ty's already seated there, a gorgeous redhead by his side. His fiancée, MacKenna Perkins.

We barely get to greet everyone at the table before the waiters fan out across the room with salad plates which everyone wolves down. Soon, we're being served our entrees. Given the choices of filet mignon, veal parmigiana, and some chicken dish, I'd chosen the beef. I hadn't known what Ellie would like, so I'd ordered the same for her. Too late, I'm kicking myself. What if she's turned into a vegan? When the plate is placed in front of her, I lean sideways and whisper in her ear. "I didn't know what you liked, so I guessed."

She grins. "You did well. I love filet mignon."

Going by the way she tucks into her meal, she's not lying.

After dessert's served and the tables cleared, the lights in the ballroom dim. As the room grows silent, an assistant coach walks up to the podium to introduce the first speaker, Coach Grohowski, who gives a rousing speech about the Outlaws' success and everyone's contribution to the big win. He follows through on his words by naming every single member of the team. Some draw applause when they stand; others get downright cheered, most especially Ty Mathews. Makes sense. He's the main reason they won the Super Bowl.

When my name's called, I come to my feet, expecting a polite reception. But to my amazement, I get an enthusiastic response. Dumbfounded, I briefly nod to the crowd and the coach before plunking my ass right back on the chair.

Once the applause dies down, Ty leans in to whisper. "Don't be surprised. They know how good you are. They expect great things from you."

I don't have a humble bone, but right now, that's my uppermost emotion. Who knew I'd be welcomed with open arms? "I'll do my best."

That's all I get to say. Oliver Lyons, the Outlaws' owner, is stepping up to the dais, and the room hushes once more.

"This is the best part," someone at our table murmurs. Every player at our table is sporting a full-toothed grin, much like a kid's on Christmas day.

I don't have long to wonder why. Upon Oliver Lyons's signal, women dressed in the Outlaws' colors spread across the room and pass out envelopes to the players. The ones at my table eagerly tear them open. Some whoop and holler when they spot what's inside. Others quietly slip the envelopes into their jackets. Ty shows what's inside his envelope to his fiancée before sharing a kiss with her.

Since I wasn't a member of the team during their winning season, I don't expect anything. But much to my surprise, I'm handed a box with my name on it. I open it up to find a key and a message inside: "Your very own Porsche Cayenne with the Chicago Outlaws' colors. Thank you for choosing to be part of our team."

Ironic, since I didn't want to come in the first place. "Wow. That's very generous."

"Oliver Lyons is a very generous owner," Ty says. "You work hard, and he will reward you." He drops his voice. "Just don't screw up."

I cut my gaze to his. "Meaning?"

"He hates scandals. Last season he fired our kicker. Granted he was a sorry excuse of skin, but he had a great leg. Didn't matter. When Oliver found out about an old college scandal, he cut him from the team."

I frown. My past history isn't exactly rosy.

"Don't worry. They know what happened at that party in Florida. They don't blame you. And San Diego involved grown women, not an innocent college kid." A shadow crosses his face, and his expression grows haunted.

"Ty," his fiancée says, covering her hand with his.

"I'm okay." He drops a kiss on her mouth.

Whatever happened with the kicker, Ty was involved somehow. Something that pains him still.

Shaking off his sadness, he turns back to me. "Just watch what you do."

"Got it."

"Good."

It doesn't take a rocket scientist to understand why they sat me next to Ty Mathews. They want to make sure I understand what's expected of me. No scandals, meaning no rowdy parties or *ménages*. I already knew it, but this year is going to suck.

With the speeches and gift giving done, the band strikes up a bouncy tune sure to get people on their feet. I turn to Ellie to ask if she wants to dance

But she's glancing at her watch. "I better go. It's getting late."

Already? I want her to stay so I can enjoy more of this evening with her. But I did promise to keep things professional, which means I have to let her go. Without fuss, without protest. "Okay. Let's get your wrap, and I'll walk you to your car."

"You don't have to do that, Brock."

"Yes. I do." I'd be a total jerk if I didn't escort her out.

After she gets her wrap, we stroll to the parking lot elevator. When the car arrives, we climb in. It's just the two of us, and I'm having a hard time saying goodbye. "Is it far, your house?"

"About a half hour drive."

The elevator stops at the P1 parking level, but before she can step out, I ask, "Are you sure you have to leave so soon? It's only a little after ten." So much for not making a fuss.

"Brock." She's wearing that same, prim schoolmarm expression she used back in the day when I didn't finish the homework she'd assigned me.

Little did she know how much that look turned me on. In fact, I'd loved it so much, I would screw up on purpose. "There's a bottle of champagne in my room. One drink?"

Her mouth scrunches. "I have to drive home."

"You've had exactly one glass of wine. Some bubbly won't be enough to get you drunk." When she arches a brow, I know what she's thinking. That I want to screw her. She's right. I do. But I'm not a horny seventeen-year-old anymore. I've got more discipline than that. "No messing around, I promise."

After thinking about it for a moment, she nods. "Okay." She holds up a finger. "One drink, that's it."

I grin. "One drink."

We ride up to the lobby level where we switch elevators. When we get to my room, there's not only a bottle of champagne, but a plate of chocolate strawberries.

"They thought of everything, didn't they?" Her face lights up with a smile.

Clearly, she trusts me. She shouldn't. I've been hard since I first saw her tonight. Given the slightest bit of encouragement, I'd gladly strip her of that little black dress and lick my way up to that sweet spot between her legs. But I can't do that. I'd vowed to behave. Desperately needing a diversion, I uncork the champagne and fill our flutes. I wait until she's had a sip before wordlessly offering her the plate of strawberries. And then I suffer the hell of the damned when her lips form a perfect "O" and bite down on the fucking fruit.

From the time she was a teenager, she's always had this effect on me. She didn't know it then, just like she doesn't know it now. Ellie was different from the other girls I knew. They just wanted to screw the star of the football team. She was sweet and gentle and kind, something I hadn't experienced much. The afternoon I found out she'd left town was the worst day of my life. It got worse when nobody knew where she'd gone.

But I can't go down memory lane. Not when it's bound to bring me pain. So I better talk about something, anything that has nothing to do with our past. "So, you have a kid?"

Her shoulders grow rigid. "Yes."

That's the third time she's tensed up when I mention her daughter. She wants to keep her personal life private. Problem is I want to know more about Ellie, more about her child. Maybe when I do, she'll let me in. "What's her name?"

She drops her glass on the table with a thud. "Can we not talk about my daughter?" There's a haunted look in her eyes. Strange.

"I'm just trying to reconnect, Ellie."

"We don't need to reconnect, Brock. Not on a personal level anyway."

I get it. She doesn't trust me. Not with my rep. I need to explain things in a way she won't become suspicious of my motives. "You're the only person I know in this whole damn town. And my only true friend is in a dog kennel."

Her gaze softens. "You'll see him soon, Brock. Surely you can make friends with some of the players. Trevor seems nice."

Trevor is nice, but once bitten, twice shy. "That would not be a good idea."

"Why not?"

"Sometimes friendships cause you to make bad decisions."

She brushes a soft hand across my arm, something she'd done in the past when I'd been frustrated or upset. "Is that what happened with Bernie Waters?"

The lineman I invited to that ill-fated party in Florida. "Yeah. I trusted him even though all the red flags were there. He drank too much. He partied too hard. And then he betrayed my trust by bringing drugs into my house." I slam back what's left of my champagne and pour some more.

"The cops knew you didn't provide the cocaine. If they thought you had, they would have charged you with a crime."

"But social media believed it. So did my team. Hell, some of the players blamed me for his death."

"I'm so sorry, Brock." Her touch strums through me, making me feel things I haven't felt for a long time.

"Me too."

"Not every player's like Bernie."

"Yeah, but with pre-season starting in three weeks, I don't have time to get to know them. Plus, I can't allow friendships to affect my performance on or off the field. So I'll just have to go it alone."

"You didn't make friends with any football players in San Diego?"

"No. I had too much to lose." I stare into my glass. "Chicago's no different. Especially, since I'm only here for a year. Next season, Ty will get his job back, and I'll move on to another team." I gulp back my drink and pour another. "No sense in getting to know the Outlaws' players." Knowing means friendship and friendship means pain. I'm better off keeping to myself.

She sips her champagne while studying me. "I shouldn't tell you this. Don't want to get your hopes up. But there are rumblings."

I gaze down at her beautiful face. "Yeah? Of what?"

"Teams that may want you to start for them next year. Of course, it will depend on your performance this season."

Glad for the change of subject, I laugh. "No pressure there."

She grins. "No. None at all."

I want to kiss that smile right on the corner, share that joy with her. Be happy this damn once.

"Oliver Lyons seems to like you."

"Yeah?"

"Aha."

"How do you know?"

"Well, for starters, he gave you a brand new SUV with all the bells and whistles."

"How do you know it's loaded."

"Because that's what he gave the team a year ago."

I grin, as I brush a curl off her face. "And here I thought I was special."

Her breath hitches. "You are. Special, I mean."

"How special?"

"Very special." Breaking contact, she walks away. Clearly, she's uncomfortable with my touch.

"The Chicago Outlaws is a very special team as well," she says, turning back around.

"Yes, it is." Where is she headed with this?

"They try hard to ensure players don't get into trouble, like driving under the influence. That's the main reason they make hotel rooms available for the players after an Outlaws team event."

I bark out a laugh. "A player can get into plenty of trouble in a hotel." I should know. I've fucked more women in my hotel room than I care to remember.

"But at least they won't drive drunk." She trails her hand across the sofa's back cushion.

I want to do the same. To her. Feel the softness of her velvety skin, taste her, breathe her in. She wants to keep her distance, but I'm like a moth to her flame. Slowly, I stroll toward her. I don't want to spook her, after all.

"Have you gotten the morality lecture in training camp?" she asks, quite unaware of what I'm aching to do to her.

I laugh, mainly to keep from following through. "Yep. In spades. They brought in a lifestyle coach. No drugs, no wild parties, no sex with underage girls, and whatever you do, use condoms." Fuck. Didn't mean to mention that. "The lecture went on and on for over three hours."

"They're protecting themselves if something happens."

"Well, they have nothing to worry about as far as I'm concerned. I intend to keep my nose clean."

"Really?" She stops stroking the seat cushion, and her head comes up.

"Really."

"What brought on this change of heart? The lecture?"

"No."

"Then what?"

"If you must know, you."

"Me?"

"Yes. When we talked on Thursday, and I heard your kid's voice." I tangle a hand through my hair. "Damn it, Ellie. She could have been mine. I was so young and stupid and horny that day. I should have stopped. I should have never let it get to the point it did." My gaze, hot and needy, finds her across the room. "I just wanted you so much."

"You wanted me?" she asks in a breathless voice.

"Yeah. You drove me crazy, you know." I let out an embarrassed laugh, without taking my gaze from her. "With your glasses and your hair tied back in a ponytail. Nothing I wanted more than to loosen the knot, toss away your glasses. Kiss you. I used to fantasize about you at night." The hell with taking it slow. I step forward until I'm standing right in front of her, breathing in her scent.

She doesn't move, or push away, but remains where she is. "You're kidding."

Unable to help myself, I stroke her silky skin, right above the wild throbbing in her throat. "Swear to God."

Her eyes are two luminous pools of brown. "But you could have had any girl on the cheerleading team."

I grin. "I did have every girl on the cheerleading team."

She steps back, her mouth scrunching in disapproval. "Figures."

Damn it. When am I going to learn? Ellie doesn't want to hear about my sexual conquests, even if they're in the past. Right here, right now, she's the only one who matters. Once again, I stride toward her. To my surprise, she doesn't skitter away. Encouraged, I gently wrap my hand around her upper arm, loosely enough she can break contact if she wants. "You were the only one who meant anything to me."

"Yeah, right," she scoffs. But her gaze projects something else—hope, excitement. Hunger. Ellie Adams wants me.

All I have to do is not screw up. I brush my thumb across her velvety skin. "I'm sorry."

"For what?"

"For being such an idiot."

She fights to hold back a smile, but the grin wins out. "Honesty at last."

I'm on a roll, so I decide to push my luck. "And I'm sorry I didn't use a condom that night." The one true regret I have when it comes to her. "But at least, I didn't knock you up. Can you imagine what a disaster that would have been?"

Her gaze turns hard and angry. She wrenches away from me and slams the champagne flute on the nearest table. "I have to go."

A second ago, she was ready to fall into my arms. What the hell went wrong? "Do you have to?"

"I don't like to be on the road after midnight. It's almost that time now." She clamps her arms around her middle, as if she's trying to hold in some pain.

Whatever it is, I caused it. "Ellie, I'm sorry if I—"

"Stop apologizing!" Her eyes flash with anger.

"Okay." Clearly, she doesn't want to hear any regrets from me. And apparently, the last thing she wants is one more second in my company. But I can't let her walk out the door by herself. "Let me escort you to your car."

"No!" She screams. "Sorry. I prefer you don't."

Is she crying? Yep, she's crying. "You're upset."

"It's been a long day, Brock. Thanks for inviting me to the banquet." She grabs her purse and wrap and, before I know it, she's gone.

I hurt her. A lot. What did I say that was so wrong?

CHAPTER 6

Eleanor

$\mathcal{P}$LEASE GOD, DON'T LET ME RUN INTO ANYBODY I KNOW. The chances might be slim to none, but life has a funny way of screwing with you. After reaching a nearly empty lobby, I rush toward the elevator that leads to the parking lot. I don't feel safe until I get into my car. Only then do I break down and cry.

So my pregnancy would have been a disaster? Of course, he'd think so. After all, he was headed for football glory at Clemson. Becoming a father at such a young age would have derailed his career. Like it almost did mine. If it hadn't been for Mama and Steve who supported me through my pregnancy and Kaylee's birth, I would have been one more pregnant teen statistic. Chances are I wouldn't have graduated from high school, much less attended college. But I did have them. And that made all the difference.

I've asked myself a million times whether I'd made the right decision by not telling him. What would have happened if I had? Would he have supported me? Or would he have refused to acknowledge the baby as his? Well, today I have my answer. He would've considered it a disaster. At the very least, he'd have resented my pregnancy. I would've surely crimped his style as busy as he was screwing his way through the cheerleading team. He might have even demanded I get an abortion, after offering to pay for it as well. After all, his family was filthy rich. Not that I would have done it. Nothing in the world could have prevailed on me to get rid of my baby.

Granted those first few years were rough. Leaving Kaylee with Mama and Steve so I could attend college was unbelievably painful. Once she came to live with me, money was tight. There were nights when all we had to eat were noodles and peanut butter for dinner. I'd felt like a total failure. But somehow we made it through. I graduated from college and law school. I have a career and a great paying job. And more important than anything else, Kaylee is beautiful, smart, and the biggest blessing in my life.

So if he thinks she would have been a disaster, well—that's his loss.

Feeling only slightly better, I put the car in drive and head home. The house is dark except for the porch light which I always leave on. After hanging my coat in the foyer closet, I walk into Kaylee's room and breathe in her pre-teen essence. I fall asleep clutching her pillow.

By the time Monday rolls around, I've regained my even footing. I refuse to let Brock's words haunt me. They belong in a past we once shared. Not the present, and most certainly, not the future. He's nothing but a client. All I need do is keep things professional. And that I can do.

Today's duties include overseeing Brock's furniture move-in. Rather than stop at the office, I drive directly to his condo since the movers are scheduled to get there by ten after they drop off some things in storage.

Unfortunately, they arrive an hour late. Having skipped breakfast, I'm starving, but hey, that's on me. With any luck, they should be done in an hour, and then I'll have time to eat. As it turns out, luck's not with me. Not by a long shot.

I'd asked my assistant to handle things in the condo, while I supervise the unloading from the lobby. At first, things proceed smoothly.

But then disaster strikes.

Massive bedposts come off the van with some medieval-looking things attached to them. As they get closer, I realize what they are. Metal chains with manacles and cuffs.

I gulp. Hard. "Oh, dear God." Why didn't they remove them?

A little, old lady and her companion stand by the front doors waiting for the movers to pass so they can exit the building. As they shuffle past the woman, her eyes grow wide. "Walter, what are those things?"

Her companion, a wizened octogenarian, covers her eyes. "Bertha, don't look."

"Walter, stop that. I can't see."

But Walter doesn't pay any attention to her. His focus is all on me. As he pushes Bertha out the door, he fairly vibrates with outrage as he stabs his walking cane at me. "Hussy. You should be ashamed of yourself."

Branded with a scarlet letter. God. This is all I need. I don't know who. I don't know how. But somebody is going to pay.

As if I haven't suffered enough humiliation, an older man is busy snapping pictures in between smirking and winking at me.

Not to be outdone, a young woman with multi-colored hair snickers as the movers stroll the manacled bedposts through the lobby.

I run toward the movers before they disappear into the elevator to see if there's something I can do to hurry them along. But then I hear a crash behind me. Fearing the worst, I turn. The contents of one box are spread helter-skelter all over the front entrance—whips, chains, dildos, vibrators, those rabbity things.

"Nice," the rainbow-colored hair woman says. Before walking out the door, she hands me a card. "Call me if you want to play."

Shoot me now. With steam practically coming out of my ears, I yell to the movers. "Pick that up!"

"Nuh-uh. Not touching that, lady," one of them says. "Not without some rubber gloves. Got any?"

While they tape the box back together, I hunt around my purse for tissues. I gingerly pick up each and every item and throw it into the box, not caring if it breaks, not caring about anything other than to get the box and me away from the gathering crowd, some of whom are pointing their cells at the scene probably videoing the whole scene. Thankfully, that's one of the last boxes, and in fifteen minutes the movers are done.

With Brock's things delivered to the apartment, I send my assistant back to work. She has no clue about what happened downstairs. There is no evidence of the lobby disaster. Well, except for all the witnesses and photos they took. Damn it. I need a drink.

But I can't indulge. I need to report what happened to Marty.

As soon as I arrive at the office, I dial his number.

"How did the move go?" he asks.

"We have a problem." Even to my own ears, my voice sounds strained. But it can't be helped. "Can I come to your office to explain?"

"Can it wait? I have a client coming in fifteen minutes." He's not in a good mood. I can tell.

"No. Sorry. I'll make it quick."

"Fine." Going by his snippy tone, he's not pleased with me. But this is something he has to know. After all, Brock Parker is his client.

With no time to waste, I mad dash it to his office.

I barely have time to sit before he's demanding. "What happened? Did something break or get damaged?" he grunts.

"No." At least as far as I know.

"So what is it?" he barks out.

"Umm, did you know Brock has a party room?"

"Like a billiard table and a bar?"

My face flushes with heat. "Like handcuffs, whips, and chains."

He sits up ramrod straight, and his chair bounces behind him. "No. I did not. How do you know this? You weren't supposed to unpack."

"The movers dropped a box containing his, err, toys, and the contents spilled out all over the entrance to the condo building. Not only that, they paraded the bedposts to his orgy bed through the lobby as well." I pause a moment to let that sink in. "The, err, restraints were still attached to the bed."

"Restraints?"

Oh, God. Do I really need to explain? "Manacles and handcuffs attached to chains."

His brow arches. Yeah, he might have been aware of Brock's life-style, but he didn't know the specifics.

"Those movers are idiots. What imbecile chose them?"

"They're on our agency's approved movers list. Don't worry. I'll have them removed and write a formal complaint, as well."

"We should sue them. They're supposed to be discreet."

"I'll get legal on it." In my opinion, there's not much legal can do. The damage is done.

"Did anybody notice?"

"Oh, they noticed all right. Some of the condo residents went so far as to snap pictures with their cells. Three guesses how long it will be before they show up on the internet."

He rubs his pate, a sure sign he's worried. "This is a disaster."

Yep. That's the word of the day.

"If word leaks out about this, that's all the social media will talk about."

"Exactly."

"If that happens, God knows if the Outlaws would keep him. Wouldn't be the first time they let go of a scandal-prone player."

Scrunching his mouth, he rubs a thumb across his lower lip. For a few seconds, there's nothing but silence.

I don't interrupt his process but sit across from him with my hands clasped in front of me. I may be disgusted with Brock and his sex toys, but I don't want his career to end, especially when I feel guilty enough already. Somehow I should have stopped what happened today.

After a minute or two, he raises his head and laser gazes me. The light shining in his eyes gives me hope. Maybe he's found a way out of this mess.

"Who knows we rented that apartment for Brock?" he asks.

"No one. I handled the arrangements. As usual, I used the agency's name to book the moving company and lease the condo. And I didn't pass on the information as to who's going to be living there to anyone, not even my assistant. Although seeing how we represent Brock and he just transferred to the Outlaws, it won't take her but two seconds to figure it out."

"At the condo building, where were you?"

"In the lobby. I sent my assistant to the condo itself."

"So everybody thinks you're the one moving in?"

"I guess." A bad feeling crawls over me.

He relaxes into his chair again. "Well, there you have it, problem solved."

"How do you figure that, Marty?" I truly have no idea how he came to that conclusion.

"The residents think you're the tenant." He grins. "You'll need to move in, of course. At least for a little while until we find Brock another place to live." He temples his hands over his middle like he's come up with a brilliant solution.

Like heck he has! "I can't move in, Marty. I have a house. A daughter," I say. "Her birthday party's this weekend!"

He waves a hand in the air, dismissing my objection. "So do the birthday party and move in on Monday."

"I can't live there!" Brock will be done with training camp in another week which means we would be sharing the same space, breathing the same air. At night. I can't do that.

His brow scrunches. "Why not?"

Do I really have to explain this to him? "Brock will be living there!"

"That place has two bedrooms, doesn't it? It shouldn't be a problem. Besides, it'll only be for a couple of weeks. A month tops." He stabs his pen in my direction. "And while you're there, you can keep an eye on him."

"What?"

"To make sure he stays out of trouble, if you know what I mean."

Yes, I know exactly what he means. "But. But." I sputter.

He glances at me over his half-frame reading glasses. "It would mean a lot, Eleanor. You play along, and I'll make sure you get a big, fat bonus check at the end of the year."

That offer shouldn't tempt me, yet it does. I certainly could use the money, not only for my student loans, but for expenses associated with the house. The hot water heater is acting up, and the roof needs replacing before winter sets in. And like he says, it's only for a little while. Surely I can handle the living arrangements for a couple of weeks. I shape my lips into what must look like a pained smile. "Well, when you put it that way. All right. But only Monday through Friday. Weekends I go home to my daughter."

"Fine." He returns to whatever he was reading when I walked in, a clear sign of dismissal.

I walk out of his office, my mind swirling with what I'll have to do to pull this off. My first call will be to my mother since I'll need her to stay with Kaylee during the week. I hate to do it, but what choice do I have? This job is too important to me. And then I'll have to explain my absence to Kaylee. I can't tell her I'll be living in Brock Parker's place. She would never understand no matter how I justified it. Which means, God help me, I'll have to lie.

CHAPTER 7

Brock

I'M SCARFING DOWN MY BREAKFAST on Thursday, when one of the assistant coaches grabs my shoulder, squeezing it lightly. "Coach Grohowski wants to see you. Stop by his office, will you?"

I've been at camp for a week and a half now. Done everything they've asked me to do. But even though it can't possibly be bad news, my heart skips a beat. I've been on the losing end of a talk with the head coach before. Been told they no longer need my services. Well, if it is bad news, might as well get it over with. I wolf down what remains of my food and head toward Coach's office.

Coach Grohowski is a huge guy. Six four. At least two seventy-five. He's seated in a massive executive chair, squinting at something on the computer. As soon as I walk in, he tosses his computer glasses on his desk and leans back in his seat. He doesn't look like he'll be dealing out any bad news. But what do I know?

I nod. "Coach. You wanted to see me?"

"Yeah. Take a seat." He points to the armchair across the desk from him. The thing's so big it doesn't even squeak when I park my ass on it.

"How are you settling in? Any issues you want to discuss?" he asks.

Yeah, like I'd be stupid enough to tell him I have a problem. "No." I grin like the Outlaws' training camp is the happiest place on earth. "Everything's great."

"Good. Got a place to live?"

He wants to talk about my living arrangements? Ookay. "Yes. Furniture's on its way. Should be here by the end of the week." Or so I've been told.

"Great. We like to have our players settled, preferably married. Any fiancée? Or steady girlfriend?" There's a hopeful tone to his voice.

Where are these questions coming from? He had to know everything there was to know about me before the trade. "Nope."

Leaning forward, he drops his elbows on the desk. "What about your date at the dinner? Eleanor Adams, was it? She seemed very nice."

Ahhh. Things are starting to get clear. Wish I could tell him Ellie and I are a thing. But we're not. Saturday night at the hotel proved that. "An old friend. Ran into her at the airport. We exchanged phone numbers. When the team dinner came up, I rang her up." I'm not lying. Everything I'm saying is true.

"Good. Good."

"Anything else, Coach?" I thumb toward the door. "I need to report to rehab."

"Nothing hurting, I hope."

"No. Like I said, everything's great."

"Good to know." He stands up and shakes my hand. When he does, he holds on to it. "A word of advice, Brock. We're very appreciative of you being here. Very appreciative. You have a great arm and you're smart. If there's anything you need, you let us know. You hear me."

"Will do, sir."

He releases my hand, but apparently, he's not done with me yet. "Now, I don't expect you to live the life of a saint. But we'd only like to see your name in the news when it relates to football. You get my drift?"

So, the purpose of this strange conversation is now apparent. He'd hoped to hear that Ellie and I were, at the very least, dating. When I didn't confirm that, I got my own personal warning. No wild parties. No sex scandals. "Loud and clear, Coach."

I walk out, quietly seething. Just how many damn lectures do I have to have? I'm a grown ass adult, for fuck's sake. I kept my nose clean in San Diego, didn't I? Well, except for that photo that got plastered all over social media. But nobody got hurt. The women in my bed were more than old enough. I have half a mind to walk right back into Coach's office and quit.

Yeah, that's not happening.

I want this job. I need this job. The Outlaws are a class organization. There's a reason they won the Super Bowl last year, and it wasn't only about skill. They truly think of themselves as family. San Diego didn't have that. It was pretty much every one out for themselves. But this team is different. They truly think of themselves as one big tribe. Not that I'll become one of them. I'll be on the outside looking in. Pretty much the way I've been my whole life.

As I leave the office, somebody approaches. A kid who looks like he's all of twelve, although I'm sure he's much older. "Mr. Parker."

"Yes."

"A package arrived for you."

"Thanks." I take the Priority Mail box with my sports agency's return address. When I open it up, a set of keys fall out, a tag attached to them with my new place's address, along with a notification that my furniture had arrived. I'd like to go check out the condo, but the team's not too keen on releasing a player during training camp, not even for a couple of hours. Thing is, as hard as I've worked I've earned a favor or two. And there's no harm in asking. I walk to the Director of Player Relations office and knock on his door.

"Come in."

"Hey, Jimmy."

He squints at me over his computer. "Brock. What can I do for you?"

"I just got the keys to my new place." I dangle them from my fingers. "Any chance I could go there tonight and check things out?"

He frowns. "Couldn't it wait? You'll be released on Saturday. That's only two days away."

"I have some exotic fish. Want to make sure they made it okay."

He removes his glasses and squints at me as he cleans them. "Never would have taken you for an aquarium fish kind of guy."

"I lived in San Diego. You learn to love them." I flash him my most honest grin.

"Oh?" He slides his glasses back on. "What are they?"

"Candy Basletts."

A grin pops up on his lips. "Sounds like stripper names."

I bark out a laugh.

"I suppose it would be okay. Just be back before eleven. Once the gates are locked, nobody gets in or out. And anybody missing at curfew gets fined $5,000."

"Got it. Thanks, Jimmy. I really appreciate it."

I don't own any damn fish. But then—-Jimmy doesn't need to know that.

CHAPTER 8

Eleanor

𝒲HAT AM I DOING AT BROCK'S PLACE? I should be home with my daughter, not in his condo passing myself off as the tenant although, technically, I now am. Originally I may have leased the place in the agency's name, but Marty requested I change it to mine to give credence to me being here. Problem is, it now looks as if I'm the owner of those sex toys and that bed with the restraints. If word were to get out, I shudder to think what would happen. But then I guess that's the price I must pay for going along with this arrangement.

I agreed to come here, partly for money, partly to save Brock's reputation. I'd told myself it would be okay. That Marty would explain the situation to Brock before I moved in. But he'd asked me to handle it. Brock has no idea I'm here going through his possessions. And that is so wrong. Whatever Marty thinks, I have no right to intrude into Brock's privacy, especially after the way I walked out on him. No. I didn't leave. I'd fled without bothering with any explanations.

Of course, Marty doesn't know about Saturday, nor is he aware

Brock and I know each other. He asked me to complete this assignment to see what kind of an agent I'll make. According to him, sports agents have to go way beyond the call of duty for the good of the client. And this is one of those times. I'll need to provide cover for Brock, and if need be, fall on the sword. Hopefully, it won't come to that.

Well, at least I'll have a couple of days before I need to explain things to Brock. He'll be done with camp tomorrow and move in the next day. It will be awkward at first, but surely he'll understand. I just need to figure out what to say to him.

In the meantime, I better get busy. This might not be my stuff, but I will be living here, and we'll need a working kitchen. I might as well put away some things. If Brock asks about it, I'll tell him it's part of the move in service. Other than dishes, glasses, flatware and a fancy coffee maker, he doesn't have much in the way of kitchen stuff. It takes me no time to empty those cardboard boxes.

Done with that task, I make my way to the guest bedroom, the one that has a regular bed. Unlike the kitchen, there are oodles of boxes here, all clearly marked. My conscience rears up its ugly head. It's one thing to put away his dishes and cutlery, it's another to handle his personal belongings. Some of the containers are labeled "suits." Maybe it would be okay to hang them up? After all, there's nothing too terribly personal about his fancy threads. Besides, they might wrinkle badly if left in their wardrobe boxes too long. In reality I'd be doing him a favor. Having rationalized my actions, I tear open one of the boxes and get busy. I've just cracked open the second one when a rattle sounds at the front door.

My breath hitches as my heart jumps to my throat. What on earth? Except for the condo management and me, nobody has a key to this place.

When steps grow closer and closer, I grab a wooden hanger and burrow deep in the closet. Whoever it is, I won't go down without a fight. But when a huge shadow looms larger than life at the opening, my courage deserts me, and I squeak.

"Ellie?" Brock steps into the light, sporting a frown.

I whoosh out a breath from the sheer relief of it. "Thank God, it's you."

"What are you doing here?"

I return the wooden hanger to the rod. "Ummm, unpacking your stuff?"

His brow knits as he stares at me. "Why?"

Think fast, Ellie. "I-I-I"—gulp—"wanted to surprise you."

"Surprise me?"

"Yes." I struggle to put on my game face. "You only have seven days between training camp and the first game, which as you know is on the road. And you'll be busy next week at the Outlaws' compound getting ready for that. Since you wouldn't have much time to unpack, I thought I'd surprise you by doing it for you." I fling my arms open wide. "Surprise."

He scratches the back of his head as if he can't quite figure me out. "Oh, okay. Thanks, I guess." His brow remains wrinkled. No wonder. Saturday, I'm storming out of his room. Thursday, I'm hanging up stuff in his closet. Can't blame him for being confused. Hope he doesn't ask about my change of heart. I don't have an answer for him.

Stepping into the bedroom, I ask as nonchalantly as I can, "How did you get the keys to this place?"

"Someone from your agency sent them to training camp, along with a note saying that my stuff had arrived."

"We did?"

He stares at me like I've grown two heads. "Yeah. Didn't you know?"

"I'd forgotten." I'd forgotten all right. Forgotten to tell my assistant not to do that. After my conversation with Marty, I'd had a chat with her. Turns out she'd known all along who'd be living in the condo. And since our standard operating procedure is to provide our clients with the personal touch, she'd followed through and sent Brock's keys to him at camp. Well, no sense crying over spilled milk. The damage is done. "You don't mind, do you?"

"Mind?"

"That I'm here. Going through your stuff."

His lips curl into that sexy grin I love. "No, I don't. You might be in for a surprise, though."

I scrunch my face. "You mean your orgy room?"

He barks out a laugh. "My orgy room?"

"Yes. Isn't that where you have your—" I can't say it a second time.

"Orgies?" He arches a brow.

That small gesture gets my motor running. But I'm here as a professional, and I can't react this way to him. Unfortunately, my body is not listening. "Yes."

"Sometimes."

My cheeks flush with heat as I picture him and several women doing the dirty deed on that bed.

He steps forward and cups my cheek with one of those big palms of his. "You should see your face right now. It's bright red."

I slap his hand away. "I just hope you sanitize those things between uses."

"My hands?" He holds them up.

"Your toys."

The corner of his mouth twists upward in a smirk. "I had a cleaning service that came in regularly."

My eyes grow wide. "And they didn't mind?"

"Mind? They loved it. It was extra money for them." His gaze bounces around the bedroom. "I'll have to find another cleaner in Chicago."

I jab a finger into the center of his very hard chest, reclaiming his attention. "No wild parties, remember."

"Oh, don't worry. It'll be only one guest. Maybe two."

"At the hotel, you said you'd keep your nose clean."

"A temporary lapse of judgment."

Should have known he was playing me. It shouldn't bother me. Yet it does. But my feelings are not important. I've been assigned keeper duties, and that's exactly what I intend to do. Aiming to put the fear of God in him, I harsh my voice and issue a warning. "Brock."

Unfortunately, it doesn't bother him in the least because he grins right back. "Ellie."

"You're disgusting."

"Darling. I'm a lot of things. Disgusting is not one of them." His sizzling gaze lands on me. "Want to take the orgy room for a spin?"

Wow! It took him all of ten minutes to proposition me. But I'm not falling for it. "I'm not going in there. No way. No how."

"Afraid you'll like it?"

"Afraid I'll catch a sexually-transmitted disease."

"Your loss."

"Uh-huh. Now about this room—"

A rat-a-tat-tat clamors at the front door, and I nearly jump out of my skin. Who on earth could that be? I'm not expecting anyone. But maybe he is. Maybe he met someone at a bar and asked her to his place for some bouncy-bouncy on his orgy bed. I scrunch my eyes and glare at him. "Did you invite someone?"

"A woman, you mean?" Without bothering to wait for an answer, he says, "No. The only chick I know in Chicago is you."

"I'm not a chick, or a honey, or whatever you call women."

"Gotcha, darling." He wraps a finger around a curl spilled over my shoulder.

Before I can tell him to stop calling me darling, there's another more insistent knock on the door.

"Maybe I should get that?" He nods toward the living room.

"No!"

He stares at me, a puzzled look on his face. "Why not?"

"Because—because"—think fast, Ellie— "You don't want anyone to know you're living here, do you? You'll be mobbed by fans as soon as they find out."

His gaze swims with suspicion. "Eleanor, what's going on?"

"Nothing. I'll get it." After freeing my hair from his grasp, I rush to the door and open it no more than an inch. "Yes."

"Hi there." The man standing on the other side is in his forties. Although he must have been fairly good looking in his youth, he's gone to seed. He's now sporting a slight paunch and a comb-over that does nothing to hide the fact he's going bald. If he's hoping his loose silk jacket camouflages his less-than-svelte physique, he's dead wrong. All it does is bring attention to his flab.

"I'm Warren Sheffield." He gestures down the hallway. "I'm your neighbor three doors down. Ten-D." He flashes a smile that reveals all of his teeth. Not a pretty sight.

"What can I do for you, Mr. Sheffield?"

"Well, thought I'd come over and introduce myself." The leer on his face tells me he's exactly what I feared. He spotted the furniture and the whips and chains and he thought he would come over and play. As if.

I stick out my hand. "Martha . . . Washington."

He lets out a belly laugh which makes his stomach quiver. Ugh.

"That's not your real name."

Granted, I should have come up with a better moniker. But how does he know it's not real? "It's not?"

"No."

"Why do you think that?"

"Because no creature as beautiful as you could have such a prosaic name."

I take umbrage to that. Martha Washington is a perfectly good handle. "It's been handed down through generations."

"All right, *Martha*. Have it your way. Guess we all must have our little secrets."

Sheesh. Patronizing much?

"Yes. Well, I have a lot of unpacking to do, so goodnight, Mr. Sheffield." I start to close the door, but he jams his foot into the opening before I can do so.

"Don't rush off, darling."

"I'm not your darling." What is it with men?

"Well, you could be. I saw some of your things. And I heard what was in one of the boxes." He smirks. He winks. He waggles a finger at me. "You naughty girl."

Where's a hole to crawl into when you need one?

His voice drops a couple of notches to almost a whisper. "We have a club of sorts in the building. You know, the kind that swings." He winks again. "We get together on Fridays. Evenings, of course. We'd love it if you would join us. Feel free to bring some of your . . . toys. Unit Twelve-B at eight. Don't be late. Toodle oooh." Waving his fingers, he slinks off.

Yeah. Sure. I'll be there. Not. I turn and run right into Brock's chest. His big, broad, hard chest. He smells like a fresh pine forest, one I'd like to roll around in while he did wild, naughty things to me, while I licked every long, hard inch of—

"What was that all about?"

Ellie. Get a grip. You're here to do a job. Not drool over the man. Struggling to regain my wits, I mumble, "Umm. A neighbor from two doors down. Warren Sheffield."

"Three doors."

"You were listening?"

"Of course, I was listening. This is my place." Not technically, it isn't. But he doesn't have to know that.

"Fine. Three doors. What does it matter? It's not like I'm going to borrow a cup of sugar from him." I push at his chest to get him out of the way, but he doesn't budge.

Instead, he brackets my body with his huge arms and cages me in. "What is he talking about when he said he saw some of my things?"

Focus, Ellie, focus. "The movers, err, dropped a box in the lobby, and some of the contents *may* have spilled out."

His eyes narrow. "What box?"

"The ones that contained your . . . toys. They also paraded your bedposts with some of those . . . things still attached."

He snorts. "Fine movers you picked."

Taking umbrage, I hitch up my chin. "I'll have you know they came highly recommended."

"Well, obviously somebody lied."

The nearness of him makes me breathless. I can't stand being this close to him. It's like I'm in a forest surrounded by trees. Big, gorgeous trees that move in strange, mysterious ways. I want to lie down on a soft canopy of leaves, and—God, not again. What is it about this man that makes me forget everything but him?

His gaze slides to the closed door. For a couple of seconds he doesn't say a thing, but then his glance bounces back to me. "Why are you here, Ellie?"

"I—I told you. I wanted to unpack your things."

"Why would you want to do that? Last Saturday, you stormed out of my hotel room, angry at me. And now you want to do me a favor? That makes no sense. Besides, you wouldn't do such a thing. Not without my approval. What the hell's going on?"

He's so intoxicatingly close I can feel the heat, the sheer masculinity of him in every part of my being, and it's driving me insane. "I, err—"

Leaning down so his eyes are level with mine, he stares right into me. "Did Marty put you up to this?"

"He may have."

"Why?"

The scent of pine is all around me, and I can't breathe without taking him in. My imagination runs wild. I'm lying in a secluded forest, naked as the day I was born while he whispers wicked words to me. Oh, God, please let it stop. Brushing a trembling hand across my face, I fight to recall what's going on. Boxes. Toys. What Warren Sheffield saw. And how much trouble I'm in.

"Okay. Fine." It's best if he knows the truth, anyway. "You're not supposed to get embroiled in a scandal, right? Unfortunately, the evidence of your lifestyle would do just that. Somebody saw your things. Warren Sheffield for one, obviously. There were others, as well. At least one of them took pictures. So there's proof. Proof that somebody would be more than glad to sell to one of those gossip rags. If anybody figures out it's you living here, it'll be all over the internet faster than I can say Bob's your uncle." I don't have to tell him how the Outlaws would react. He knows.

He strides away, anger evident in every step. "Damn it. Just as things were starting to look up."

His scent's still in the air, but not as strong. I take a long, deep breath to regain my equilibrium. "It sucks. I know." He may be a horn-

63

dog. He may have lied at the hotel, but I don't want to see him suffer. "You can get through this without anybody finding out."

He swivels back to me. "How?"

"You have one more day of training camp, right?"

"Yes."

"And when camp ends, you'll be living here."

He nods.

I take a deep breath. "I'll be living here too."

"Why would you do that, Eleanor?" His brow knits, but his question emerges in a soft, low tone.

"To stop anyone from finding out you're the tenant." Before he has a chance to say something, I rush through my next words. "If anybody gets nosy about who's renting the place, they'll find my name on the lease, not yours. And it was me they saw in the lobby. Everything points to me. I'm nobody famous, so if it gets out about the furniture and stuff, it'll be no biggie." That's right. Play it off like it's not that important.

During my explanation, his expression clears up. "So." He grins. "We'd be sharing the place?"

"But not the same bed." Gotta make things crystal clear before he gets the wrong idea. "It's a two-bedroom condo, Brock. I'll be in one, you'll be in the other. Privacy shouldn't be a problem."

"Uh-huh." He doesn't sound like he wants privacy.

Tough. I'm willing to share the condo, but I'm not jumping into his bed. "I'll be here Monday through Friday. Go home on weekends. Days, you'll be at the Outlaws' compound. I'll be at work. We'll only run into each other at night. Saturday and Sunday, you'd have the place to yourself."

"Sounds like you've worked everything out."

"I try."

"Only one problem with your plan. I'm bound to run into people. In the elevator. The parking lot. What if somebody recognizes me?"

"Not if you adopt a disguise."

"A disguise?" He scoffs.

"Yes. I got you a wig. Dark, shaggy hair. You'll have to wear sunglasses and a hoodie."

"It's eighty degrees out there. They'll think I'm out to rob them, for fuck's sake. And why would I wear sunglasses at night?"

"Because that's what cool people do?" I venture.

"Ellie. Be serious," he says in a not unkind tone.

"I am. Look, you'll be leaving at the crack of dawn, right?"

"Something like that."

"Nobody will be out that early in the morning. Even if they are, they'll be half asleep. Chances are they won't notice you."

"You do know I'm six four and weigh 210? And my face has been plastered all over the news? How the hell do you think nobody will recognize me?"

"You wear your wig and sunglasses and keep your hoodie over your head, and they'll ignore you. If someone's stupid enough to comment, mumble 'hangover.' They'll leave you alone after that."

"And in the evening?"

"Keep your head down. If anybody gets in the elevator with you, get off a couple of floors up and walk down."

"Not sure that's going to work, sweetheart."

I ignore the sweetheart bit, seeing how I'm trying to convince him to go along with my plan. "Do you have any other suggestions?"

He thinks about it for a little bit. "Maybe I could find another place, fully furnished."

"You could. But there aren't any closer to the Outlaws' facility. Believe me, I looked."

"Somewhere farther away then."

"You'd spend an hour or more in traffic. Each way. Chicago traffic is a bear. Do you really want to spend all that time on the road, especially after a long day of training?"

He tangles a hand through his sandy blond mane. "No."

I know that gesture. It means he's considering my argument, or at least listening to it. So I press on. "I know this is not the best situation, but it will only be for a little while. If you're worried about me cramping your style, don't worry. I won't."

"That's not what I'm worried about. I don't mind sharing the condo with you."

I thought that would be his number one objection. After all, he can't bring his honeys or chicks to his pad if I'm here. "Then what's the problem?"

"I want to come and go as I please, not play incognito like some cheap character in a bad spy movie. Is that so hard to understand?"

"No, it isn't." He does have his pride, after all. But it'd be for his own good. "Look, I know this is not what you want. But it won't last long. We can start looking for a house for you right away. Just let me know what you want."

"I'll need one with a big yard for Butch."

"Yes, but I need to know what style house you'd like—contemporary, colonial, Victorian?"

"Doesn't matter. Chances are I'll only be here for a year."

I could tell him that it matters, that you never know what fate will bring. But he's not likely to listen. Not now when he's as upset as he is. Better I point him in the right direction and let him decide where he wants to live. "How about I have my realtor contact you? She helped me find a house that fit my budget in a great neighborhood. I'm sure she can help you."

"I guess that would work." He doesn't look too happy about it, but I think he'll go along with the plan. "In the meantime, what about Butch?"

I didn't even think about his dog. "What about him?"

"He can't live here. Look at it. The place is too small for him."

"Couldn't you leave him at the dog kennel until you find a house?"

"No. I can't. I called to check up on him. He tried to escape so they have him caged up most of the time. That's not going to work. He needs room to run around. And a big backyard."

"I may be able to help." God, I can't believe I'm saying this. I can't believe I'm thinking this.

His head comes up at that. "How?"

"Butch can stay at my house. I have a big yard and Mama will be there during the week." She'd already agreed to supervise Kaylee while I'm at Brock's place. "Weekends, he can be with you."

"Your mom won't mind?"

"No. She won't. She'll already be watching Kaylee, and she loves dogs."

"Kaylee? Is that your daughter's name?"

Darn it. I shouldn't have let that slip out. "Yes."

Head down, he meanders around the living room, mulling things over, until he comes to a stop directly in front of me. "You sure it wouldn't be an imposition?"

I try hard not to breathe. "Positive."

Acceptance rolls over his face. "Then I guess that would work. Thank you. I'll spring him from the dog kennel and bring him by this weekend."

That can't happen. "No!"

"Why not?"

"I'm having a birthday party for Kaylee on Saturday. A bunch of giggling girls, a slumber party. It would not work."

"Next weekend then. Although I hate for Butch to stay at the kennel another week."

"Okay." Kaylee won't be there when he drops off Butch. She'll be at camp for two weeks. I'll have to hide all her photos before he comes by, though. "I'm glad we worked that out."

"Thanks, Eleanor. I really appreciate it." The relief in him is palpable. He was really worried about his dog. He never agreed to go incognito, though.

Baby steps, Eleanor. Rome wasn't built in a day. I'll need to figure out a way to convince him. In the meantime, we can do something about his things. "Want to finish unpacking?"

"Yeah."

"Great. You take the orgy room, and I'll finish up with the guest bedroom."

He props his hands on his hips. "You do realize you've been putting my things away in your room?"

I do now. "I was not going in the—"

"Orgy room?"

"That's right."

A lopsided smile pops up on his face. "Stick in the mud."

I answer with a grin of my own. "Pervert."

In the end he moves his things and his boxes into the orgy room which leaves me with little to unpack. Once done, I head out, happy with the way things are working out. With any luck at all, we'll sail right through this.

CHAPTER 9

Brock

a WEEK AFTER TRAINING CAMP ENDS, I head to the kennel to pick up my best bud. Going by the cleanliness of the place and the healthy-looking, happy dogs, the place is run professionally. So, no complaints there. But Butch being caged up for most of his day, even if it was for his own good, doesn't sit right with me.

As soon as he spots me, he does his wiggly-butt dance.

"Hey, bud, how you doing?"

"Woof."

"Yeah, I'm here to spring you. Did you miss me?" More rump-shaking tells me he does.

Rather than bring the spiffy Porsche Cayenne the Outlaws gave me, I drove my SUV which arrived at training camp, no worse for the wear, a couple of days ago. Not only does it have Butch's very own seatbelt, but he's familiar with its smell. So even though he's in a strange, new city, hopefully, he'll think of it as home. After settling his bill and thanking the staff, I snap him into the car's restraint and plug Ellie's address into the GPS. Soon we're flying down the highway on a bright, sunny day. With my best friend sitting in the back, slobbering all over the seat, everything's right as rain.

"They treat you good back there, bud?"

His gaze narrows with reproach. "Rawr."

"Yeah, I can see they starved you to death." He's actually gained a couple of pounds. No wonder. Except for two scheduled outings a day, he wasn't running around. But his coat's healthy and his eyes are bright, so the place did their job of keeping him healthy and well fed.

"Soon you'll have a new backyard to explore. With trees and squirrels." I have no idea if Ellie's backyard has such critters, or even trees, but it can't hurt to mention them. "You'll like that, boy, won't you?"

"Aaaaooooo." Yeah, he's happy to have been sprung. Or maybe he's just happy to be with me.

I fire up the audio and find his special song, "Who let the dogs out?" and soon, we're howling along with the tune.

Forty minutes later we arrive at Ellie's house which sits on a corner lot. Not big by any standards, but extremely well kept. The lawn's mowed, the hedge's manicured and the rows of flowers in front of her home bloom in profusion.

Holding tight to Butch's leash, I walk up the path to the front door. I barely have time to knock before the door swings open to reveal Ellie standing on the other side and an older version of the woman I knew as her mother next to her. Both are wearing aprons. The scent of something yummy hits me—apples if I'm not mistaken.

"Brock," Ellie's breathless voice surprises me. Did she sprint for the door? Or is it something else?

I nod to both of them. "Ellie. Mrs. Adams."

"It's Mrs. Jensen now, Brock, but please call me Ruth. Come in."

I wipe my feet on the welcome rug and turn to Butch. He's a pure breed pit bull, so he can appear a little intimidating. But I've trained him well. "Wipe your paws, bud."

Tongue hanging out, Butch swipes at the welcome mat. "Good boy."

Ellie smiles and Ruth outright laughs. "What a well-mannered dog."

"Thanks. He's very gentle." I reassure them. I don't want them thinking Butch is a threat of any kind.

"I can see that," Ruth says. "I made something for him. It contains eggs, peanut butter, and whole wheat. Is it okay if I give it to him?"

The tension I'd been holding eases out of me. If she's gone through the trouble of cooking for Butch, he's going to be all right. "He loves peanut butter."

She retreats to the kitchen and returns with a bone-shaped treat. As soon as he sees it, Butch's eyes light up.

"Sit," I command. When he does, I praise him. "Good boy."

She extends her hand with the treat. As if he knows he must be on his very best behavior, he very gingerly takes it from her fingers. But once it's in his mouth, two bites and it's gone.

"He loves it, thank you."

"We baked some apple pie. Would you like some?" Ellie says smiling.

All this time she's hung back, quietly observing Butch. Can't blame her. She has a young daughter. Before she lets Butch into her house, she has to make sure he's well behaved. But seemingly he's passed the test. Otherwise, she wouldn't be putting out the welcome mat.

"We can eat on the back porch while Butch checks out the yard."

"Yes, please." I'm not about to turn down that offer. The food at the Outlaws' facility is great, but nothing beats the taste of home cooking.

As soon as Ellie opens the door to the back porch, Butch makes a beeline for the huge oak tree in the back of the yard to baptize it.

"Just marking his territory," I say.

"Boys will be boys," she says with a grin.

"I have yet to lift my leg and pee on a woman." Standing in the screened-in porch with the sun dappling her face, she's breathtakingly beautiful. I ache to touch her, to feel the softness of her skin, but I can't do that. Not when she wants to keep things professional. She's made that perfectly clear this week at the condo.

"And thank God for that." Her smile reminds me of past happy times. Before I marked her and ruined our friendship forever. I want to return to those carefree days when we joked around. Well, I joked around. She was all business then, just as she was a week ago. Maybe it's not too late to be friends again. I can only hope.

"This is amazing," I say, glancing around.

With its white wicker love seat, two rocking chairs and chimes tinkling with the breeze, the wraparound porch reminds me of many southern homes. So do the white stools, the containers overflowing with pansies, and a fern that sits in a golden pot in the corner. The backyard itself is beyond spectacular. An array of blue, yellow and pink flowers grows wild next to the fence that separates their yard from the one next door. But the main attraction is definitely the oak tree from which a rope swing hangs.

"We like it," Ellie says, taking a seat on one of the chairs, while I park myself on the roomy two-seater.

Behind us, the door swings open and Ruth emerges with two slices of pie.

Ellie taps the rocker next to hers. "Join us, Mama."

"Can't. I have to keep my eye on the food, honey. Would you like some coffee, Brock?"

"Yes, please. I take it black."

"How about you, Eleanor?"

"No, thanks, Mama."

After Ruth brings my coffee, Ellie and I watch Butch who's busy exploring the yard. When a squirrel scurries across the grass, Butch races after it, hoping to catch him. But it's faster than him, and soon it's scampering up the majestic oak, leaving him literally barking up the tree.

"He's in heaven." I relax into the love seat. Butch's exactly where he should be, and so am I.

Ellie side glances me. "You were worried, weren't you?"

"Yes, I have to admit I was. I didn't know if he'd like the place, or if you would be okay with him. Butch is the closest thing I have to family."

"What about your father?"

"He passed away during my last year in college."

"I'm sorry. I didn't know."

It's no wonder she doesn't. I didn't make a big deal about it. When his lawyer called to tell me he'd died, I went home to bury him and came right back to school the next day. "Don't be. I hardly noticed. We were never close." I fork off another piece of the scrumptious dessert and savor the taste. "Your mother always made the best apple pies."

Taking the hint I want to drop the subject, she bites into her slice.

The scent of something delicious wafts in the air. Not apples. At least not anymore. "Whatever your mom is cooking, it smells great."

"Chicken pot pie. Most Sundays, she comes over with enough dinners to feed Kaylee and me for the entire week."

"She comes here and cooks?"

"Usually she brings home-made meals she's frozen for us. But this weekend Steve's at a convention in Boston. Since she needed to meet Butch, plus, of course, she wanted to see you again, she decided to fix the food here."

"That's nice. She's nice." I never once saw my mother in the kitchen. Heck, I barely saw her at all. She had staff who cooked, cleaned, and took care of me. When my nanny told me she'd passed away, I shrugged and continued playing with my toys. You can't grieve over what you've never known.

I polish off the rest of the pie and drink the last of the coffee while Butch runs around the yard, acquainting himself with the place. It suddenly occurs to me that sitting here next to Ellie is as close to heaven as I'll ever be. I swallow past the lump in my throat.

Her head turns in my direction, concern clear in her gaze. "You okay?"

"Yeah. Just a crumb."

Seeming to accept my explanation, her gaze swerves back to Butch. "You don't have to worry about the plants. None of them are poisonous."

"He won't eat them. He just likes to smell them." Now that I've gotten my emotions back under control, I go back to reassuring her about Butch. "In case you haven't picked up on it, he's pretty tame."

"I can see that." Her brown-eyed gaze glows with contentment. She's happy in her home, with her life. Much as I'd like to get closer, the last thing she needs is the bad boy who time and time again screwed up.

Not wanting to overstay my welcome, I come to my feet and grab our empty plates and my cup. "I better go."

"Already?"

Is that a wistful tone I hear? No. It can't be. She's just being polite, that's all. "I want to take Butch for a run in the park. I haven't seen him in forever."

"Of course." In one fluid move, she unfolds from the chair and stands. It's only now I notice she's not wearing any shoes. My imagination runs wild with images of Ellie naked on my bed while I bury myself inside her. I've never forgotten that one stormy night. Never forgotten the cinnamon scent of her throat, the sweet taste of her skin. Predictably, I get a hard-on.

"There's one close by with a dog run. Turner Park. Just up the street."

"Right." I gotta get out fast before she notices my erection. Or worse, her mother does. I walk to the kitchen, where Ruth is up to her elbows in dough, rest the plates and cup in the sink. "Thanks for the pie and coffee."

"You're welcome," Ruth says, rinsing her hands.

I push open the back porch door and yell, "Butch, come here, boy." When he reaches me, I snap the leash on him. He doesn't fight it. He knows the leash will lead to a walk.

With Ellie and Ruth trailing behind us, we head toward the front.

"I bought this dog food he likes. It's in the SUV. I'll drop it off when I bring him back. If that's all right."

Ellie nods. "Of course."

"We'll be here," Ruth adds.

I don't know how to bring up the subject, so I just come right out with it. "I'd like to pay you for the dog sitting."

Ellie jumps in with, "You don't have to."

Ruth's response is much stronger, "Absolutely not."

"Please. You're going through so much trouble."

"No trouble at all," Ruth says. "I love dogs. We had a Labrador

Retriever back home, but he passed away shortly before our move to Chicago. For one reason or another, we haven't adopted another one. It'll be fun to watch over Butch."

I have no doubt I'm leaving Butch in good hands. Not that I expected any less from Ellie or her mom. They were class acts then and are still so now. "Thank you. Nice seeing you again, Ruth. Thanks for the pie and coffee."

"Anytime." Something buzzes in the kitchen, and Ruth excuses herself to go attend to whatever it is.

I tell myself to get out fast. But a curl has fallen across Ellie's face. And the need to touch her is more than I can stand. Unable to help myself, I reach over and tuck it behind her ear. My hand languishes at the feel of her soft skin.

"Where's your daughter?" I ask. My voice is pure gravel.

"Computer camp." She sounds breathless again.

"She's smart, isn't she?"

She smiles from ear to ear. "Oh, yes." Clearly, she takes great pride in her child.

I search around the living room for a photo of her kid, but there isn't one. "How old is she again?"

"Tw-ten." Her face flushes as my fingers drift down her throat. Before I have time to pull her to me and kiss her the way I'm aching to, her phone rings. She retrieves it from her apron pocket. "It's her. I have to take it."

That's my cue to leave. "Thanks again. I'll bring him back in a couple of hours."

She clutches the cell to her chest as if she's trying to hold her daughter close. "Enjoy your afternoon with him."

"I will."

Once the door has closed, I don't leave right away, but stand on her front porch, gazing at her house, wishing for something that can never be.

CHAPTER 10

Eleanor

MAMA EMERGES FROM THE KITCHEN, wiping her hands on her apron. The look on her face tells me it's not cooking she has in mind. "Honey, you have to tell him about Kaylee."

"That's not happening, Mama."

"She's his daughter. He has a right to know."

"He doesn't want a daughter, or a son, for that matter."

"How do you know?"

"He told me at the Outlaws' banquet. He said how glad he was he hadn't gotten me pregnant. That it would have been a disaster." My heart aches from that memory.

"Well, of course, he would have felt that way at the time. He was seventeen, only a kid. But he's a grown man now. He probably feels different about a child."

"No. He doesn't. He lives, breathes, and eats football. He barely has enough time for Butch, and you saw how much he loves his dog. How much time do you think he'd have for a kid he never wanted and didn't know he had?"

"That's not the point, and you know it."

Yeah, I know. The point is he is Kaylee's father, and he needs to know. But how can I bring myself to tell him? He still craves his party lifestyle. What if he got visitation rights? Where exactly would he take her? To a place where his orgy room reigned front and center? I shudder to think of Kaylee wandering around his house and finding that bed, those "toys." Such a thing might scar her for life. I can't tell Mama about that room, so voicing those reasons is not happening. I take another approach.

"How am I supposed to explain him to Kaylee, Mama?" When Kaylee turned four, she asked me about her father. I told her he wasn't around. Four years later, when she'd been old enough to understand, I'd explained her father hadn't been interested in being a daddy, but that she had a mommy, a grandma, and grandpa who loved her dearly. She'd felt bad for a time, but eventually she'd rebounded. It had helped that her best friend didn't have a father in the picture either.

Many of her friends here in Chicago have single mothers as well, so being a kid with a missing father's no big deal. And she has had a father figure in Steve, Mama's husband. He's always been there for her —birthday parties, family celebrations, holidays. Just this year, he'd gone to a father-daughter dance with her. I don't think she's minded the lack of a dad. But I honestly don't know how she feels deep down inside. It's something we don't talk about.

With Brock back in my life, though, I can no longer ignore the reality of him. But the thought of explaining him to Kaylee is more than I can deal with. So the easy answer is I don't. What she doesn't know won't hurt her.

"She's smart, Eleanor. If you sit her down and explain your reasoning, yes, she'll be angry at first. But eventually, she will forgive you. She loves you too much to resent you for long. You need to tell him first, though. You want to know exactly where he stands before you talk to Kaylee."

"Mama, you're the wisest woman I know, but this time you're wrong."

She shakes her head. "You're plumb scared, that's what you are."

I hitch up my chin. "Scared of what?"

"Scared you'll lose your daughter. Most of all, you're petrified you'll lose Kaylee to him."

"Why would I? She hates football."

"Football has nothing to do with it. He's her father. She needs to know, and so does he."

"No."

She whooshes out a hard breath. "You've always been stubborn. How are you going to manage when he picks up or drops off Butch and she's here?"

"She won't be. First off, she's at camp for two weeks. After she comes home, I'll take her to the movies or the art museum or shopping for school clothes when he comes by."

She folds her hands in front of her. "And I guess it'll be me waiting for him?"

"You don't mind, Mama, do you?" I hate to ask so much of her, when I've already done it so many times. But I'd do anything to keep Brock and Kaylee from ever meeting.

"Of course not. But—"

"Thank you." I hug and kiss her before she can say something else. "It should only be for a couple of weekends. He'll find a house soon enough, and then Butch will be gone."

She glances at me with sad eyes. "Eleanor, I know you mean well, but it's not going to work, honey. Things have a way of coming out."

"I'll make it work." After all, I have an entire week to come up with a plan of action for Kaylee and me.

But as it often happens, fate intervenes. What seemed challenging becomes downright daunting when I get a phone call from Kaylee's summer camp. She's seriously sprained an ankle and needs to come home.

I rush to northwest Illinois where Camp Kikamoo is located. I'd specifically chosen the place because it was away from civilization. With Kaylee growing up in urban settings, I wanted her to experience the outdoors. She hadn't been too gung-ho about it until I mentioned she'd also be learning computer programming. Then she'd been rarin' to go.

When I arrive, the camp director welcomes me. After apologizing profusely for Kaylee's injury, he personally escorts me to the medical suite. When I spot Kaylee sitting on a bed with her ankle in an air cast, I almost lose it. She's being a brave little soldier, but going by her quivering lip, she's hurting.

As carefully as I can, I hug her. "Sweetheart, I'm so sorry this happened to you. How are you feeling?"

She chokes back a sob. "It hurts, Mom."

The man standing next to us seems too young to be a doctor, but that's exactly what he is.

After the camp director introduces him, he pulls me aside, probably so Kaylee can't overhear our conversation.

"Is it serious? Her injury?" I ask.

"We took her to the clinic in town where we took an X-ray. As far as I can tell, it's a simple sprain. But she may have strained a ligament. Her doctor will probably order an MRI to either confirm or rule it out."

"Why didn't you perform that procedure?"

"The clinic doesn't have the equipment. It's a small town."

"Mom. I want to go home."

A quick peek at her tells me the faster we get on the road the better, but not before I finish with the doctor. "In a moment, honey." I turn back to the physician. "Has she been given anything for the pain?"

"Ibuprofen. 200 milligrams." He nods toward Kaylee. "We just gave her a dose, so she'll be fine on the way home. She'll need to take it three times a day for the next seventy-two hours or so, and she'll also need to rest her ankle and keep it elevated at all times. I recommend you have her visit her doctor tomorrow or no later than the next day. He can treat her going forward."

The thought of keeping Kaylee in bed or the couch immobile is not going to be easy. But it's got to be done. Hopefully, not for long. "How long will her foot remain in a cast?"

"Her doctor would know the best time to remove it. It could be as little as a couple of days. But it could be longer as well."

No help there. "Okay. Thank you, doctor."

The camp director and the medic escort us back to my car while a camp counselor brings up the rear with Kaylee's duffle bag. Before we head off, I call Mama to give her a status report. She's been worried sick ever since I got the call.

"Do you want to stop and get something to eat?" I ask Kaylee once we get on the road. The drive home is at least three hours, and she might be hungry. "We can go to a drive-through, if you wish." I'm not a fan of fast food, but needs must.

"No, Mama. I just want to go home."

"Okay, sweetheart."

"So other than the sprained ankle, did you get to enjoy camp?"

Her head spins toward me. "It was horrible, Mom. I thought I was going to learn computer programming all the time. We did for two days, but then they dragged us out of bed at six. Six, mom! The birds weren't even up yet. And they made us climb this humongous hill."

The hill she's talking about did not look that big in the photos. But then, I wasn't there.

"Coming down, I tripped over a stupid rock and twisted my ankle. Now the rest of my summer's ruined. I'll be hobbling on these dumb crutches and this stupid boot for weeks." She's not normally a drama queen, but she is hurting, so it makes sense for her to vent her feelings.

"Now, honey, that's not what the doctor said. The boot might come off in a couple of days."

"I hope you're getting your money back, because that camp seriously sucked."

"The camp director did mention I'd get a partial refund." Makes sense since she didn't stay there for the entire two weeks. She barely made it through four days. The GPS announces another turn ahead. Thank God it's summer and still daylight because I would not want to be on these back roads late at night. When I finally reach the main road, I breathe an easy sigh. I'll have to fight the Chicago congestion when we get closer to the city, but for now, the traffic's manageable.

The tension seems to drain out of Kaylee as she spends the rest of the drive on her cell texting with her friends.

"Meghan says 'Hi'. She wants to know when she can come over."

"Let's wait and see, honey. You're supposed to be getting some rest, and I'll have to get you into your doctor's tomorrow. Maybe Saturday?"

"Okay." Her fingers fly on her cell some more. At least there's nothing wrong with them. Thank God.

After what seems like forever, we finally pull into the garage. A frenzied scratching on the door that leads to the kitchen catches Kaylee's attention. Her gaze bounces to me, eyes wide open. "What's that?"

With all my attention focused on Kaylee's injury, I'd forgotten to tell her about Brock's dog. "Butch."

"Who's Butch?"

Resigned to what's coming, I turn off the ignition. "You remember Brock Parker? The football player my firm represents?"

"Yes."

"Well, his dog's staying with us."

"What? Why?" We've never had a dog, but Mama did. So Kaylee's familiar with them. Of course, Mama's was a Labrador Retriever who mainly sat around and scarfed up food. Butch is a lot more active, as I've found out during the last few days. He loves to play catch and tug-o-rope with the toys Brock dropped off for him. But with Kaylee being on crutches, it could be a recipe for disaster.

"Butch needed a place where he could run free. Apparently, he didn't get much of a chance at the dog kennel. And since we have a nice big backyard, I offered to take him temporarily."

"What kind of a dog is he? He sounds . . . big."

No wonder she thinks that. Butch's scratching has turned into mad howls.

"He's a Pit Bull."

"You wouldn't let me have a Yorkie because it'd be too much trouble. But now you bring a Pit Bull into the house. Those things are huge."

"He's really gentle, honey."

"Mom. I'm on crutches. I'll trip over him."

"You're supposed to rest in bed, remember."

"What if I have to go to the bathroom?" The one full bath in the house can only be reached from the hallway. So she might run into Butch when she has to go.

"If he becomes a problem, I'll get a doggie gate. But grandma will make sure he doesn't stray in your direction."

"Grandma's here?" For the first time, her face lights up. Doesn't surprise me. She's always had a special relationship with her grandmother.

"Yes. She's watching him. It's only for a little while. I promise." I walk to the passenger side and help her to her feet. "Stay here. Let me make sure Butch is secured."

But when I open the door a smidge, Butch jams his nose into the opening and bellows a couple of big breaths.

"Mama?" Where can she be? "Can you leash Butch?"

I wait patiently until I hear her hurried steps. "Sorry, honey. Nature called." She snaps the leash on Butch and reels him back, but Butch is super strong and he's not obeying her.

Oh, please God, let him go with Mama. I don't want to have to call Brock and tell him this is not working out.

"Butch. Sit," Mama commands.

Thankfully, he does.

"It's okay to open the door, Eleanor. I have him."

I slice it open until the space is big enough to walk through. And then I hurry back to Kaylee and help her maneuver the steps to the garage door.

As soon as Butch sees her, he whines, straining at the leash.

"Don't you dare jump on me, dog." Kaylee shoots him a death glare.

As if by magic, Butch plops his entire massive body on the floor. Well, I'll be darned. Reckon he knows Kaylee's no one to mess with.

"How are you, sweetheart?" Mama asks, embracing Kaylee with her one free arm.

"Been better, Grandma." Kaylee buzzes Mama's cheek. "Thanks for asking."

"Why don't we go to your room, so you can get off your feet," I say. The sooner she's on the bed, the sooner she can rest that ankle.

"Okay."

Once I have her settled, I retrieve her duffel bag and bring it to her room. "You want me to unpack your things?"

"Okay." She must be in pain when she's allowing me to go through her clothes.

After I'm done, I turn to her. "Does it hurt?"

"A little."

"The doctor said you could take ibuprofen, right?"

Her mouth scrunches. "I'm not doing drugs." She's always been careful about what she ingests. So it stands to reason she wouldn't want to take something that might harm her.

"Sweetheart, they're not drugs." Well, technically, they are. But that's not what she means. "They're sold over the counter. Anyone can buy them. And you already took them at camp."

"Yeah, the doctor caught me at a weak moment."

"Honey, you don't wish to be in pain, do you, plus they'll help you heal faster. Isn't that what you want?"

She shrugs. "I guess."

A scratch at the door interrupts us and she lets out a long, suffering sigh. "It's that beast."

"He's probably worried about you." One thing about Butch. He has a sixth sense. Earlier in the week, I'd made a pit stop to deliver groceries to Mama. The incipient sinus headache that had skirted around the edges all day had become full-blown. After I'd taken my medicine and laid down on the couch for a few, he hadn't left my side until it was gone.

"How can he be? He just met me."

"He has a big heart, honey. Do you want me to let him in?" Sooner or later, she'll have to make peace with him. If she doesn't, he'll have to go. And I'd really hate for that to happen.

"Okay, but he can't climb on the bed."

"I agree."

After I slice open the door, Butch advances into the room. He must know he has to be on his best behavior because he practically crawls in on all fours.

"There. You've seen me. I'm fine. Now go away."

Rather than leave, Butch lies down on the rug next to her bed.

"I think he wants to stay, sweetheart."

Her gaze cuts to me. "Whose room is it anyway?"

"Yours, honey. He won't hurt you. He just wants to keep you company."

"He better not eat something. Meghan's dog ate the couch."

"Meghan's dog is a Newfoundland, as big as their house. And Butch is very well behaved. Aren't you, boy?"

"Woof."

Kaylee's lips twist. "He's barking."

"That's the way he talks."

She doesn't appear to be the least convinced.

"He's really sweet. Wait and see. You'll like him. I'll feel better knowing he's watching over you, especially when I'm not around."

Kaylee stops the pity party and her head jerks up. "Not around? Are you going somewhere?"

I'll need to stick close to the truth; otherwise, she'll smell a rat. "I have a work assignment which means I'll be gone Monday through Friday. It should only be for a couple of weeks."

"That seriously sucks, Mom. I need you."

"Grandma will be here to watch over you, and I'll be home on weekends. That's not so bad, is it?"

Right on cue, Mama knocks on the door. "Hello, sweetheart. How are you feeling?"

She pouts. "It hurts, grandma."

"Well, I have something that will make you feel a whole lot better. Sweet tea and some peach pie."

Mama settles the tray on Kaylee's lap.

"Thank you, Grandma."

Mama drops a kiss on Kaylee's forehead. "Anytime, sweetheart."

I wait only long enough for her to take a bite of the pie and a sip of the tea before asking, "How about you take that ibuprofen now?"

"Okay. If you insist," she mumbles through a bite of the pie.

"Woof."

"See? Even Butch approves."

She side eyes him when she swallows the ibuprofen, but she doesn't protest.

When she's done with the food and drink, I carry the tray back to the kitchen where Mama's cleaning up. "I'm going to stay the night, Mama. I'll sleep on the couch."

Mama props one hand on her hip. "No, you're not."

"Kaylee needs me."

"Chances are she only has a sprain. And all she needs is to rest and elevate her leg. If she needs anything else, I can handle it."

"I'm staying and that's that."

"Honey, she'll survive. And you need to do your job."

"Not tonight, I don't. My daughter needs me."

"Hmph." She turns back to the kitchen. "Stubborn as always."

"Yes, ma'am."

Done wiping the counter, she swivels back to me. "Did you get something to eat?"

"No. Kaylee wasn't hungry."

She points to the stool next to the kitchen island. "Then sit, and I'll fix you a plate."

"Thanks, Mama. Kaylee might want some as well. Let me check." That peach pie is certainly not going to tide her over until morning. But when I peek into her room, I find her fast asleep, Butch right where I left him on the rug next to her bed. "Good boy."

He softly thumps his tail on the floor as he gazes at me with his soft, brown eyes.

I lean down and pat his head. "You take good care of her while I'm gone."

His low "woof" seems to say, "Don't worry. I got this."

Now if his master were only this compliant.

CHAPTER 11

Brock

A WEEK OF LIVING WITH ELLIE is a special kind of hell. How could I have thought I could handle this arrangement? When I spotted her at O'Hare she'd knocked me for a loop, and at the Hilton, she'd taken my breath away. But when I bared my soul in my hotel room, she'd run away. And, of course, now she thinks I was playing her. Mainly because I practically told her, even though that's the farthest from the truth. So I can't blame her for keeping her distance.

I told myself I could deal with it. After all, it would only be for a couple of weeks. But seeing her, smelling her, hearing her hum some tune while she drifts around the kitchen is driving me insane. I should have nixed the plan, but, damn it, my future's riding on it. So, whether I like it or not I'm stuck here, slowly going insane.

She has no clue how hot she is. Which is pretty much par for the course. She was pretty oblivious in high school as well. Not that I noticed at first. After all, we ran with different crowds. Me with the jocks; her with the nerds. But when she became my tutor, everything changed. Everything about her turned me on. The dark-rimmed glasses that shaded her luminous eyes. The long mahogany hair that fell across her face. The soft, pink lips that made me want to kiss her until she begged me to stop.

Somehow, I'd managed to hide my attraction, until that stormy night when I couldn't stop myself from putting my hands on her. And now years later, she's turned me inside out again. I thought I could deal with it. But I just can't. I may be older, but not wiser, at least as far as my raging hunger for her is concerned.

Hopefully, I won't have to live in this torture chamber much longer. Ellie's realtor has lined up a couple of ready-to-move-in houses for me to check out on my day off. With any luck, I can do a quick close and move in within a couple of weeks. In the meantime, Butch is happily chasing squirrels up the tree in Ellie's backyard. So everything's under control. Except when I'm around her and sporting a permanent hard-on.

Last night, I'd gotten a reprieve when she hadn't come home. But, of course, I kept wondering where she'd gone. Who she'd been with. Hell. I can't win. Damned if she's here. Damned if she's not.

I open the front door to find her in the kitchen making dinner. She doesn't appear her usual cheerful self. Maybe this crazy arrangement is wearing her down too. Or maybe, just maybe she misses her boyfriend. She never said she had a man in her life. But I can't believe a woman as gorgeous as her doesn't have a lover. Even with a young daughter, she should find time to date.

"You're here," I say.

"Where else would I be?"

"You didn't come home last night."

Her mouth goes tight-lipped. "I had somewhere else to be. And this is not my home."

Don't ask. You're not her keeper. "Where were you?"

She turns off the fire on the stove and glares at me. "None of your business, Brock."

"None of my business?"

"Yes. My life is my life. And you have nothing to do with it."

"Fine. I'll be in my room."

All I get back is silence. Not even a "Good Night."

Just as well she stopped talking to me. With only two days before the Detroit game, I need to study their defense strategy. If I can get Ellie off my mind, that is. She's looking downright fuckable in a t-shirt and a pair of shorts that come down mid-thigh and toenails painted fire-engine red. God, how pathetic am I to be turned on by her damned toes?

As soon as I reach my room, I strip and toss my clothes in the hamper before heading for the shower. I don't need to get clean. I'd done that at the compound. But to make it through the night, I'm going to need a hand job. Otherwise, I'll spend the night tossing and turning with a serious case of blue balls. But the quick release does nothing for me. Frustrated, I yank my hair, almost tearing off chunks by the roots. I need to find a new place to live. Fast.

Butt naked, I slip into bed and grab my iPad to focus on the game tapes. Detroit's tackle is the fucking size of a mountain, and a mean son of a bitch. Not only that, he's fast and he'll be rushing from my left side. Since I don't want my head torn off anytime soon, he'll need to be double teamed. I'm making notes on tactics when a faint sound reaches me. Someone's rapping on the condo's front door. Who the hell could it be? Except for Marty, no one knows where we live. I crack open my bedroom door and listen in.

"Hi there."

I've heard that voice before. The turd.

"Hello, Mr. Sheffield." Why did she go and answer the knock? She could have ignored the idiot.

"It's Friday."

"I know. It comes around every week."

Laughter. "Did you forget my invite?"

"No. I didn't forget."

"We have a sex swing." He says it sing-songy, like that's supposed to tempt her.

"Oh?"

"And a latex mattress."

"Ooookay." She probably has no idea what that means.

"A member of our club brought back an aphrodisiac oil from Brazil. When applied properly, she swears it'll give you the Big O in three minutes or less."

"How very interesting."

Having heard enough from this slug, I stomp to the living room and swing the front door open wide. "I can make her come in two."

"Oh, my." Warren's eyes widen and the corners of his lips tick up. The little turd swings both ways, does he?

"Martha's not interested. So scram." Reaching over Ellie's head, I slam shut the door.

She whirls around and slaps my bare chest. "You idiot!"

"What?"

"He saw you. In *my* apartment. What is he going to think?"

"That I'm playing hide the salami with you. What's the big deal?"

"What's the big deal? He knows about *your* orgy bed, *your* toys. And now he's seen *you*. How long do you think it'll take him to spread the news that the Outlaws' new quarterback is living in a den of sin?"

"Den of sin?" I croak. "I'm living the life of a fucking monk. Besides, he won't tell. If that idiot knows anything about football, I'll eat my shorts."

Her gaze cuts down to my groin, and her eyes grow wide. No wonder. I'm naked and sporting a super-sized hard-on. "Oh, wow."

Damn if my cock doesn't grow bigger.

Face flushed beet red, she says, "Maybe you should put something on."

"This is my place, and I'll walk around any damn way I please."

She crosses her arms and shoots me a death glare. "I'm living here too, and I'd appreciate a little modesty."

"I'm going back to bed. Care to join me?"

"No."

"See?" I spread my arms wide as I walk backward. "A monk. That's what I fucking am." I slam the bedroom door behind me. Jaysus. I don't know how long I can take this.

By the time I leave in the morning, she's gone. Good. Last thing I want is to see Ellie in those skimpy shorts. It's Saturday, which means she'll spend the entire weekend with her kid. Not that I'll get time to enjoy the solitude. The team's flying off to Detroit this afternoon.

After a light workout at the Outlaws' compound, the team heads to the airport. In the mood I'm in, I really don't want to talk to anyone. I head for the back of the bus and stare out of the window, hoping whoever sits next to me gets the hint. But no such luck.

Trevor plops his six seven frame next to me. "Not looking too good there, Parker. You're not coming down with something, are you, because we need you in tip-top shape?"

He's right. I look like crap all right. The dark circles under my eyes clear evidence of my tossing and turning all night. "Nope. Right as rain. I've been staying up late studying Detroit's defense, that's all." It's the truth. I have.

"Well, you better get a good sleep tonight. Tomorrow's game day."

"Sure thing." As it turns out, that's exactly what I do. Not having the temptation of Ellie sleeping in the next room, I zonk out as soon as my head hits the pillow.

After breakfast the next morning, we head for the Detroit stadium. Since this is the first game of the pre-season, I'm rarin' to go. Coach puts me in for the first half, and I throw for three touchdowns and run in one. The final score is 44-12. Elated does not begin to describe me. Now that we've won the first game, the monkey's off my back. I can win with this team too.

Back in the locker room, a jubilant Trevor slaps me on the back. "Man, you were on fire out there. Save some for the regular season, will ya?"

"Will do." Pretty pleased with myself, I'm eager to celebrate. Alone. After we land in Chicago, I pick up a supreme pizza and a six-pack of cold brews on the way home. Without Ellie there, I can well and truly kick back. But when I walk into my place, she's there in the living room. Not cooking, not cleaning, not doing anything but sitting on the couch, wearing another damn pair of skimpy shorts and a halter top.

All worried eyes, she jumps to her feet. "Hi." She sounds tentative, as if she's unsure of my greeting. As well she should be.

Her being here is not good. I'm jazzed from our win. Adrenaline's kicking through my veins. I need to handle my shit, before I do something I'll regret like lay her on the couch and fuck her brains out. I walk to the kitchen and drop the pizza and beer on the counter to get myself under control. Once I'm reasonably sure I won't tear her clothes off and bend her over the kitchen chair, I turn around. "What are you doing here, Ellie?"

"I came to apologize."

"For what?" I bark out.

"For Friday. I'm sorry I yelled. I was upset about . . . something. And I let my temper get the better of me."

"What were you upset about?"

"It's personal."

"Fine. Apology accepted. Good night." Abandoning my dinner and beer on the counter, I head toward the bedroom. Anything not to see her, smell her, heck, watch her breathe.

I barely make it two steps past her when she says, "You don't sound like you've accepted my apology."

Whirling back, I bark out, "What the hell do you want from me, Ellie?"

She spreads her hands wide. "I don't know. Something more than goodnight, I guess."

"Such as?"

"Honesty. Sincerity."

She refuses to tell me what she was doing Thursday night and she wants *me* to spill my guts? Fine. I strut forward until I'm looming over her. "You want honesty? You want sincerity?"

"Y-Yes." She doesn't sound so sure anymore.

But I'm fucking tired of holding back, of pretending, of living a celibate life. Strutting forward, I back her up until she's flush against the wall. "How about this for honesty? I want to fuck you. I want to taste that sweet spot between your legs. And then I want to ride you all night long until you cry for me to stop. Is that honest enough for you?"

Her eyes grow wide. She really has no idea how much I fucking want her.

She swallows hard, but then her chin comes up, challenging me, questioning my motives. "That's just lust talking."

I slap my right hand on the wall. "Damn right it's lust."

"Well, I'm sure you can find some bimbo who'll jump at the chance to go to bed with you. Just drop in at the nearest bar. I believe there's one at the corner."

"And there's the rub, darling." I lean forward to breathe in the sweet intoxicating scent of her, and my cock comes to life. "You're the only one I want."

"Yeah. Right." Her mouth twists with derision.

"You don't believe me." I wind one of her curls around my fingers, play with it, like I want to play with her.

"No, I don't." That stubborn chin does things to me.

"Then answer this. Why didn't I bring someone home tonight, huh? I could have easily done what you said."

"You're probably exhausted after the game."

"Only played the first half; had plenty of time to recuperate. You want to know why the only things I brought home were pizza and beer?"

"No. I don't." She turns her face away from me.

But she's not getting away from me that easily. She's not hiding from me anymore. I gently grab her chin and swing it right back to me. "Bullshit. You're dying to know."

"Fine. I'll bite. Why?"

"Because you're the only woman I want. The only one I need." I lean forward and lick the throbbing vein on her neck. God. The taste of her.

"Don't do that." She pushes against my chest as if she wants me to stop. But there's no stopping me. Not anymore. I've burned for her for too long.

I prop my left hand on her other side and cage her in. We're doing this my way.

She tries to move past my arm, but I won't budge. "Please let me go." She begs.

"Not in a million years."

Her gaze finds me, pleads with me. "I can't. We can't."

"Oh, darling, of course we can." I breathe in the intoxicating scent of her. Honeydew, honey melon, honey . . . something. Damn if I don't grow harder. "You want me. You know you do."

"I don't."

She's lying, and I can prove it. I play with her nipples until her breath comes out in short bursts. I rub my palm across her wet pussy until she pushes back against my hand. "Ahhhh."

She can deny it all she wants, but her body's telling a different tale. I curl my lips into a triumphant smile. "See?"

Trembling, she says, "Please, Brock, back off."

Feeling generous, I give her just enough room to breathe.

She takes in big noisy gulps, as if she can't quite get enough air into her lungs.

Why she's denying herself, denying us is beyond me. "Don't you miss having a man between your legs, Ellie?"

Still breathing hard, she licks her lips. "N-no."

My nostrils flare.

"I d-don't want you."

Oh, she wants me all right, and everything I can give her. But maybe, just maybe, she doesn't want to want me. Because she's got somebody else. "Do you have another man in your life? Is that where you were on Thursday? Did he fuck you?"

She stops breathing hard long enough to glare at me. "You're a pig."

That doesn't answer my question. But I don't give a fuck. Not when she can't hide her attraction for me. The heat coming off her, the pheromones, the dilated pupils, her tight little nipples beneath her top. All clear signs of desire. I don't care if she has another man in her life. She's mine. And I'm going to prove it to her once and for all. "Maybe, but you want me."

"No."

"That's the third time you've denied me. Aren't you tired of lying, Ellie?"

"I'm not lying."

I take my time studying her. She's shaking. Clear proof she desires me? Or evidence she's scared of me? God. How did we get to this point? I'll be damned if I force her to do something she doesn't want. Disgusted with myself, I step back, giving her the space she needs. "Leave, Ellie. Go on. Get out of here." I pick up the duffel and trudge toward my bedroom before I do something we'll both regret.

Behind me, the front door closes as she makes her get away. Well, that's it. She's gone. And she won't be back. Fine. I lived without her for close to thirteen years. I can live without her again. Even if it kills me.

CHAPTER 12

Eleanor

I RUN TO THE ELEVATOR as if all the hounds of hell were chasing me. When I get there, I push the down button, once, twice, three times. Not that it will make it come any faster. I pace back and forth so I won't have time to think. So I won't have time for regrets. But it doesn't do any good. My thoughts hound me anyway.

I play back what just happened. Brock pushing me against the wall, touching me, demanding I admit my need for him. Time and again I denied him, and time and again my body made a liar out of me. Every day we've lived together, I've fought against my desire for Brock. I want him plain and simple. Always have. Always will. But I can't succumb to this madness. It would destroy my career if anybody found out.

"But he's not really your client." The devil on my shoulder whispers. "He's Marty's."

"Semantics, Eleanor," my professional self roars back. "He's the agency's client and sex with him is strictly *verboten*."

So what if it's forbidden? Who'd know? He wouldn't tell, and I'd take that secret to the grave. Would it be so wrong to go to bed with him? To enjoy each other for one night? So we'd both get what we want?

"What about me?" my dignity demands. "Regardless of what he said, he doesn't want *you*. He wants only what you can give him. Sex."

So what? Don't I want the same thing? To get as much pleasure from him? After all, what's good for the goose is good for the gander.

The car arrives, and the doors slide open. Inside, a woman glances at me expectantly. Thing is, I can't make myself climb in.

"Are you coming?" she asks.

"No. I-I forgot something."

The doors close and the elevator zooms off, taking with it my last chance of salvation. But then, I never said I was a saint.

I shut down the voices in my head and retread the path to perdition. Along the way, I figure out just what to say should Brock ask. Which he won't. More than likely, he'll just pick me up and throw me on the bed. And I'll love every second of whatever he does to me. Without further thought, I drive the key into the lock, rush in, knock on his bedroom door. "Brock?"

When there's no answer, I take a deep breath and step inside the den of sin. He's not there, but the water's running in the bathroom. He must be taking a shower. The reprieve gives me time to reconsider. He doesn't know I'm here. I still have a chance to leave. To save myself from this colossal mistake.

I remain rooted to the spot.

The water shuts off. An eternity later, Brock strolls into the bedroom, towel slung around his neck, wearing only his skin. And what gorgeous skin it is. Well-muscled chest, brawny arms, massive legs. Rampant cock. He's hard and getting harder. But then, why wouldn't he? I'm staring at it like it's manna from heaven, and I've been starving for far too long.

He strides forward, like a feral creature stalking his helpless prey. But then, isn't that exactly what I am? Helpless. God knows, I have no defenses when it comes to him. I might as well run up the white flag of surrender.

But there's something wrong. He's upset I'm here. His gaze tells me so. "Did you forget something?" he asks.

My mind. I lost it over you. But I can't say that. He already has the advantage. I can't hand him any more ammunition. I have to take another tack. Clutching my hands in front of me, I adopt my most businesslike tone. "I've reconsidered our situation."

He arches a brow. "What situation is that?"

"You're a man. I'm a woman. We're living in the same space."

He folds his arms across his chest and widens his stance. "Go on. I'm listening."

Somebody should paint him like that. He is so unbelievably beautiful. Eight-pack abs, sculpted pecs, massive thighs. And a treasure trail that travels down to the most masculine part of him. The one that's telegraphing in no uncertain terms what it wants. "You have . . . certain needs. And as busy as you are, you haven't had a chance to . . . satisfy them."

He doesn't say anything. His mouth is one rigid slash.

"So, I thought." God. This is a lot harder than I thought it would be.

"You thought?" he prompts.

"You scratch my back. I'll scratch yours." The words rush out of me.

His brow wrinkles. "What's that supposed to mean?"

Blowing out a breath, I say, "We have sex."

His gaze narrows. "Why?"

"I just told you. You, me"—I point to him and me—"we have certain needs."

"Ahh, so it's *we* now. Thanks for the clarification."

"You're welcome." This is the weirdest conversation I've ever had about sex. Not that I've had many.

"So did these certain "needs"—he freakin' air-quotes them—"suddenly surface in the last ten minutes."

"Yes. No."

"Which is it? Yes or no?"

I cock my hip and drop my fist on it. Honestly. What is wrong with him? He should have picked me up and thrown me on the bed by now. "No. They were always there."

"Ahhh. When did you realize they were "there"?" Air-quotes. Again. I'm going to kill him.

"At the elevator."

"Not before?"

"No."

"And you want me now?"

"Yes."

"But not before?"

"Yes. No."

I forget to breathe while he tilts his head and studies me for what seems like forever. "Sorry. This is not going to work out." He turns and walks away.

I race after him and somehow manage to plant myself in front of him. "Why?"

Anger flashes in his eyes. I was wrong. He's not upset; he's furious. He steps forward to tower over me. "When I fuck a woman, it's because she wants me all the time, not when it's convenient to her."

My breath hitches. He's punishing me for denying him. But he's also punishing himself. Because he wants me. Badly. His erection is living proof. He won't give in easily, though. Not unless I give him a reason to. And it starts with speaking the truth. "I do want you all the time, Brock."

"Yeah? Fucking prove it."

"How?"

"Get naked. Right now."

"I thought you'd want to strip me." My words are a mere whisper.

"Not this time." He struts toward the bed and, face up, he spread eagles his powerful body on it. "Put on a good show."

Bastard. I should walk out right now. Leave him like that, hard and aching. But I don't. I want him too much. When I reach for my shorts, he stops me. "Nuh-uh. Start with your top. I want to see your tits."

I don't know how; I don't know when. But he's going to pay for this. The halter top snaps in the front. Wanting to get this humiliation over as soon as possible, I attack it with zest.

"Nuh-uh. Slowly. Like this." His hand goes to his cock and he pumps it at a glacial pace.

My eyes practically fall out of my head. I've never seen a more beautiful thing than Brock pleasuring himself.

While his hand strokes his shaft, I free the prongs one at a time. When the last one's done, I shrug and the top lands at my feet.

A drop of dew eases out from the crown of his cock. I want to take him in my mouth, suck him, lick him. But I can't do that. At least not until he's done torturing me.

"Cup your breasts, Ellie. Play with them."

My sex life has been pretty rudimentary. Almost nonexistent fore-play followed by basic sex. Nothing like what he's demanding of me. But if he wants a slow striptease, that's exactly what he's going to get.

My way.

With the day as hot as it's been, I'd tied back my hair. Reaching up, I rip off the band, let it dangle from my fingers. Once I have his full attention, I rub it across my nipples. The tips perk up, and I roll back my head and moan. "Ohhhhh."

No longer concerned with his cock, he sits up, his eyes glued to my breasts. Done with the first act, I snap the band, before slowly rubbing it across my pussy. This time the moan's real. Oh, dear God. Who knew this would feel so damn good.

He's panting. His cock's grown longer, thicker. How is that even possible?

I toss the band to the floor and move on to act two. While slowly undulating my hips, I slip down my shorts. Right, left. Right again.

He gulps. Hard. A lot more moisture leaks from his cock.

I kick out of my shorts, leaving me in nothing but my bikini panties. Turning to the side, I raise the hem and flash him a sneak peek of my ass.

"Fuuuuucccccck."

With my back to him, I grin. I take good care of that ass. I run, do squats. I know it looks good.

"Turn around, Ellie." His voice's pure gravel.

I do as he says, but when he reaches for me, I dance away.

"Ellie." His brows thunder down. "Come here."

"Nuh-uh." Two can play at this game, stud.

I slowly strip off my panties, revealing my pussy an inch at a time. When it's bared for him to see, I shimmy the panties down, kick them to the side.

"Ellie," he grits out. "Come the fuck here."

I roll a finger over my lips, suck it into my mouth, pull it out. Wet and shiny, it gleams in the muted light of the room. I slick the finger down my throat, through the valley between my breasts, roll it around my belly button, and skim my way down to my clit.

But before I get there, he grabs my hips and pulls me on top of him. "Witch."

"We going to have sex now, Brock?" I ask in my most innocent voice.

"You better believe it."

"Ooooh. Can't wait." He's going to topsy-turvy us and drive into me, I just know it. As wet as I am, I don't need any foreplay. I just need him in me. Right now.

But to my surprise, he doesn't. Instead, he brushes a lock off my face. "You walked willingly into my den of sin, Ellie Adams."

Yes, I did.

"I'm keeping you."

I wiggle my pussy against his cock, so he knows I'm fully on board with his plan.

His lips quirk into that take-no-prisoners, pirate smile I know so well. But his gaze softens as he cups my cheek. And then ever so slowly he kisses me. The kiss is soft, tender.

It shouldn't have much of an impact. And yet it sets me ablaze. Who knew he had that in him?

But soon, the kiss turns incendiary. His tongue tangles with mine. Wanting more, I curl my hand around his neck and kiss him back hungrily, furiously with every repressed longing of mine. As I kiss him, I grind against him, communicating what I need. When the heat of his cock presses back, I go up in flames.

"Please." No clue what I'm asking for.

But he does. His big hands mold my ass, presses my pussy against his long, hard cock. Hungry for what he's dishing out, I rock against him, and his cock hits my sweet spot. "Oh, God. Yes." I groan.

I breathe him in. Hard to say which scent turns me on more—the fresh pine scent of his soap or the randy, earthy male of him. I nibble every inch of skin my lips can reach. He tastes of sin and heat and delicious man.

His arms tighten around me. His hands knead my ass, my side, my breasts. "You're so fucking hot, Ellie. I can't get enough of you."

Returning the favor, I palm as much of his ass as I can reach and squeeze. A thrill runs through me when he grunts in my mouth.

"Make love to me, Brock."

I don't have to ask him twice. He rolls me over until I'm lying on my back.

He strokes a finger up and down my clit. "You're wet."

And about to get wetter. "Uh-huh."

"I love your body."

"You do?" I'm confused. The women he's gone out with? They were all curvy. Granted, I'm not rail thin, but I have few curves to call my own.

"Yes." His irises glow crystal bright. He leans in to nip my waist, rasp his tongue over a hip. When he brushes a rough thumb over my sensitive clit, I almost come off the bed.

"Easy, babe." He lays a strong hand over my trembling belly. "We have all night."

Yes, that long I can promise him.

He comes off the bed and kneels on the floor. And then he widens my legs and pulls me toward him. I'm spread eagled before him and served up as his feast. His tongue finds my aching pearl. All warm breath, he suckles, gently at first, more insistently when I moan. Oh, sweet God in heaven. Beneath his clever tongue, I writhe, clench my hands on the sheet while I fight the urge to beg for more.

"You're beautiful here too, Ellie. Such a pink and pretty pussy." He slips a finger into me. "So tight. How long has it been?"

Oh, hell. I'm not 'fessing up to that. It's too embarrassing. "A while." I roll my hips, silently asking for more.

He stops what he's doing and stares at me. "How long, Ellie?"

I don't want to share that with him, but he won't go on until I do. "Law school. Okay?"

"That must have been what? Three years ago?"

"More like four," I say, peeved about this interrogation.

His brows knit. "Why?"

"I have a kid, Parker." I huff out.

His smile would make all the angels in heaven sing. And a few devils in hell. "Yes. I know."

"It's not like I could leave her alone and go off on a date."

"I want to apologize." He pulls out the finger and traces a circle around my clit.

I squirm wanting more. "What for? It wasn't your fault." Tired of this conversation, I urge his hand back to the task. "Now, go on."

He slides the first finger back into me, and then a second. He thrusts gently as if he fears hurting me.

But that's not what I want. Knowing what he's capable of, I urge, "Harder. Faster."

A light glows deep in his eyes, as my panting echoes in the room. I bite my lip to keep from begging him, even though it's too late.

The blood pounds through my veins as he keeps up the relentless pace. Everything in me quakes. My core tightens. A flame rises within me, threatening to burn out of control. I'm a mere millisecond from orgasm when he does something with his fingers, and I come harder than I ever have in my whole life. While I'm still shaking, he stretches over my head and grabs a packet from his night table. I watch silently while he slips the condom over his cock.

His fingers graze my thighs, and his mouth follows. Once more he teases my folds apart, finds my core again, leans down to suckle me. "Ready?"

Unable to say a word, I can only nod. The power of speech has deserted me.

The excitement builds once more when he circles my pearl with his tongue and laps up every drop. Shameless, I wrap my hand around his head and grind into his greedy mouth. Everything tightens in me, and I keen short, desperate cries. I can't believe I'm coming again. He spears me with his tongue and I come apart, squirming on the bed, screaming his name.

I'm still lost in the mindless aftermath, when he rises above me, presses his massive erection against my opening and thrusts. The pleasure is so intense, I arch off the bed, moaning.

As sweat pours off him unto my heated skin, he fucks me with a hard and steady rhythm. His breathing tells me he's in control. The bed's bouncing below us, so I curl my legs around his hips to keep me tethered to him. When his pace grows faster and he sinks deeper, I clutch his arms. He shifts to a slower speed, pulls out and turns me face down. Thrusting into my pussy from behind, his hand reaches around to find my pearl and then, God help me, he flicks my clit. I scream and convulse around his cock.

It takes him no time to follow. Sweaty, bellowing hard breaths, he collapses on top of me. "You're mine now, Ellie Adams. I'm never going to let you go."

I don't have the breath to deny him.

CHAPTER 13

Brock

*I*N THE MORNING WHEN I WAKE UP, SHE'S GONE.
Her absence is unexpected since I usually head out before
her. But maybe there was something at the office she needed to do.

At the Outlaws' compound, my focus is not on practice, but on the
things we did last night. But I pay enough attention to the drills that
nobody notices. Rather than join the team for dinner, I rush home to
her. I want more time with Ellie. More time with the woman who's
rapidly becoming an indispensable part of my life.

I walk in the door, expecting to see her, but she's not there. Could
something have happened? She'd been upset over whatever happened
on Thursday. So maybe it's more of the same? I dial her number to
find out if everything's okay, but she doesn't pick up.

Tuesday's my day off and I'm to go house hunting. Before heading
off, I call Ellie again with the same outcome. I'm worried enough to
give Marty a call. If anybody would know that something happened to
her, it would be him. Using the excuse I'm checking in, I casually
inquire about Ellie, but Marty's response tells me nothing's wrong
with her. So why isn't she returning my calls?

Briefly, I entertain the idea of dropping by the sports agency. After all, it wouldn't be an unusual thing for an athlete client to do. But I don't have the time. Not with the number of houses her realtor has lined up for me. As it turns out, she's a real gem. She's found exactly what I'm looking for. Big houses with big yards where Butch can run free. They're gorgeous, really, any one of them would do. Problem is, none of them has the thing I want most—Eleanor. After I bid goodbye to the realtor, I head back to the condo, hoping against hope that Ellie will be there, but she's not.

Being a glutton for punishment, I call her again. But like the last fifteen times, she doesn't pick up.

Much as I don't want to, I have to face the facts. What we did Sunday night meant nothing to her. Or maybe it'd been too much.

After all those years of longing for her, I'd ridden her all night long. Done my level best to satisfy myself, without asking once if she wanted it as well. She hadn't complained, but I should have paid more attention to her needs.

I really fucked up this time.

Over the next three days, rather than head home after practice, I remain at the compound with the excuse of watching game tapes. Anything to avoid walking into an empty apartment. But when the game tapes roll, I don't absorb anything in them. I'm too busy lashing myself over what I did. Or rather, didn't do.

I'd promised I'd make it good for her and then I'd become a ravening beast. Taking, not giving. Pleasuring myself, not her. No wonder she doesn't want more of the same. After the way I behaved, she probably regrets what we'd done, much as she had thirteen years ago. More than likely she thinks she made a huge mistake. So she's taking the easy way out and not coming back to the condo at all.

Saturday finally arrives, and with it, travel day since it's an out-of-town game. We win against a particularly difficult team, but it doesn't bring the elation the first win did.

"What's wrong with you, man?" Trevor, my seat flight buddy, asks. "You should be ecstatic. We won."

Out of all the players on the team, he's the one I've gotten closest to. Maybe because I depend on a great center to hand me the ball. "Nothing's wrong."

"Yeah? Well, you look like you lost your best friend."

I shrug. "Nah, just tired, I guess."

"Man, that pass to Johnson was a thing of beauty."

"Thanks."

"At this rate, we're sure to make the playoffs."

"We've got a long ways to go, Trevor."

"Yeah, but you're the real thing." He side glances me. "We were worried about you, you know."

That gets my attention. "Really?"

"Yeah. Some of the players believed you weren't serious about the game."

"Even after I took San Diego to the playoffs?"

"Yeah, even then. But it's turned out all right."

"Yeah. It has," I say, without much enthusiasm.

Other players come by to shake my hand, smack me on the shoulder, and deliver the same message, "Great game." For once, I feel welcomed. This is what I wanted. A team that made me feel at home. So why am I not more elated?

A little after seven, our flight lands in Chicago. We climb on the team bus that will take us back to the stadium. Most of the players have someone waiting for them. But there's no one there for me. No one missed me while I was gone.

I drop the duffel bag on the passenger seat of the Porsche Cayenne SUV, crank on the ignition. When a wave of sadness rolls over me, I drop my forehead on the steering wheel. I'm so fucking tired of being alone.

I got to see Ellie. Get things straightened out. Whether she wants to or not, we're going to sit down and talk. I can't call ahead, and she won't pick up the phone. The only way to do this is to drop in unannounced.

CHAPTER 14

Eleanor

"IS BROCK PARKER COMING OVER?" Meghan, Kaylee's best friend, asks. She'd come to visit Kaylee, ostensibly to find out how she's doing, but I'm guessing her real reason was to meet Brock. Well, she's bound to be disappointed.

"No. Not tonight." Because of his away game, Brock didn't have Butch for the weekend. Rather, he'd arranged for Butch to remain with us. Even if he wanted to do a quick drive by to see Butch, it's late. He'd never be that rude.

His fifteen phone messages would suggest he might have another purpose for dropping by, but I know better. I'd given him exactly what he wanted and now he wants more of the same. And that's not happening. I'm not about to compound the colossal mistake I'd made.

It had been earth-shattering what we'd done. There's no other way to describe it. He'd taken me in every way he knew how, most new to me. For hours, he'd tasted me, savored me, ridden me. And I'd loved every second of it. When dawn arrived, every bit of me hurt. It'd been more difficult than I can say to crawl out of bed, dress quietly in the dark and leave. But it was the right thing to do. Before we get caught.

Before I lose my job. Before I fall in love with him. Too late. I never stopped loving Brock. But I've lived without him all these years. I can live without him again.

"Oh." Meghan's definitely deflated. She'd hoped to meet her crush. But she's not seeing him in person if I have anything to say about it.

"Let's make popcorn," Kaylee says, walking into the kitchen. Although the MRI revealed her injury was only a sprain, the orthopedist recommended she wear the air cast, at least for another week. He'd also traded her old-fashioned crutches for a hands-free one which has made her more mobile and a lot happier.

"'K," Meghan responds. Still despondent, she follows Kaylee into the kitchen.

After the popcorn is done, the girls will probably go back to giggling, Skyping their friends, painting their toenails. Typical pre-teen girl stuff.

I, however, have some work to do. So I head to my study to catch up.

No sooner do I get there, than there's a knock at the front door. Who on earth could it be? I'm not expecting anyone.

"You want me to get it, Ms. Adams?" Meghan yells.

Before I can say no. I hear a squeak. "It's him."

A bad feeling crawls over me. "Him who?"

"Brock Parker. He's gorgeous."

Dear God. Barefoot I run out of the study in a fruitless attempt to stop her from opening the door.

But it's too late.

The sight of Brock standing on the porch makes my stupid heart skip a beat.

"Hi," Meghan says, twirling her hair.

"You must be Kaylee," Brock responds with that killer smile of his.

Giggling ensues. "Oh, no. I'm Kaylee's best friend, Meghan." More giggling.

I reach the living room at the same time Kaylee emerges from the kitchen, popcorn bowl in her free hand.

Meghan points to her best friend. "That's Kaylee."

Oh, fuckity, fuck, fuck. Brock's gaze zeroes in on Kaylee. And the smile on his face vanishes in an instant.

Having no idea of the disaster brewing, Kaylee greets him. "Hi, Mr. Parker. Nice to meet you."

"You're Kaylee?" His gaze narrows. His lips tighten.

She rolls forward on her hands-free crutch until she's about a foot away from him. "Yes."

It's so obvious they're related, even a blind man could see. Meghan might be flighty but the resemblance is not lost on her. Her gaze bounces between the two of them, and her silly grin disappears. "Oh. My. God."

"Meghan, don't." I beg.

To no avail. She whirls on Kaylee, scowling. "Why didn't you tell me?"

Confused, Kaylee says, "Tell you what?"

"That he's your father."

A look of horror rolls over Kaylee's face. "What? No."

"Here I made a fool of myself, blathering about how hot he is. And he's your dad. Your dad, Kaylee. This is so embarrassing." Her complexion's a mottled shade of red.

Kaylee turns to me, tears shimmering in her eyes. "Mom? Tell her, he's not."

I have to gain control of the situation, so I say the only thing I can. "Girls, go to Kaylee's room."

"I'm leaving," Meghan says, and then she hisses at Kaylee. "I'm not speaking to you again. Ever."

"Let me walk you home." I offer halfheartedly.

"No, thank you. I live only three doors down." And with that, she flounces out, slamming the door behind her.

The expression on Kaylee's face breaks my heart. She appears frightened, confused. I need to explain things to her. But not now. Now I have to deal with Brock, who looks ready to blow. "Kaylee, please go to your room. We'll talk later."

She doesn't move.

"Please, Kaylee." I'm barely hanging on.

Brock waits only long enough for her door to slam shut before he erupts. "Why didn't you tell me?"

I pray with everything in me that somehow I can bluff my way through this. "Tell you what?"

"That Kaylee's my daughter."

"No, she's—"

He holds up his hand, palm facing me. "Stop. Just stop."

Not much I can do but obey.

"She's the spitting image of me. Same hair, same eyes. Same lick of hair sticking out of the top of her head."

"Lots of people—"

"Fucking stop, Ellie," he yells.

I pinch my lips together. "I don't allow cursing in this house."

"Oh, yeah. But you allow lies, deceit, betrayal."

"I never betrayed you. We weren't even dating. It was just one night."

"That's all it takes. That's all it took." He gestures in the direction Kaylee took. "Clearly."

"I was your tutor."

"We were a hell of a lot more than that. We were friends, Ellie."

"No, we were not."

He tangles a hand through hair the same shade as my daughter's. "You told me you were okay."

I stomp over to his side. "What was I supposed to say? That you knocked me up?"

"Yes!"

"You were headed for football glory. Last thing you wanted was a child. You said it yourself at the Hilton. It would have been a disaster if you had a kid."

"I could have done something."

"Like what? Pay for an abortion?" I jerk up my chin.

"God. No. I would have never asked that of you. I could have helped with expenses."

"How? You had no money of your own. It was all your father's."

"I would have begged, borrowed or stolen. I would have crawled to him for money for my kid." Unable to stand still, he strides up and down the living room, eating up the space.

"He never would have given it to you."

He whirls back around. "Oh, yes, he damn well would have. All I would have had to do is threaten him with a scandal. That's the last thing he would have wanted. He would have handed over the money to shut me up." He marches forward until he's towering over me. "God. All these years, Ellie. I could have made life easier for you. I could have made life easier for her."

Butch nudges Brock's hand, licks mine. He's trying to make peace between us. What does it say about us that a dog is more mature than we are?

"Yelling at each other won't solve anything, Brock. You better go. I have to talk to Kaylee." And somehow make her understand.

A gamut of emotions roll across his face—anger, frustration, helplessness. He closes his eyes and takes a deep breath. When he opens them again, there's a measure of calm there. "Maybe we should both talk to her."

"No!" He can't step into the role of her father. I won't allow it.

A cold anger seems to settles within him as he points a finger to me. "You're not shutting me out of her life. That's my child in there."

I hitch up my chin. "Watch me."

He taps his chest with a closed fist. "I have rights. Rights I will exercise, legally if you force me."

"Get out. Get out now." I push at him, but he doesn't budge. Only when Butch whines again does he move toward the door.

With his large hand on the door frame, he fires one last salvo at me. "I want to talk to my daughter, Ellie. I'll give you twenty-four hours to explain things to her. If I don't hear from you, I'll contact my lawyer, and we'll settle this in court." And then he storms out, slamming the door behind him.

In an effort to calm down, I take a deep breath before heading to Kaylee's room. Butch, ever the peacekeeper, tags along. As soon as we get there, he jumps on her bed and licks her face.

She's not having any and pushes him away. "Get away from me, you stupid dog."

But I can see her heart's not in it, and when he does it again, she lets him.

Butch glances at me, a clear message in his big, brown eyes. 'Do something.'

"He's my father, isn't he?" When I don't answer quick enough, she screams. "Isn't he?"

"Yes, he is."

"Why didn't you tell me? Why did you lie to me?"

"I thought it was the best thing to do."

"He didn't know?"

"No. I never told him. He was seventeen, Kaylee, a senior in high school. He had his whole life ahead of him. I didn't want to ruin his future."

Her breath hitches, and a sob escapes her. "You mean like I ruined yours?"

"No, sweetheart. You didn't. I wanted you from the first."

"How could you want me? You were seventeen with *your* whole life ahead."

"But I had one thing he didn't have. A great mom. Grandma made sure we were okay. We moved to another town where nobody knew who I or your father were. Her support and Steve's allowed me to finish high school, attend college."

She swipes at the tears streaming down her cheeks. "But why didn't you tell me once I was old enough?"

I clasp my hands to keep them from trembling. "By then the lie had grown so big, I didn't know how to tell you."

"If he hadn't come to Chicago, I would have never known, would I?"

Her tear-streaked face breaks my heart. "No. I would have never told you."

She takes a shuddering breath. "I need to be alone right now."

What did I expect? That she would throw her arms around me,

hug me and tell me she understood? No. I didn't. Still, her rejection hurts. "Come on, Butch."

"Let him stay."

"All right." I walk out, closing her door softly behind me.

As soon as I step into the hallway, my held tears rain down my face. I deserve every accusation, every reproach from her. Plain and simple, I screwed up. Once she was old enough to understand, I should have told her. But I didn't. I was too afraid her love would turn to hate. Which is exactly what's happening now. And, unfortunately, she's not the only one.

CHAPTER 15

Brock

"THE GM WANTS TO SEE YOU," the assistant coach says after Wednesday's practice ends. I don't have to guess what he wants to talk about. It's all over the internet. The kinder posts refer to me as an absentee father. The harsher ones brand me a deadbeat dad who abandoned his kid to party his way through the NFL, all while his child lived in abject poverty. A bit extreme, but they have a point.

I did party my way through the NFL. My child may not have grown up poor, but she and Ellie lived through hard times. More than likely, Ellie had to borrow money for law school. At least that's one thing I can take off her plate. I can pay off her student debt. If she'll let me. Right now, that doesn't seem likely. She won't even return my calls.

I've phoned her at least ten times in the last two days. Not once did she pick up. I left message after message. Demanding at first, then threatening her with a lawsuit. The last few times, I downright begged. But just like before, she ignored them all. Damn it. I want to see my daughter. That's not too much to ask, is it? I want to talk to her. Get to know what she's like. It won't be easy, I know. But I need to make some kind of a connection with her. I don't want to miss any more years of her life than I already have.

I trudge my way to the GM's office and knock on the glass panel. When he yells enter, I stick my head in the door. "You wanted to see me?"

"Yes, come in. Close the door, Brock." Not only is he present, but so is Coach and Oliver Lyons, the Outlaws' owner. I'm truly in deep shit.

The GM slides a copy of some sports gossip rag across his desk. The headline reads 'Brock Parker, Deadbeat Dad.' "Is it true?"

Not wanting to miss a word, I carefully read the article. The last thing I want to do is lie. The situation is bad enough as it is.

"Kaylee Adams is my child," I admit.

One of them hisses a breath. Don't know who since I'm reading the article again. I got the gist first time around, but I want to know how far the slanderous rag has gone.

Once I've caught all the salacious innuendos, I glance up. "I didn't know. Eleanor never told me."

"How could that be?" The GM's lip curls in disdain. "This thing happened while you were both in high school, didn't it?"

"This thing?" I spit out. "You mean Eleanor's pregnancy?"

"Yes. Sorry." He waves his hand in the air in an apparent apologetic gesture. "Didn't mean it as an insult."

The coach stares at me stone-faced. Oliver Lyon's expression is easier to understand. Disgust covers it nicely. He doesn't have to say a word for me to understand my position on the team is on the line.

Damn it. I'm not at fault here. I'm not the bad guy. But I've got to get my temper under control if I'm to come out unscathed. I breathe deep in an attempt to calm down. "She left midway through her senior year. She wasn't showing yet." A logical explanation which just happens to be true.

"Well, that's something." The GM leans back into his chair, as the tension eases out of him. "We can spin this. Blame it on the mother."

I pound his desk. "The hell we are." There goes my calm.

"Care to rephrase that, Brock," Coach Grohowski says, in a quiet tone. That's not good. Everyone knows it's better when he yells at you.

I count to ten to regain command over my temper. Once I'm reasonably sure I won't bite off somebody's head, I say, "You're not blaming Ellie. And neither am I."

"Brock, you're in serious trouble here," Coach says, not unkindly. "The notoriety can hurt the team, end your career. We need to do something."

"We?" I scoff. "You don't need to do anything. This is mine to fix. I'll handle it. I'll make it right."

"You want to come out of this smelling like a rose," he says. "Otherwise . . ."

He doesn't have to say it. The look on the owner's face says it all. If I don't fix this, I'll no longer have a place on the team.

CHAPTER 16

Eleanor

"ELEANOR, COULD YOU STEP INTO MY OFFICE?" Marty, my boss. Three guesses what he wants to talk about, and the first two don't count.

It'd taken no time for Meghan to spread the news that Kaylee was Brock Parker's daughter. Heck, she'd probably texted the information to her friends on the way back to her house. Once the cat was out of the bag, it had spread like wildfire on social media, and the gossip rags had wasted no time setting their news hounds loose on the story. Within a day, they'd found out how Brock and I knew each other, and that he'd never paid child support. The reports had been vicious, some of them branding him a 'Deadbeat Dad.'

Not content with hurling insults at Brock, my house phone has been ringing nonstop; so has my cell. They'd even managed to track down Kaylee's number and my mother's. She'd called in a panic on Monday. "Honey, I'm getting calls about Brock and Kaylee."

"Don't say anything!"

"I haven't, sweetheart. I know better than that. I just thought you should know."

"Thank you, Mama."

"What are you going to do?"

"Nothing."

And that's exactly what I'd done the last two days. But now it seems that option has been taken away from me.

Marty and I had tried to prevent a scandal, but it found Brock anyway. No wonder Marty wants to talk to me.

The gazes of most everyone in the agency follow my every step as I walk on shaky legs to Marty's office. When I reach it, I'm not surprised to find two of the firm's senior partners there as well.

"Close the door, Ms. Adams."

God. If Marty's calling me by my last name, it's a lot worse than I thought. Am I going to lose my job?

"Please take a seat." Marty is sitting on one of the easy chairs next to the couch where the two partners are perched like vultures eager to pounce.

As carefully as I can, I fold into the matching seat.

"Thank you for coming. The reason we asked you here is that we need to broach a sensitive subject with you."

In other words, the 'sensitive' subject will be discussed with care, something I truly appreciate. "All right."

"Are you aware of the rumors swirling in the media about Brock Parker and you?" he asks.

I lace my hands to keep from breaking down. "Yes."

"Is it true?"

"There's so much information flying around. Anything in particular you'd like to know?"

"Is he the father of your child?"

Ahhh. The crux of the matter. There's only one answer I can give. "Yes. He is."

One of the senior partners jumps in. "You didn't see fit to let Martin know you had a relationship with Brock Parker when we hired you?"

"There was no relationship. I hadn't seen him in over ten years."

"Come, come, Ms. Adams. Whether you hadn't seen him in ten

years is immaterial. You had a child with him," he thunders on. There goes the polite approach. But then he's got a reason to worry. The brewing scandal may impact the agency in negative ways.

"I didn't think it mattered."

"It matters, Eleanor," Marty says, not unkindly. "Some media outlets claim Brock never provided child support. Is it true?"

"Yes."

Marty hisses in a breath.

I hurry to explain. "It's not what you think. He never knew he had a child."

His eyes practically bug out. "You never told him?"

"No."

"From the media accounts, you were in high school when this happened. How could he not know?"

"My mom and I moved out of town before my pregnancy showed."

Silence reigns while he processes the information.

"Well, if he didn't know it then, he certainly knows it now," Marty says.

"Yes, he does."

"Is he willing to pay child support? We can work with that."

I knew that question would come up, but I don't have an answer. At least not one that will satisfy them. So all I can reveal is the truth. "We haven't really talked about it."

His brows scrunch together. "Why not?"

I swallow hard. "I haven't taken his calls." Along with the media, Brock had rung me up a bunch of times.

For several seconds, they stare at each other, probably thinking what an idiot I am. The tension in the room's so thick, you can cut it with a knife.

But before it gets to the breaking point, Marty says, "Can we have the room, please? I'd like to speak privately with Ms. Adams."

The two senior partners come to their feet, but before they exit, one of them fires one last salvo. "Fix this, Ms. Adams. Otherwise, you'll no longer work here."

My stomach lurches. I can't lose this job. I have a mortgage and school loans to pay. More than that, if they let me go, no sports agency in the world would hire me. I'd be forever known as the woman who destroyed Brock Parker's career.

As soon as the door closes behind them, Marty says, "Don't mind him. He's still living in the Stone Age."

"I'm so sorry, Marty." I keep my head down while tears rain down my face. "I never intended for this to happen."

"I know you didn't." He offers me a box of Kleenex and waits until I compose myself.

"You have to talk to Brock. You know that, right?"

"Yes." The keeping-my-head-in-the-sand-hoping-the-problem-goes-away approach hasn't worked. Not that it ever had a chance. It was just wishful thinking on my part.

"Brock has a quite notorious past. I don't have to tell you how much damage this scandal would do to his career."

"I know."

"I'm sure he'll want to provide child support."

I nod, wiping a tear from my cheek. "More than likely."

"Good. Good. Now, once you get things worked out, you'll need to make a joint statement. I'll help you draft it, if you wish. It's going to hurt, but you'll need to come clean about hiding your daughter's existence from him. You're thrilled you reconnected, blah, blah, blah. And he'll be paying child support for all those years he missed. You get my drift, Eleanor?"

He's calling me Eleanor again. That's a good sign, right? "Yes, Marty."

"Okay, now." He pats his hands on his thighs, a gesture he often makes when things have been settled to his satisfaction. "I'll let you return to your office so you can call Brock."

I come to my feet and take a step toward the door.

"Oh, one more thing. The sooner you make that joint statement, the better. We don't want to give this story any more oxygen than it already has."

With my back to him, I nod. "Of course."

But as it turns out, I don't get a chance to call Brock. He's already in my office waiting for me. As soon as I step in, he comes to his feet. His face reflects a myriad of emotions—anger, concern. But mostly, resolve. "We have to talk," he says.

"I know."

Before I can say anything else, my assistant knocks on the glass door. I hadn't checked in with her on the way back, mainly because I was in a daze. But something tells me I really should have.

"Come in."

She dashes in, an apologetic look on her face. "Sorry to interrupt." She hands me a note. "Your mom called while you were with Marty. She says to call her back right away. It's urgent."

My stomach lurches. "Thanks." I grab my cell from my desk and dial mom's number. She picks up before the second ring.

"What's wrong? It's not Kaylee, is it?" She'd endured the gossip storm at her school for the last two days, but today she'd begged off with the excuse of a stomach ache. I hadn't the heart to deny her.

"No. She's fine. It's a mess of photographers, about twenty of them, in front of the house. Snapping pictures, trampling over the bushes. Butch's going crazy. He's tearing at the front door trying to get to them. You better come home, honey."

"I'll be there as soon as I can. Whatever you do, don't let Butch out." He might be mild tempered, but he's still a Pit Bull. He's so protective of us, he might do some serious damage to those photographers.

"What's wrong?" Brock asks, looking just as worried as I feel.

I summarize Mama's end of the conversation. "How did they find out where I live?"

"It's not that hard, Ellie. Not when you live, eat, and breathe tabloid journalism."

Angry about the invasion of privacy, I lash out at him. "Is that what you call it?"

"No. I call it trash. But it's lucrative trash. They make a lot of money from these stories."

"Well, it sucks." My life's going off the rails, and I don't know how to get it back on track.

"Yeah, it does." He touches my shoulder. "Ellie, let me come with you."

Not happening. "I don't think so." I shrug him off. "It would make things worse."

"How can it be any worse?"

He does have a point. But I'm not convinced he'll improve the situation.

"You don't want them there, right?"

I nod.

"Well, from personal experience I can tell you they won't leave until they get something. I can give that to them."

I rub a hand across my brow against the incipient headache blossoming there. "Like what?"

"A statement from me while I'm standing in front of your house. That way they'll get a photo and copy."

Given how much experience he's had with these types of things, I have to trust his idea will work. It's worth a shot anyway. "Okay. Let's go with that." I grab my purse and briefcase. On the way out, I tell my assistant, "We're headed home. Please call Marty and let him know that Mr. Parker is with me."

She nods, but her gaze zeroes in on Brock. So does everyone else's. Seems most of those working here have found a reason to hang out around my office. The only thing that's missing is the popcorn so they can enjoy the show.

But I don't have time to worry about that as we head out the agency's front doors. Once in the elevator, I punch P4.

He hits P1, the visitors' parking lot. "I'll drive. We'll use my SUV."

"My car—"

"—will be fine staying here overnight."

They have pretty good security in this building, but I'm not leaving it behind. "Brock—"

He jams his hand into his front jeans pocket, probably to retrieve his keys. "Your car's too small for me, Ellie."

He would bring that up now.

"And you only have a one-car garage. We can't both park in it, and

I'm not leaving a souped-up Outlaws' Porsche Cayenne on the street. Or here for that matter."

He's right. I know he's right. Why am I finding it hard to breathe? I grab the handrail to keep from shaking. I hate all that is happening. I hate not being in control.

Stepping into me, he cups my cheeks. "Everything's going to be all right."

"Is it?" My voice has grown breathless, as it so often does when I'm around him.

"I'll make sure of it, sweet girl." He brushes his lips against mine.

His kiss calms me, soothes me. I want more. But the doors open to the P1 level, and there's no time.

As we exit the elevator, he curls his hand around mine. "We can talk on the way."

My shoulders snap rigid once more.

Strangely enough, once we're underway, he remains silent. Maybe he changed his mind about talking. Or maybe he's thinking about what to say. Either works for me since it's given me a chance to find a measure of peace.

"I want to see our daughter."

Ah, he was figuring out how to phrase things. "Well, you're going to get your wish. She's home."

He briefly takes his eyes off the road to glance at me. "I want to help support her. Financially. I figure I owe about ten—no, that can't be. How old is she?"

"Twelve. She just turned twelve." One of the few outright lies I told him.

"I owe you twelve years' worth of child support."

"You don't have to." I blurt out, even though I'm totally wrong.

"Yes, I do, Ellie. I want to do this. I need to do this. For her sake as well as mine."

He's right. Morally and legally, he should pay. It's just, once he does, she won't be all mine. A part of her will belong to him. But then, it always has. I just refused to acknowledge it.

Rather than respond, I stare out the window wondering how

everyone at home is coping. I never wanted this to turn into a three-ring circus. I tried so hard to avoid a scandal. All to no avail. "They're not going to stop, are they?"

"Who?"

"The paparazzi, the media."

He drops one of his big hands over mine and squeezes. "They will. Once we work things out, they'll have nothing to talk about, and they'll move on to the next story."

My gaze cuts to him. "You think so?"

"I know so."

He should. He's lived through enough notoriety to know.

"I'd like visitation rights, Ellie."

My breath cuts short. "You going to take her to the dog park once a week, too?"

He juts out his jaw. "That's a cheap shot."

He's right. I'm more mature than this. "Yes, it was. Sorry." I pick at my fingernail polish. "Marty talked to me this morning. A couple of the senior partners were there as well."

The GPS announces a turn and he pulls the car onto the exit ramp.

"What did they have to say?"

"Basically? Fix this or you'll get fired."

"They won't do that."

My gaze cuts to his. "Why not? I screwed up. I should have told them about you." I turn my head to the window so he won't see the moisture pooling in my eyes.

"If you had, would they have hired you?"

"I'd like to think they would have. But who knows?" I can't wallow in the what ifs, not when the present demands a solution. "Marty suggested we make a joint statement to the press."

"All right."

I retrieve a legal pad from my briefcase to jot down some ideas. For a few minutes, I list the important, salient points. "Okay. Here's what I have so far. You didn't know you fathered a child. But now you're eager to get to know her. You're paying back child support. Anything else?"

"I think that covers it. For now."

"What do you mean for now?"

"We'll have to settle some things between us, Ellie. Legally. I need to confirm I'm her legal father. Which means a blood test. We'll need to meet with lawyers to draw up visitation rights, custody rights."

Oh, hell no. "Visitation rights are one thing, but I'm not sharing custody with you."

"Why not? I am her father."

"You met Kaylee five minutes ago, and now you want the part of her father?"

"I've always wanted a family."

"Funny way you went about it," I scoff. "What with your orgy room and all."

That remark should have silenced him, but it doesn't faze him one bit. "They weren't the type of women you have a family with."

"Did you use condoms with them?"

"Every single time. You were the only one. The only one, Ellie."

"Am I supposed to believe that?"

"Have I ever been sued for child support?"

"Not to my knowledge."

"I haven't. I always used protection."

Okay, so he always took precautions. But that's neither here nor there. He'll have a bigger issue to deal with as far as Kaylee is concerned. "She'll fight you. Last thing she thinks she needs is a father."

"Doesn't matter what she thinks or does. I intend to take responsibility for her. Be reasonable, Ellie. If anything happens to me, I want her to inherit what I have. It'd be a lot easier if she were my legal daughter."

He's not going to give in, no matter what I have to say. And I'm too exhausted emotionally and physically to argue about it at the moment, so I punt. "I have to think about it."

His jaw juts out. "There's nothing to think about. I'm going to do it. Whether you like it or not."

This is a disaster. "She's scared, Brock. Her whole world has been turned upside down."

"I know it won't be easy, but I won't give up. Whether she, or you for that matter, don't think she needs a father, she does. I know what it's like to grow up with an absent parent. I don't want that for my daughter. I've lost twelve years of her life, I don't intend to lose anymore." And that, as far as he's concerned, is that.

We arrive home to find about a dozen photographers parked outside my door. When we pull into the driveway, a feeding frenzy ensues as they trip over one another to get the best shot. Only when the garage door closes behind us do I take a deep breath.

We walk into the house to find Mama cooking on the stove and Kaylee eating at the kitchen island.

As soon as we step into the kitchen, Kaylee shoots Brock a death glare. If looks could burn, he'd be seared on the spot. "What's *he* doing here?"

"He's your father, Kaylee. Show some respect."

She has the grace to blush.

"Hello, Kaylee." He keeps his proper distance, probably because he's got no clue what to do. Meeting a daughter is one thing, meeting a twelve-year-old who's royally pissed at you is another.

Butch comes racing up and jumps on Brock.

"Sit, boy."

But for once, Butch doesn't obey. Nudging Brock's knee, he pushes him toward the living room.

"It's okay. No one's going to hurt anyone."

As if he's ceding his role of protector, he plops on the floor next to Kaylee, probably trusting Brock to handle whatever's happening outside.

"Well, I'll be damned," Brock says. "He's guarding her."

"He's been glued to her side since she came home from camp."

Brock turns to me. "What happened to her?"

But before I have a chance to answer, Kaylee interrupts, "I'm right here, you know. You can ask me."

"Sorry. What happened to you?" he asks her.

"I tripped over a stupid, dumb rock and sprained my ankle."

"Is it serious?"

"It's only a sprain, but the doctor wants me to keep this stupid cast on for a whole week."

"Well, that's for the best. Otherwise, you might make it worse. Just rest it and take some ibuprofen. You'll be right as rain in no time."

She squints at him. "Did you ever suffer a sprain?"

"About five of them. None of them were any fun, so I know what you're going through." He grins, probably because he's in safe territory discussing his injuries.

Thank God they have something in common.

"What are you going to do about the invading horde?" Kaylee nods toward the front yard.

A small smile flits in and out of Brock's lips. "I'll talk to them."

"I'll come with you," I say.

"No. It's best if you stay inside." When I start to protest, he adds, "For now."

He walks out the front door and stands in the path leading up to the street. I rush to the living room window, crack open the curtain, and listen to what he's saying. His speech is short and to the point. He tells them they're trespassing on private property and they're making his daughter and dog very nervous. And then he asks them to leave. Unfazed, they pepper him with questions. After answering a couple, he promises to have a longer statement the next day. But right now they need to go.

When none of them move, he lowers the hammer.

"If anyone's around in fifteen minutes, I'll call the police and have you arrested. If you persist with this invasion of privacy, I'll have you and your publications banned from the Outlaws' approved media list."

Upon hearing that statement, most of them hightail it out of there, but a couple of diehards move their beachhead to the sidewalk. They'll be sitting out there all night, because I'm not coming out for the rest of the day. Maybe ever.

Having accomplished his goal, Brock walks back into the house. "They're gone."

"Some are still out there," Kaylee says, tapping the app on her phone, the one that came with our security camera system and clearly shows some photographers still hanging out.

"They'll get tired soon enough when there's nothing to see."

"Would you like something to eat, Brock?" Mama asks. "I made some chicken and rice."

"That would be lovely, Ruth. Thank you."

"How about you, honey?" she asks me.

"No, thanks, Mama. I ate at the office."

While she ladles a portion from the cooking pot onto a plate, I set out a placemat and cutlery on the kitchen island. He drops on a stool next to Kaylee, who's quietly eating while sneaking bits to Butch.

"So, Kaylee, what grade are you in?"

"I'm going into seventh grade at Larmoor Junior High."

"Your mother tells me you're really smart."

She shrugs while playing around with her food. "I guess."

"You get that from your mother. I pretty much sucked at most classes."

"Guess you were too busy with football."

"You're right. I was."

"I suck at sports. Mama, may I be excused?"

"Sure, honey."

He reaches out to help her stand.

"I can do it. Thank you." She rests her leg on her hands-free crutch and rolls toward her room, with Butch bringing up the rear.

Once she's disappeared from view, Brock lets out a long breath. "Boy."

"Told you it would be hard."

Ruth pats his hand as she serves him a full plate of food. "You did fine, Brock. She'll come around."

But will she? That's to be determined. Kaylee's got a stubborn streak in her a mile long.

Mom loosens her apron strings and hangs it on the peg on the wall. "Well, I better go. Got some pies to bake for the church fair. I'll be back tomorrow, honey." She buzzes me on the cheek.

"Thank you, Mama."

"Good seeing you again, Brock."

"Thanks, Ruth. Appreciate the food."

"Anytime." And with that, she exits through the back porch door. She usually parks by the side of the house and comes in through the back gate. Hopefully, she won't run into any paparazzi out there.

Once she's gone, Brock glances off into the distance, as if he's seriously considering something. "You know, the more I think about it, the more I believe holding a press conference won't be enough."

"It won't?"

His glance rolls over to me. "The Outlaws' owner is worried about my tendency to create a scandal wherever I go. When I told him I would handle it, he was very honest. He doesn't believe I can change. So I'll have to make him believe I can."

"And how would you do that?"

"Obviously, I'll have to take a drastic step."

Alarm bells go off. "What drastic step?"

His gaze lands on me. "I think we should get married."

CHAPTER 17

Eleanor

"GET MAR-MARRIED?" My stomach flip-flops. Good thing there's nothing in there; otherwise, it would have come back up. "Are you crazy?"

"No. Not at all. In fact, I think it's the sanest decision I've made." He calmly takes another bite of Mama's chicken and rice, as if he hasn't totally upended my world. "That should solve all our problems, don't you think?"

Yelling won't do any good. I have to discuss this rationally, logically with him. Well, as logically as I can given the fact he's insane. "How?"

"Marrying you will prove I've given up my wild partying days and settled down into domestic bliss. The Outlaws' management will love that." He grins like it's the most brilliant idea he's ever dreamed up. "With any luck, the media will stop writing about my personal life and focus on my football stats."

On the verge of hyperventilating, I rush to explain. "We don't need to marry, Brock. If I acknowledge you're Kaylee's father and you're providing child support, that'll take care of your problem."

For a couple of seconds, he chews over my suggestion. But then he shakes his head. "I don't think so. Oliver Lyons will keep waiting for the other shoe to drop, especially after word gets out about my 'orgy room.'"

"It hasn't gotten out so far."

He turns toward me, and I get the full effect of his green-eyed gaze. "Well, with all the publicity, do you honestly believe that little turd at the condo, what's his name—"

"Warren Sheffield."

"You think he won't find out? As soon as he figures out who's living in that condo, he'll blast it all over social media. And it won't take the tabloids a nanosecond to spread it far and wide." He helps himself to more chicken and rice before pointing his fork at me. "They'll drag you into it as well."

"Me? I haven't done anything."

That sexy grin of his curls over his lips. "Oh, I wouldn't say that. We did plenty on Sunday, didn't we?" He punctuates his question with a wink. Bastard.

I bow my head and pick at my nail polish. If I keep this up, I'm going to need a coat of Floozy Red or Scarlet Tramp to go along with my new fallen woman status. "That was just a one-time thing."

"Not if I have anything to say about it." He manages to inhale another healthy portion of Mama's food and waggle his eyebrows at the same time.

Is he ever going to be serious? He thinks marrying me would be one big lark. Of course, he does. Not only would it solve all his problems, he would have a readily available sex partner. Someone he could screw all night long. That thought shouldn't sound appealing, yet it does. What is wrong with me? Do I really want to play bouncy-bouncy on his bed? Have him do all the things he did to me and more? I shiver. Yeah, I would. But I'll need more than that if I'm to agree to this. "Okay, fine. Let's say for the sake of argument, I say yes. If we get married, and that's a big if, your playboy problems would be solved. But what do I get out of it?"

His mouth twists with disdain. "Money, you mean?"

"I don't want your money, Brock," I snap back. "If I had, I would have demanded it years ago."

His brow clears up. "You should have. Why didn't you?"

Unable to meet the question in his eyes, I stare down at the floor. "I couldn't."

"Why?"

"Because—" How do I explain I didn't want him in our lives?

"That's okay. I understand." The bleakness of his tone prompts me to raise my head. And I'm floored by his expression. He knows why I never contacted him.

"You were busy with football and . . . everything else."

"I would have made time for our daughter, Ellie. I would have loved having her in my life."

"How? When?"

"Football season lasts only a few months. Plenty of other time to spend with her."

"She was too young to be away from me, Brock. And she would have never understood. Heck, she barely understands now."

He scrubs a hand over his face. "No sense hashing over the past. What's done is done."

He's right about that.

"Look. You're in hot water with your agency, right?"

He had to remind me. "Yes."

"Well, if you marry me, you won't be. Simple as that." Done eating, he strolls to the sink, rinses his dish and drops it into the dishwasher. He then folds his arms across his chest and leans back against the kitchen counter. Sexy does not begin to describe those roped arms and wide chest of his.

But I can't be sidetracked by his powerful body. "How do you figure that?"

"Well, for starters, I'll walk if they do anything to harm your career."

"You would?"

"You better believe it. And that's only for starters. If they so much as give you the side eye, I'll spread the word among my teammates about how they treated you. They would not look kindly upon sports agents who mistreated my wife. Plus, the agency might have a harder time signing new players, especially ones who came from my Alma Mater."

"I can't believe players would sever their relationship with my agency. It's one of the best in the business."

"Trust me. Some would. If there's one thing players respect is families." He strolls back to me, that slow swing of his hips drawing my gaze, along with the rest of him. Why am I fighting this? He could be mine, in bed and out. Fine. I'm in. But first, we need to set some rules.

"One more thing."

"Yes, darling." He says, cupping my cheeks.

"While we're married, you don't screw around with anyone."

"Oh, Ellie girl, don't you know? There's no other woman for me." He brushes his mouth across mine, and I tingle down to my toes.

"Yeah, right," I whisper against his lips. He might ooze honesty, but I know what he's really like. "Promise me, Brock."

He makes the sign of the cross over his heart. "I promise. I'll treat you right, especially in bed. We had a great time Sunday night, didn't we?"

My face grows hot as I recall the things he did to me. And everything I did to him. "Yeah, but that was just—"

"Sex?"

"Yes."

"No. It wasn't." His hands slide down to my ass and lift me. After dropping me on the counter, he rubs his hard cock against my pussy.

"Oh." I widen my legs to give him better access. There's only so much temptation I can withstand.

He kisses my lips, nibbles my jaw. "I've had lots of sex, Ellie girl. What we have? It's special."

"I bet you say that to every woman who hops in the sack with you."

"No, I don't."

"Uh-huh." I don't believe him for one second.

"Most of those women were looking to score with an NFL player so they could brag about it to their friends. It meant nothing to them or me." He kisses my fingers, one at a time, the last one he licks, same as he did Sunday in bed. "But you are different. You've always been different."

God. Why am I falling for his malarkey? Sooner or later, he'll want his freedom, because Brock Parker can't be true to one woman. No matter what he says. And the last thing I want is more heartbreak. I've had enough to last a lifetime. So as much as I want to say yes, I can't. I push away from him. "Sorry. This is not going to work out."

He rubs his hands up and down my back, and I practically melt in his arms. "It doesn't have to be forever, you know."

Well, that makes sense. He would think that way. And that is something I could agree to. "Only long enough to get over this hump, then?"

"Exactly." He gives me his most brilliant smile, as if I'm a dull student who's just caught up. "We'll have to give it a go for at least a year. Until I'm through with this season and signed on to a new team. Then we can put out a statement. A mutually agreed story about how things didn't work out. In the meantime, we'll just enjoy ourselves." He waggles his eyebrows.

"Pervert." I whisper against his mouth.

"Stick in the mud." He kisses me and everything fades away. I've never been able to be this close to Brock and not melt.

"Oh, God, that's just gross." Kaylee.

Busted by my own daughter. I hide my flushed face against his shoulder.

Brock's thumb strokes my throat as if to say, 'Don't worry. I got this.' "Get used to it, kid. I just asked your mother to marry me. And she said 'Yes.'"

"I didn't," I whisper against his chest.

"Yeah, you did," he murmurs right back.

"Uggh." Kaylee clatters away, probably to hide in her bedroom again.

I glance up into his gorgeous face. "Told you she would be a hard nut to crack."

His mouth quirks. "Guess what? So am I. Hard I mean."

He lifts me off the counter.

But when he pulls me toward the hallway, panic sets in. "What are you doing?"

"Taking you to bed?"

I yank back and stop our progress. "With Kaylee in the next room? Are you insane?"

"Is that going to be a problem?"

"Yes!" How could he think I could have sex with my daughter only a few feet away?

"Then we'll have to find a bigger house."

Like hell, we will. "I'm not moving." I might be willing to get married, but I'm not chucking my whole life for him.

CHAPTER 18

Brock

THE THREE-RING CIRCUS, otherwise known as our press conference, gets scheduled for two days later. Over two hundred media representatives eager to cover the juicy scandal have camped out at the Outlaws' compound. But only those credentialed with the team's PR office are allowed in, which should keep out most of the gossip rags.

The day of the press conference, Ellie and I wait in the PR office until it's time for the briefing to begin. Having suffered through several media frenzies, I know what to expect. Ellie, on the other hand, is practically jumping out of her skin. Unable to remain still for long, she paces up and down the office, arms wrapped around her middle, eyes darting around the room.

"They won't bite, you know?"

"Right."

"That's my job."

The glare she shoots at me is hot enough to singe. "You're disgusting."

"But you love it." When she doesn't return another snappy one-liner, I know I have to do something to calm her nerves.

Taking her hand, I lead her into the nearest office. Thankfully, the place is empty. Whoever it belongs to, he's probably dealing with the press.

I rub her chilled hands between my own. "You're one block of ice."

"I don't know why I'm so nervous. It's not like I haven't attended a press conference before."

"Because you know how brutal the questions can be." I drape my jacket around her shoulders. As big as it is, it comes down to her thighs.

She burrows into me, seeking my warmth. "Thanks."

I stroke her back to get her circulation going. "I won't let them browbeat you, you know, and neither will the head of Public Relations." She'd insisted on taking questions with the hope it would stop them once and for all. Even though I have my doubts, I went along with her plan.

Taking a step back, she glances up. "It's not the questions that worry me."

"Then what does?"

"That I'll snap at them. Say the wrong thing."

I chuckle as I hug her to me. "You won't."

"How do you know that?" Her words rumble against my chest, and everything's right in my world.

"Because you are the consummate professional. And you'll know exactly what to say." I drop a kiss on her lips. Wish I could do more. But now's neither the time nor place.

Someone raps on the door. "Mr. Parker? Ms. Adams? They're ready for you."

"Be right out," I yell.

We wind our way through the media office into the press conference room right next door. As soon as we walk in, a flurry of camera clicks go off.

The head of PR greets us from the dais. "Brock, Ms. Adams. Please come up and take a seat."

Holding her hand, I lead her up to the steps to the raised platform used for after-game interviews. Not only is the head of PR there, but so is Coach Grohowski and Oliver Lyons, the owner of the Outlaws. For that matter, Marty's here as well, although he's keeping a low profile in the back of the room.

The PR director introduces himself, Coach Grohowski, and Oliver Lyons before he spells out the rules of the conference. "Brock Parker will make a brief statement, and then he'll take some questions." He turns to me. "Brock."

"Thank you."

When I stand, Ellie removes her jacket, but I tell her to keep it on. I don't want her to get cold. I drop a kiss on her lips, and another barrage of clicks go off.

"Hello." The statement I prepared along with the Outlaws PR and my agent rests on the podium in front of me. The few words written there are not nearly enough to express what I'm feeling. I have to make things crystal clear. I owe Ellie that much. "Some of you, okay most of you, are wondering about my relationship with Eleanor Adams."

She gives me the side eye because she knows I'm going off script.

"I met Ellie at Stonewall Jackson High. She was one of the smartest girls I knew. All straight A's. Me, on the other hand? Well, I was too busy with football to pay much attention to school. And Macbeth was kicking my ass."

Laughter rolls around the room.

"You know the NCAA rules. If you don't maintain a C average, you can't be drafted to play college ball. So I needed to improve my grades. A friend told me about a girl that tutored students. So I hired her to help me out. It wasn't easy. I was stubborn as a mule, but she didn't give up on me. I got a B+ on my midterm. First time I'd gotten such a high mark. She went from being my tutor to being my friend. And before I knew it, I'd fallen for her. But halfway through our senior year, she left. I didn't know it at the time, but her Mama was getting married and her fiancé had gotten a new job out of town. I asked everyone—the school, my friends—if they knew where she'd gone. But nobody had a clue."

I grip the edge of the dais as I recall the pain of the day I realized I'd never see her again.

"I went on to college, but I never forgot the sweetest girl I'd ever known." I glance back to see her eyes filled with tears. "You see, I'd truly cared about her. But I'd never told her so. The rest you probably know. I attended Clemson, made it all the way to the Championship game. During my last year in college, I was drafted by the Florida Manatees. Later on, I got transferred to the San Diego Missionaries."

The gazes of the journalists bounce between Ellie and me. One thing for sure, they're not bored.

"When I heard I'd been transferred to the Chicago Outlaws, the top team in the nation, well, I was elated." A choked sound reaches me. Ellie. It has to be. A quick peek at her confirms it. She's biting down on her bottom lip to hold back a laugh.

I gotta make this story good, pour on my Southern charm, to keep her from getting sad again. "Well, imagine my surprise when I spot the little lady herself waiting for me at the airport. Whoo-boy! She almost knocked me off my feet."

She's rolling her eyes. I can feel it.

"Never one to pass up an opportunity, I asked her out. You might remember seeing her at the banquet a couple of weeks ago?" Some of the journalists nod. Good. They were paying attention.

"Now, let me be clear about this. She attended as a favor to me. You see, she works for the agency that represents me and wanted to keep things professional. So much so that when I asked her out again, she turned me down. Yeah, she pretty much busted my heart into a million pieces."

"Oh, for Pete's sake." Her voice is low enough only I can hear.

I place my hand over my chest as if I'm still feeling the pain. "So, I gave in. What else could I do? I'm a gentleman after all." I turn to Ellie. "Aren't I, darling?"

"Sure thing. Sweetheart." Her saccharine smile might fool everyone else, but it doesn't fool me.

"I couldn't stop thinking about her, so I thought I'd give it one more try. After the Minnesota game, I dropped by her place. And there I got the surprise of my life. A daughter I knew nothing about."

Her demeanor grows somber, as every eye zeroes in on her. Some questioning, some downright nasty.

Knowing my future is on the line, with her, with the team, I turn serious. "Now I got to be honest here. It hurt that she'd never told me. That she'd chosen to raise our daughter with no assistance from me." I take a deep breath, let it out.

"But I understand why she did it. She knew about my reputation, my partying. She didn't think that would be a healthy relationship for her child. So she made the hard decision to keep the baby secret from me."

Half of the audience glares at Ellie, but the other half appears sympathetic.

"Our daughter takes after her Mama. She's beautiful and smart. And that's all I'm going to say about her. As journalists, you're curious about what's going on, but we need privacy while I get to know our daughter. Ellie and I would prefer you don't intrude while we work hard on becoming a family."

"What about child support, Brock? Are you going to pay for that?" someone in the back of the room yells. So much for waiting for the Q&A.

"Every penny and then some. I've already set up a college trust fund for our daughter. She won't have to worry about expenses when she goes to school. Every penny will be taken care of."

"What about Ms. Adams? Are you going to pay her?"

Ellie jumps to her feet and pushes me out of the way. "No, he's not. He doesn't owe me a dime."

I wink at the audience. "Whoo-eee. She's something else, isn't she? She's an independent, self-sufficient woman to her core who refuses to take money from me."

"Why didn't you tell Brock about his daughter?" a woman reporter, one of the few in the audience, asks.

"Because, err—"

I wrap an arm around Ellie's waist. "Tell the truth, honey, don't be shy."

"Well, I knew about Brock's, err, lifestyle. And I didn't want to expose my daughter to it." She pretty much paraphrases what I just said.

"Can you blame her? I was a horndog plain and simple."

"Was?" somebody asks. "Have you changed your ways?"

"I'm glad you asked that question. That's very perspicuous of you," I say.

"Perceptive," Ellie says.

"What?"

"Perceptive, not perspicuous."

I grin. "See how smart she is. She's always teaching me." I cover the microphone so only she can hear. "Of course, in the bedroom, it's another story."

Her face turns a bright shade of red.

Needing to put her out of her misery, I take my hand off the mike. "Shall we share our news with them, sweetheart?"

Her gaze roams over the gaggle of reporters. She knows they won't leave us alone until we tell them what's going on. "Yes."

"I asked the little lady to marry me. And she said yes."

If the noise was deafening before, it's nothing to the sudden eruption of sounds in the room—camera clicks, voices yelling questions. Ignoring it all, I tell her, "Show them the ring, darling."

She holds up her right hand which sports the six-carat solitaire diamond I bought the day before. It's way too big for her, but we didn't have time for a fitting.

"When's the wedding, Brock?"

"As soon as possible. I can't wait to make her my bride." I squeeze her to me.

"You're not getting married just to quiet the rumors?"

I grow dead serious. "Absolutely not. I'm marrying Ellie because I love her and always will." And with that, I swing her into my arms and give her the hottest smooch possible. As always, she melts. "And she loves me. Don't you, darling?" Seemingly, I left her speechless, because all she does is nod.

"All right. That's enough," the head of PR interrupts. "You got the answers to your questions and—"

His voice fades as one of the assistants rushes us off the stage and out a side door to the parking lot. Although some reporters apparently figured out which one was my car, they're not being allowed near it by the team's mountain-sized security guys.

After opening the door for Ellie, I climb into the Porsche Cayenne and we head out.

"How are you doing?" I ask her. She seems her usual self, but it can't help to ask.

"Okay. It wasn't as bad as I thought."

"You did good."

"Well. I did well." Her correcting my grammar gets my motor running. But then what doesn't? Everything she does turns me on.

Pretty satisfied with my own performance, I ask. "So how did I do?"

"You really want to know?"

"Absolutely. I value your opinion."

"I never heard so much horse pucky in all my life."

I grin. "Maybe. But I had them eating out of my hand."

CHAPTER 19

Eleanor

USY REPLAYING THE PRESS CONFERENCE in my head, I don't pay much attention to the road. Only when he pulls into his condo parking lot, do I realize where we are.

"What are we doing here? Shouldn't you be dropping me off first?"

He turns off the ignition key and leans back in his seat. "We need to talk."

There's no shortage of subjects. The press conference. Our wedding plans. But there's no time. At least not now. "I need to go home, Brock. Kaylee will be there soon."

"Your mom's at your house, isn't she?"

"Yes, of course." She's supervising Butch who's become ultra-protective. If anybody so much as rings our doorbell, he goes nuts. "But she'll leave as soon as Kaylee arrives." Of course, Mama will stay if the paparazzi are still hanging out, but I'd just as soon not impose upon her more than I already have.

"The press still camped at your door?"

"Some." I fetch my cell from my purse. "Should I call an Uber?"

"No need. I'll drive you home. Let me grab a few things first."

"What things?"

"Clothes, toiletries, my shaving gear."

Clueless, I ask, "Why?"

"Because I'll be staying with you."

"What?!!!" I'm not ready to have him move in this instant. I need time to prepare, to come to terms with the reality of Brock in my house. "You can't do that. Not today."

"Ellie"—he cradles my jaw in that big hand of his—"now that we've announced our engagement everyone will expect us to live together. And going by the strong media presence at the press conference, they won't stop camping out at your door. At least, not until our wedding. So I need to be there, living with you. If I don't, it'll be all over the tabloids."

I only have two bedrooms. "Where would you sleep?" Silly question, I know.

"With you, of course."

Brock in my bed holding me, kissing me, making love to me every night. I'm not ready for this. "No."

"Ellie, be reasonable."

I can't imagine how Kaylee will react to Brock in our home. I've never, ever brought a man to the house. "It's not right. I have a daughter."

"*We* have a daughter."

"We're not married."

"Yet."

"But. But."

"It'll be fine, sweetheart, you'll see."

"I'm not your sweetheart."

"Yes. You are." Crooking a finger, he lifts my chin and brushes his lips against mine. He nibbles the corners of my mouth, suckles my lower lip, and everything in me goes liquid. Our mouths, tongues, teeth tangle in a frenzy of lust. His hand climbs down to the hem of my skirt. Before I know it, his fingers are brushing my thighs, pushing my panties aside, teasing my pussy. Silently begging for more, I push against his fingers, until he thrusts one inside. I ride him until another finger and a third join the first. I want to come. I need to come.

"I want to taste you."

Oh, God. He is a devil. "Here?"

"Back seat." He barely waits for my 'Yes,' before helping me to the rear. He opens his driver's door and crawls in with me. The panties come off, and his mouth covers my pussy. His fingers continue what they started, while he slicks his tongue over me. I clutch his hair, as he tongues me, bites me, drives me wild. With such expert handling, it takes me no time to come.

Gulping in air, I slick sweaty hair off my face. That's when I catch the time. "We have to stop. Kaylee." That's all I can manage.

Breathing hard, he rests his forehead on mine, as he brushes his hard-on against me. "Of course."

I know what he wants, and I'd love to return the favor, but we have to get home. Our daughter's needs come first.

At his condo, he spends little time filling his suitcase. But then, as many away games as he's played, packing must be second nature to him.

We arrive home to find no paparazzi at our door. Maybe they got their fill at the press conference. Yeah, right. They'll probably be back the next day.

Inside, Kaylee's seated by the kitchen island eating a bowl of something with Butch at her feet.

"Did Grandma leave?"

"She headed out as soon as I got home. She had some food shopping to do." She squints at Brock. "What's *he* doing here?"

After the press conference and sex in Brock's car, I find myself lacking in parental patience. "*He* is your father, and he's moving in."

Frowning, she awkwardly comes to her feet. "It would have been nice to have gotten some notice."

I start to respond, but Brock gets there before I do. "If you want someone to blame, that would be me. I sprung this on your mother."

I can't allow him to take all of the responsibility for this decision. That

146

would only make Kaylee dislike him more. "And I agreed." I walk up, put my arms around her. "Honey. You're right. We should have told you. But things are moving kind of fast. I hope you can accept them when they do."

Staring at the floor, she shrugs.

Not really a response, but at the moment, it's the best I can hope for. In time, I pray she'll accept Brock's presence in our lives.

After rinsing and dropping her dish in the dishwasher, she turns back to us, "I saw your press conference."

"How on earth did you do that?" As far as I know, the press conference was not live.

"A YouTube channel showed the whole thing."

Brock's gaze seems to say 'Told you so.'

"Thank you for not bringing me into it. It's bad enough at school as it is."

"What's happening at school?" Brock asks, his Papa Bear instincts seemingly kicking in. Who knew?

"Nothing," Kaylee says. "Shouldn't have mentioned it. Well, I better leave you alone. I'm sure you have wedding plans to discuss." And with that, she rolls out of the kitchen and disappears into the hallway that leads to her room.

Brock's worried gaze follows her. "Is she going to be all right?"

"Yeah. She will. She's a strong kid."

He tangles a hand through his hair. "Shouldn't we, I don't know, talk to her or something?"

"I will, later on. But right now, she needs some space."

"You sure?"

"Positive." More than likely, she doesn't want to air her feelings in front of Brock. It'll take time for her to come to terms with him.

After dinner, I knock on her door. "Kaylee? May I come in?"

"Okay."

She's sitting up on her bed, laptop on her lap, and Butch next to her. "He's not coming in too, is he?"

"No. He's watching a football tape to prepare for Sunday's game."

She rolls her eyes. "Is that all he can think about?"

"It's his job, honey. And he's very good at it precisely because, among other things, he studies game tapes."

"Oh."

I drop on the corner of her bed. "We haven't had a chance to discuss things since Sunday. Anything you want to talk about?"

She doesn't respond right away. But then, "I was wondering . . ."

"Yes."

"Well, you and Brock hadn't seen each other for years, right?"

"Yes."

"So when did you. I mean, how did you . . ."

She can't quite figure out how to ask, but having anticipated the question, I'm prepared with a response. "After he arrived in Chicago, we discovered sparks were still there."

"Ookayyy. But when exactly did you discover this?"

This is the tricky part, but I figured out an answer that should work out. "You remember that dinner he invited me to?"

"Yes."

"It happened that night." Since she was at a sleepover, she wouldn't know I hadn't spent the night at the hotel with Brock.

"So, why didn't you tell him about me then?"

There's no good answer to that, so I can only go with the truth. "Our reconnection was so fragile, it didn't seem the right time."

"Aha."

She doesn't believe a word I'm saying, and who can blame her?

"You want to know what I think?"

"Yes, sweetheart. I do."

"You're getting married because it got out he's my father, and he got into trouble with his football team."

I can't disagree. That's exactly why we're getting married. Well, that, and the fact I'd probably get canned from my job.

"But—" she adds.

"But what?"

"You're happy when he's around."

"I am?"

"Yeah. Your face lights up, and you smile more."

Huh? Somehow I thought we were always arguing. Except for the times he teases me about something, and I laugh. Maybe Kaylee has a point.

"So, I'm willing to go along with the flow. Just don't ask me to smile pretty for the cameras."

"I won't." That much I can promise her.

With our wedding in two weeks, I throw myself full tilt at the planning. Marty encourages me to take whatever time I need, but I don't want to abuse the privilege. So I try to arrange for everything after hours. The church is easy. Kaylee and I are regular attendees. The reception, however, is another matter. You just don't snag a reception hall that will hold 350 guests on two weeks' notice.

But a couple of days after we announced our engagement, the Outlaws' Event Coordinator calls to offer her services. I'm no fool. Knowing a lifeline when I see it, I clutch it desperately to my chest. Before I know it, she's booked the Chicago Hilton which is more than glad to host our reception. Guess when a wedding comes with all kinds of free publicity, you tend to say yes. I'm sure it doesn't hurt that the Outlaws regularly drop a small fortune at that place.

Not only does she take care of the reception, but everything else as well. So in the end all I have to worry about are my wedding gown and Kaylee's bridesmaid dress. You'd think with practically every detail taken off my hands, I'd just lay back and chill. But the opposite happens. The closer the wedding day gets, the more jittery I become. And then People magazine calls, asking if they can feature our fairytale wedding in their weekly spread.

Kaylee's reaction is predictable. "Fairytale wedding? Honestly, Mom."

"Yeah, I know, honey." I agree, trying to keep my objections at bay. The whole thing is ludicrous. But what choice do I have? His team and my sports agency are loving all the publicity.

Finally, the wedding day arrives, and before I know it, I'm standing in front of my priest.

"Dearly Beloved, we're gathered here today . . ." Father Sullivan's voice fades away as he speaks the words that will unite Brock and me in holy matrimony.

How on earth did I get here? One minute I'm kissing Brock, the next I'm getting married. Well, it's too late to back out now even if I wanted to. Which I mostly don't.

I glance back toward the congregants. His entire football's team is here with their wives or significant others. We'd made it a kid-friendly wedding so some brought their children as well. Kaylee is my maid of honor and Trevor, Brock's center, is his best man. The height differential is ludicrous. Kaylee comes up to his middle of his chest. But both of them, thank God, are taking it in stride.

At least Kaylee and her best friend made up after Meghan came over to apologize. She said she was sorry, that she shouldn't have yelled. And that's all that matters. With everything that's going on, Kaylee needs someone her own age in her life.

"Eleanor Ruth Adams, will you have this man to be your husband; to live together with him in the covenant of marriage? Will you love him, comfort him, honor and keep him, in sickness and in health; and, forsaking all others, be faithful unto him as long as you both shall live?"

This is really real, isn't it? "I will."

"Brock James Parker, will you have this woman to be your wife; to live together with her in the covenant of marriage? Will you love her, comfort her, honor and keep her, in sickness and in health; and, forsaking all others, be faithful unto her as long as you both shall live?"

Someone in the audience snickers, probably at the faithful line. But Brock ignores it.

"With all my heart, I will."

Oh, geez. He didn't have to add that, did he? It's not in the script.

Before I know it, Brock's taking my hand in his. "In the name of God, I, Brock James Parker, take you, Eleanor Ruth Adams, to be my wife, to have and to hold from this day forward, for better, for worse, for richer, for poorer, in sickness and in health, to love and to cherish until we are parted by death. This is my solemn vow." He sounds so sure of himself, so sure of me, so sure of this marriage. How could he? It's going to last all of five minutes.

When I repeat the same vow and get to the love and cherish part, he squeezes my hand. He's pretty thrilled to be getting me out of this deal. No clue why. It's a mystery to me.

"Eleanor Ruth Adams and Brock James Parker, having witnessed your vows of love to one another, it is my joy to present you to all gathered here as husband and wife." He turns to Brock. "You may kiss your bride."

Brock's arm slides around my waist and pulls me to him. Rather than a chaste kiss, he full out frenches me. Right in front of God and everyone. I fight with every cell in my body not to respond. We need to keep this somewhat PG-rated, after all.

Only when Father Sullivan whispers, "You'll have enough time for that later, son," does Brock let go.

He turns and whoops, punches his arm in the air. And then he strides up the aisle so fast I have a hard time keeping up with him.

The Outlaws' event manager booked a pretty good band for the reception. For our first song, we dance to "The Way You Look Tonight." As he gazes into my eyes with his full of love, tears spring to mine. Who knew Brock was such a good actor?

The buffet tables practically groan with the mountains of food on them. When it's time for the toast, Trevor makes a surprisingly sweet one. But when it's Brock's turn to say a few words, he floors me.

> Drink to me only with thine eyes,
> And I will pledge with mine;
> Or leave a kiss but in the cup,
> And I'll not look for wine.
> The thirst that from the soul doth rise
> Doth ask a drink divine;
> But might I of Jove's nectar sup,
> I would not change for thine.

He gets an enthusiastic round of applause for his ditty, though I doubt most of them understood it. "That was beautiful. Where on earth did you find that poem?"

"Ben Johnson. A contemporary of Shakespeare, I believe." And he winks.

Close to midnight, we make our getaway. Mama, Steve, and Kaylee already retired to the two-bedroom suite that Brock booked for them, but the party's in full swing doing a conga line.

When we get to our suite, he carries me over the threshold before dropping me back on my feet and kissing me. "All alone. Finally."

"Yes." No idea why I'm so nervous. It isn't like it's the first time we've had sex.

"Do you need help getting out of your gown?"

"Please." Although I'd removed the train after the ceremony, I'm still in the silk organza gown. As beautiful as it is, I don't want to damage it. Maybe Kaylee would like to wear it on her wedding day someday.

He slowly, methodically unhooks the dress. After he's released the last prong, I lean on his arm and step out of it. And then I lay it across the sofa in the front room of our suite.

"You don't want to hang it?"

"No. The weight of the gown will damage the lace."

"You looked very beautiful today."

"So did you." The black tuxedo suits his blond hair and green eyes.

He cups the back of my neck and kisses me. I'm surprised not by the hunger or passion but by the trembling of his lips. He's as nervous as I am.

"Can you unhook the corset too?" I whisper against his mouth.

"You're so slender. Why would you strap yourself into this thing?"

"So the gown would look better. I only intend to marry this one time, so I wanted to look perfect."

His hands pause. "I never thought about that."

"About what?"

"That you would marry only once. You're a great mom. Don't you want more children?"

"Babies demand a lot of attention, Brock. With my career, I can't afford the time."

"You could hire a nanny."

"That's not happening."

"Take a sabbatical then. I'm sure they'd hold the job for you."

"Yeah, right! You know what happens to agents who go on the mommy track? They get relegated to the back office to do grunt work when they return. I didn't sweat over three years of law school to work at a lower pay. I have school loans and a mortgage to pay."

"No, you don't."

I twist around and face him. "What do you mean?"

He retrieves an envelope from his jacket and hands it to me. "My wedding present. One of them, anyway."

I open it to find two sheets of paper, both marked "Paid in Full."

"You paid off my mortgage and my school loans?"

"Surprise!" He grins.

"How could you?"

His happy smile crumbles. "I thought you'd be pleased."

"I'm not. We never agreed to this."

"Of course, we didn't. You never asked for a dime. Ellie, I make millions playing football. Contrary to popular opinion, I haven't spent that much. On top of that, I have a really good investment manager who's more than tripled my income. I can afford a few measly dollars for you to be debt free."

"I wish you'd told me."

"If I had, it wouldn't have been a surprise, would it?"

"I can't accept this." I hand the papers back to him.

But he won't take them. "Yes, you can. If not for yourself, for Kaylee. You'll have more money to spend on her."

A sore point with me. There have been times when I hadn't been able to get something she wanted. "She has everything she needs."

"I'm sure she does, but wouldn't it be nice to afford it when she asks for something."

"Like what?"

"Well, in four years, she'll be sixteen. I'm sure she'll want a car. Oh, by the way." He dangles a key fob in front of me.

"What's that?"

"Your other wedding present."

"What is it?"

"A silver Mercedes Benz with all the bells and whistles."

I'd been drooling over one for the longest time. Wishful thinking on my part because I'd never be able to afford one. "How did you know?"

"Your mother."

Of course, Mama would have told him. "Thank you." I take the fob from his hand. He's given me these extravagant thoughtful gifts, and I have nothing for him. I turn my head to the side to keep him from seeing my tears.

Crooking a finger, he turns my chin to face him. "Ellie, what's wrong?"

"I didn't get you anything."

Shaking his head, he cups my jaw in his hand. "Of course, you did. You gave me a beautiful daughter."

A watery grin slips out. "Yeah, I did, didn't I?" Not quite done with my tears, I sniff.

He cocks his head to the side and flashes that devil-may-care grin of his. "I know what you need."

"What?"

"Us naked on that bed."

"Doing naughty things, I suppose?"

"Very naughty."

When I laugh, he picks me up by my ass and walks toward the bed. "We've only got twenty-four hours before I have to report back to camp, and I mean to spend every last minute worshipping this hot little body of yours."

"At some point, we'll need to eat."

"We'll order room service, and I'll feed you in bed."

"And shower."

"Nuh-uh. For the next day, I want you to smell just like me."

CHAPTER 20

Brock

$\mathcal{I}$'M STARVING, NOT FOR FOOD BUT FOR HER. The scent of her skin, as always, makes me want to devour her whole. I have to stop myself from attacking Ellie like the beast I am. But I'm still fully dressed while she's almost naked. And something has to be done about this.

"Should I undress you?" she asks, her eyes luminous.

"Do you want to undress me?"

"Very much."

"Okay." Even though I'll suffer the tortures of the damned with her hands on me.

She slides her hands underneath the tuxedo's jacket. I end up helping her since it's a tight fit.

"Rented or yours?"

"What do you think?"

She cocks her head to the side as she considers her answer. "Rented. I didn't see a tuxedo when I put away your clothes in the condo."

"Wrong." I brush a thin line of hair from her lips. "I had it custom made. I didn't want to wear a rented suit on my wedding day."

"But you'll never wear it again." Her eyes narrow. "Unless you're planning to get married again?"

"No. Once is more than enough for me." She has no idea she's my one and only.

"So, why?"

"Because today's special, and I wanted to wear a suit especially made for the occasion."

The vest comes off next. Her dainty hands attack the seed pearl buttons, and they roll off their holes one by one. By the time she gets to the lowest one, I'm hard enough to pound nails. "Hurry."

"Why? You took your time."

"Because I'm hard as stone, sweet girl." I promised myself I'd keep my hands off her while she completed this task. But I don't think I can.

She peeks up at me through smoky lashes. "Patience is a virtue."

"Of which I have none." I lean forward, nibble her neck. But she pushes me back to slide off the vest.

The bow comes off easily. For a second, she dangles it from her fingers before she tosses it . . . somewhere.

The shirt studs come off at a glacial pace.

"You're killing me, Ellie."

"You'll survive."

Once the last one is gone, she slides her hands beneath my shirt. When her cool touch comes into contact with my hot skin, I hiss out a breath.

She yanks down the shirt trapping my arms and bares my chest. With an impish look in her eyes, she wets her index finger with her tongue and circles my right nipple.

"You're playing with fire." My voice's pure gravel, but I can't help it.

"I know." She stands on her tiptoes and circles her tongue around one nipple. While her fingers tease the other.

I snake a hand around her nape and bend down to suck her tongue into my mouth, nibble at her lips, bite down. My hand wanders down to her sweet breasts. But she pushes me back again. "I'm not done."

We're standing right next to the bed, so all it takes is one push for me to land backward on the bed. While I lie prone, she removes my shoes and socks.

She releases the belt, whips it in the air. And then she unsnaps my waistband, lowers my zipper, and snakes her hand within to grab her prize.

"Oh, my. What a big boy you are."

"I'm not a boy." I roll her over and proceed to devour her the way I've been wanting to most of the damn day. I lick, nibble, bite my way down to her core. When I get there, I widen her legs and settle down to feast on her. The honey-sweet taste of her pussy is beyond delicious.

"Ahhh." She wriggles beneath my assault, grabs my hair and wiggles under me.

I don't know how much longer I can stand doing this, so I stand and toss off the rest of my clothes. I grab a condom from the stash I'd stored in the night table and roll it over me while she silently watches.

I lift her hips and position my hard cock over her opening. "Ready?"

She nods.

I ease into her slowly. As big and as hard as I am, the last thing I want to do is hurt her.

Our coupling sounds loud in the confine of the room and so do her moans. "Faster, Brock."

"You sure?"

"Positive."

"Hang on."

She wraps her arms around my arms, and I go for it, surging into her with every ounce of my being. She's blazing hot and so, so wet. For me. For everything I can give to her.

"I'm coming, Brock."

So am I, but I don't want to get there. Not just yet. Not before her.

I don't have to wait long. Her whole body grows rigid as she dissolves. I follow her into paradise.

I collapse on her but immediately roll over taking her with me. As much as I weigh and as tiny as she is, I could hurt her. I clutch her to me as our breaths bellow.

"How was that?" I ask.

"I'll let you know as soon as I catch my breath."

CHAPTER 21

Brock

EVEN THOUGH THIS IS THE PLAYERS' REST DAY, I don't get the time off. Instead, I spend most of the day doing social media. With the team being 4 and 0, you'd think there'd be lots to talk about. But turns out the media's main interest is my married life. Seems like people love hearing how the love of a good woman reformed the league's bad boy. I'd love to say no to spending the day doing interviews, but I can't. Not as helpful as the Outlaws were with our wedding reception.

Once the interviews are done, I head home. I step into the house to find Kaylee studying in the living room, Butch by her feet. "Your mom home?"

"She ran to the grocery store. Should be back soon."

As soon as she says that, the sound of the garage door opening reaches me. Two minutes later, a breathless Ellie stumbles into the kitchen, carrying two heavy bags of food. "You're here!"

I walk toward her to take the bags off her hands. "Yeah. I cut out early. They understood. Newly-married man and all that. Need any help?"

"Yeah. You can help me put away the groceries."

"Okay."

She directs me to put some things in the cupboard; others in the refrigerator.

"I thought I'd have dinner on the table before you got home. But don't worry, it'll be done in a jiff," she says, snapping on a retro red and white apron Betty Crocker would be proud to wear. But when she has trouble with the tie in the back, she turns to me. "Can you . . . ?"

After I tie a perfect bow, I whisper in her ear. "I'm sure whatever you make will be delicious, but I didn't marry you for your cooking skills." And then so she understands exactly why I married her, I haul her into me and kiss her.

"If you guys are going to do that, I'm going to leave the room."

"Go ahead." I toss over my shoulder while keeping Ellie close.

But Kaylee remains exactly where she is.

Ellie frees herself from my embrace. "You shouldn't tease her like that."

"Who's teasing?"

She shoots me a look with 'Behave' written all over it.

Okay, I get it. She's uncomfortable with PDAs in front of our daughter. But Kaylee's got to get used to it. Because I intend to hug and kiss Ellie a lot. It wouldn't hurt to schedule some private time, though.

"Do you think you could get your mom to stay here a couple of days next week?"

"Why?" she says, slinging some chicken into a pot.

"So we could go have some sexy times at the condo." I rub my hand across her delicious, round bottom. With the kitchen island between us and our audience in the living room, I'm pretty sure Kaylee can't see us.

"Shhhhh. Kaylee will hear."

"You liked the den of sin. You know you did." The night we made love, I'd tied up Ellie and spanked her sweet ass. She'd loved every second of it.

She giggles. "It was kind of fun."

I've never heard that sound from her before. Not even when she was a teenager. She was such a serious little thing.

After dinner is done and the dishwasher's running, we sit in front of the TV to watch some baking show she and Kaylee love.

After a while, I whisper in Ellie's ear. "I'd rather do something else."

"Oh, God. Shoot me now. You guys going to have sex?"

That girl has the ears of a bat.

"Kaylee!"

"That's what married people do," I say.

"That's disgusting. I'm going to my room." And this time she follows through. She flounces out leaving us alone in the living room.

"Is she going to spend the rest of our married life hiding in her bedroom?"

"She's a tween. That's what they do."

"A tween?"

"Meaning in between a girl and a teen."

We can't keep walking on tippy toes around Kaylee. Sooner or later, she'll need to accept our intimacy. And I know just the way to do it. "Does she have headphones?"

Her brow scrunches. "Yes."

"Let's make sure she puts them on."

"What?"

I pull her to her feet. "Follow my lead."

The double bed in Ellie's room is not big enough for the two of us, but we'll make it work until the King-size gets delivered next week. But it does have one great feature. A nice, big, oak headboard.

"Get on the bed. On your knees."

"What are you going to do?"

"It's not what I'm going to do, but what we're going to do. If there's any damage, I'll take care of it. Okay?"

Her eyes grow big as saucers.

I bang the headboard against the wall. "Moan."

"What?"

"Moan."

She does.

"Louder."

"Oooohhhhh."

"Now, yell my name."

A wicked glint shines in her eyes as she realizes what I'm doing. "Oh, my God, Brock. Oh, that feels so good. So good. Harder." She's clearly getting into the act, but then she giggles and that may spoil the whole effect.

I kiss her and cover her mouth. "No giggling." I spank her bottom, one, twice, three times.

And that gets her motor running. She keeps up the yelling, the moaning, screaming my name and a couple of saints while I rhythmically bang the headboard against the wall.

After fifteen minutes, I slowly dial it down. And then I strip the both of us and quietly, tenderly make love to my wife.

When dawn comes, I roll out of bed. After a quick shower, I kiss Ellie, who's still fast asleep, probably exhausted from our lovemaking. I walk out of our bedroom to find Kaylee parked by the kitchen island, a smoothie in her hand.

"Good morning." I head for the kitchen counter to grab some caffeine since I can't function without it. To my surprise, the coffee's already made.

"I brewed it while you were in the shower."

A peace offering? Maybe. "Thanks." I pour the java into a cup, add in cream until it's the shade I like.

"You guys were awfully loud last night."

Where's she going with this? "Were we?"

"The way you were going at it, I should have a little brother or sister in no time." She's made of tough stuff, my daughter.

But I'm tougher. "God willing."

She squints. "I'm not going to take care of it."

Leaning back against the counter, I sip the fragrant brew. "You won't have to. I'll hire a nanny."

She scoffs. "Yeah, right. That's not going to happen. Mom would only allow Grandma to take care of me."

Ellie had shared some of Kaylee's upbringing, but I'm curious to hear her side of it. "What happened after you were born, Kaylee?"

"Well, obviously I was too young to remember, but we all lived in the same house—Mom, Grandma, Steve, and me. While Mom attended community college, Grandma watched over me. When I turned two, Mom got a partial scholarship to Duke University and transferred over there. But I was too little to go with her, so I remained with Grandma. She hated being away from me. Although she tried to hide how sad she was, one day I caught her crying in her car. That's my earliest memory of her."

Damn it. If Ellie had told me, I could have given her money so she could have hired a nanny and kept Kaylee with her. But from what Kaylee says, she wouldn't have allowed that.

"When I turned four, she couldn't stand being away from me anymore, so she brought me to Durham. We lived in this tiny one-bedroom apartment, slept on the same bed. Every once in a while, she'd make this big production number out of eating noodles and peanut butter. I loved it."

"Did you?"

"Yeah, I did. Weekends, Grandma would visit so Mom wouldn't have to worry about me while she studied."

"I wish she'd told me about you. I could have made your lives easier."

"It was fine, Br—I mean Dad." She doesn't seem comfortable with the dad bit.

I take another coffee sip. "You call me whatever feels comfortable to you, except Mr. Parker. That just sounds odd."

She grins. "Then Brock it is."

"Fine." Can't expect for her to call me dad when I've been her father for all of five minutes.

Her brow scrunches. "I don't have to change my last name, do I?"

"Only if you want to."

"I don't." She hitches up her chin.

She might look like me, but that gesture is pure Ellie. Seen her do that a million times.

"Can I ask you a question?" she asks.

"Sure."

"How was Mom as a teenager?"

Tit for tat. She opened up about me. So I need to do the same about her mom. Can't really fault her for her curiosity. "Pretty much the same as she is now. Only younger."

"Was she always so serious?"

"Yes. She studied all the time. Got straight A's in school."

"You hired mom as a tutor."

"I did. I wasn't doing too well in English. Had a problem with Shakespeare. Macbeth to be exact. One of the football players on my team told me about her. So I asked her to tutor me. Every Thursday from six to seven."

"And you studied the whole time?"

"Yes."

"When did I happen?"

I drop the empty coffee cup in the dishwasher to give me time to think. Would Ellie like me to answer that question? "You should ask your mother about that."

"I already did. She won't tell me."

Kaylee should know how she was created. If I were her, I'd want to know. So I go with my gut. "I got a B plus on my midterm exam. First time that had ever happened. So I went to her house to celebrate. There was a monster of a thunderstorm that night, violent enough to rattle windows and down trees. When the lights went out, she panicked. She tried to cover it up, but I knew."

"Mom's not comfortable in the dark. That's why we have a whole slew of flashlights around the house."

"She had one, but the battery was dead. She was so frightened. I put my arms around her to comfort her and . . . " I'll leave the rest out. Can't really discuss the birds and bees with a twelve-year-old.

"You conceived me."

I nod.

"Was that the only time you two . . . ?"

This is fucking awkward. But she deserves to know. "Yes."

"Wow."

Wow, indeed. I push away from the counter. "Do you need a ride to school? I can drop you off."

"No. I'm good. I take the school bus. But thanks."

I sling my duffel bag over my shoulder and head toward the front door.

Before I get there, she says, "Brock?"

I turn to face her. "Yes."

"Mom's happy now. She wasn't before."

I nod. "Thanks for telling me." I intend to keep Ellie happy. Whatever it takes.

CHAPTER 22

Eleanor

TWO WEEKS OF MARRIED LIFE HAVE BEEN, WELL, MAGICAL. There's no other way to describe it. Brock comes home for dinner most every night, even though the team prefers he eat at the facility. He says he loves my cooking. But he doesn't fool me. It's something else he loves.

Family life.

You'd think he'd be bored to tears with our daily routine, but he seems to treasure the moments, even the simple ones, like cleaning up after dinner, and watching television together. Sometimes, Kaylee joins us, but most times she gives us privacy. Good thing because Brock won't stop kissing me and holding hands. He leaves the more private stuff for the bedroom. And the really wild things to the condo. I never thought I'd enjoy being tied up and spanked. But, God help me, I do.

Tonight, we're watching one of my favorite cooking shows, and it's bread week. Before too long, the participants are measuring and mixing ingredients. As they do, the tension builds in him. What is it about a cooking show that turns him on?

Leaning into me, he whispers, "I love the way she's pounding that flour."

"It's called kneading." I correct him.

"The way she digs her fingers into the dough, forces it into submission." As he speaks, his hand softly strokes my shoulders. When my breath catches, his fingers explore my aching flesh, finding the erotic spots that set my body on fire. When his efforts turn to unbuttoning my blouse, I protest, "Kaylee."

"She's in her room." He nibbles the bare expanse of skin he's exposed and heat streaks down to my pussy.

"Ahhhh." I should tell him we need to take this to our room, but right now I'm loving what he's doing too much to ask him to stop.

His fingers cup my breast, play with my nipple, and I tip back my head to give him more room. When I do, he leans over to suckle my nipple. As he tastes me, I grow liquid.

"Sweet Ellie," he breathes over my trembling belly. "You want me to fuck you?"

Oh, God. Yes. But, "Not here."

He stands, hauls me into his arms, and carries me into our room. When we get there, he takes his time stripping me, stroking me, licking me, until I'm quivering and aching for him.

"You want me, Ellie?"

Bastard. "You know, I do."

He spreads his arms wide and offers himself to me. "Then get me naked, woman."

Aaargh. He is the devil. As tall as he is, I have to stand on the bed to get his shirt off. Once his magnificent chest is bared, I climb down and unbutton his jeans, unzip his fly and pull. When the jeans and boxers come off, he kicks them to the side, and I'm left to gawk while he stands there in his glorious masculinity, his cock flying high and proud. Unable to withstand the temptation, I splay my hands across his hips and take him into my mouth.

He groans. "God, Ellie. You're killing me."

I don't care. I want the taste of earthy, randy male in my mouth. He rests his hands on my head and sways back and forth with deep, shallow strokes as I suck, lick the life out of him. I dig my nails into his ass. When he grows even bigger, I know his orgasm is near.

"I'm coming, darling."

That's all the warning I get before his heat spurts into my mouth, so much that some spills out to dribble down my chin. Once I've licked every bit of his essence, I glance up. The look of ecstasy on his face is something I will treasure forever.

"Get on the bed." He growls.

Without hesitation, I clamber backwards on the mattress, aiming for the center. But he doesn't want me there. He grabs my legs and pulls me to the edge. Widening my thighs, his mouth clamps over me and suckles, teases, licks my pussy. I teased him, so now it's his turn to torture me. As wound up as I am, it takes me no time to orgasm. Only then does he rise and push me deeper into the bed as he rises over me, like the god he is, and in one strong thrust spears me. He's so big, he takes my breath away. But I wouldn't have him any other way.

The next morning, I wake up, sore as hell. A hot shower eases some of the aches and pains from our lovemaking. Thankfully, neither Kaylee nor Brock are present as I make my walk of shame. But Mama is. She stands by the kitchen counter, drinking a cup of tea. "Morning."

"Morning."

"Sleep well?" Her knowing smile tells me she knows exactly how I spent my night.

"Yes." My face flushes. Why, I don't know. It's not like I'm fooling around. I'm married to Brock, for heaven's sake.

Thankfully, she takes pity on me. "You want some coffee? I just made a pot."

"No, thanks." Pride drives me to make a quick getaway. "I'll grab some at work." I thoroughly regret my decision on the long drive. Coffee would have made the ride easier.

I arrive at the office to find a message from a stranger on my office phone.

"Mrs. Parker. This is Horace Watkins. I'm calling about a very important matter regarding your daughter. Could you please return my call at 312-555-2400?"

Kaylee! Did something happen to her? In a panic, I hang up and dial Kaylee's cell. She picks up on the first ring. "Mom?"

"Are you okay?" I sound alarmed, but it can't be helped.

"Yeah. I'm fine. What's wrong?"

"Nothing, sweetheart. I just got a weird call."

"About me?" Should have known she'd figure it out.

"Maybe." I can't say anymore since I don't know why Mr. Watkins contacted me. "Let me call him and find out. Love you."

"Oh, okay. Love you too."

Darn it. Too late I realize I should have phoned the school, not her. But in my panic, I didn't think things through. Taking a deep breath, I dial Horace Watkins' number. A receptionist picks up. "Turner and Watkins Law Group. How may I direct your call?"

A law firm? "Yes, I'm returning Horace Watkins' call. My name is Eleanor Adams, err. Parker."

"Yes. He's expecting your call. I'll put you through."

A couple of rings later, a man's voice answers. "Mrs. Parker?"

"Yes."

"Horace Watkins. Thank you for returning my call."

Eager to hurry things along, I ask, "Your message said it concerned my daughter?"

"Yes. It's good news, Mrs. Parker." He must have picked up on my anxiety.

"Oh?"

"How much do you know about William Parker?"

The name strikes a chord, of course. "He's my husband's father." That's the extent of my knowledge.

"That's right. He passed away several years ago."

"Brock told me."

"Before his death, he created a trust fund and made his son the sole beneficiary. The trust assets are mainly comprised of stock in Creighton Pharmaceutical as well as William Parker's private fortune.

The latter alone is quite valuable." Doesn't matter. Brock wants no part of it. "Do you follow the pharmaceutical industry, Mrs. Parker?"

"No. Not really."

"Well, Creighton Pharmaceutical has done quite well. Its shares have quadrupled in value since its original offering."

"That's . . . great?" Where is he going with this? He must know Brock won't touch the money in that trust, no matter how much it's worth.

"Mr. Parker also made a provision for your husband's children, should there be any."

Now he has *all* my attention. "He did?"

"Yes. A certain amount was bequeathed to each child of your husband's upon his or her birth, as well as certain milestones, such as high school and college graduations, and legal marriages."

"Oh."

Mr. Watkins clears his throat. "As we understand it, your child, Kaylee Adams, is Brock Parker's daughter. Is that correct?"

"Yes. She is." The entire world learned that fact at the Outlaws' press conference, so it's no surprise Mr. Watkins did as well.

"Glad to hear it." He sounds almost relieved. "Her legacy has been accumulating since her birth, and she's due quite a tidy sum."

"How much?"

"Twenty million."

I choke. "Dollars?"

A small chuckle on his part. "That's right."

That much money would set up Kaylee for life. She'd never have to worry about making ends meet. But there's one thing I don't understand. "Why are you calling me instead of Brock?"

"We've approached Mr. Parker, but he won't accept the bequest."

Brock did what? I don't care how lousy his relationship was with his father. You don't pass up that kind of money, not when it's meant for Kaylee. "I'll need to talk to him. Can I get back to you tomorrow?"

"Of course, Mrs. Parker. Once you do, let us know how you wish to proceed."

Although my first inclination is to call Brock and ask him if he's lost his mind, I can't discuss this over the phone. The conversation is bound to be volatile. Kaylee can't overhear it either. So there's really only one place we can talk. The condo.

I check my watch. He's in practice, which means he doesn't have his phone close by. After I call Mama to make sure she can be home for Kaylee, I leave a message for Brock asking him to meet me at the condo after work.

That night, he strides into the place, sporting a grin a mile wide. He's probably anticipating another sex romp. But he's going to be very disappointed.

His gaze cuts to the kitchen where I have something on the stove. "You're cooking dinner?"

The couple of times we've come to the condo since our wedding, food was the last thing on our minds. "Yes, a casserole. We need to talk."

His gaze grows worried. "About what?"

I fold my arms across my chest. "I got a call today from Horace Watkins."

His grin disappears. "He shouldn't have phoned you. I told him I wanted no part of it."

"You turned down $20,000,000 for Kaylee without consulting me?"

"Yes."

I stomp toward him and smack his chest. "How dare you do such a thing?"

"I don't want my father's money. I didn't need it all these years. And I certainly don't need it now. I can provide for Kaylee. I can provide for you."

"That's not the point. That money can ensure her future, her children's future. She doesn't have to suffer through hard times." I'm so angry I'm practically hyperventilating.

His voice softens. "Like you did?"

"Yes."

He cups my face. "I'm so sorry I wasn't there to make your life easier."

"I'm not blaming you, Brock. It's my fault. I should have told you."

"Ellie, my father's legacy. I don't want it."

I gaze up at him, pleading. "So don't take it for you. Accept it for Kaylee. Please." He's lived in the lap of luxury since birth. His parents may have been emotionally distant but they made sure he never wanted for anything. He was clothed, sheltered and fed. Although he empathizes with my situation, he's got no idea what it means to be poor. "You don't know how difficult it is to juggle bills; to choose between the rent and the electric bill, because you can't pay both; to weep for joy at the grocery store because the spaghetti is on sale and you have two more dollars to spend on food."

"I'm sorry."

"Nor do you know how badly I felt when I had to deny Kaylee every time she asked for a toy." I grit my teeth. "I swore by almighty God once I got a job, she would never want for a thing. And I've come through on that promise. She's a happy, well-adjusted child."

"Yes, she is." He wipes the tears from my face.

"So if there's any way I can help it, I'll be damned if I let you keep that money from her. Don't you see? That's her ticket from poverty and want and need."

He envelops me in his strong arms as I bawl my eyes out. "Hush, sweetheart."

But I'm so wound up, it takes me several minutes to regain my composure.

He drops a kiss on my head. "Very well."

I sniff one last time. "Really?"

"Yes. If it means that much to you."

"Thank you." I fling my arms around him and kiss him full on the mouth.

"How long 'til that casserole is done?"

"About forty-five minutes."

"Well, then." He carries me to the den of sin where we spend the rest of the night making long and boisterous love.

CHAPTER 23

Brock

FOOTBALL SEASON ROLLS ALONG in a Chicago freezing tundra cold enough to freeze your nuts. We make the playoffs, but lose the conference championship game. Although disappointed, I have no regrets. I know I've done my best.

With the season over, I know what's bound to come. Sure enough, a week after the loss, Coach calls me into his office. Ty Mathews' doctor has cleared him to play. So come fall, he'll return to his starting quarterback position. I'm too good to let go, so he'd like to offer me the backup position. I thank the coach for his honesty and tell him I'll think about it. No sense burning your bridges unless you have a better one to cross. He nods in understanding. After the success I've had this year, he knows I can get a better deal.

He comes to his feet and holds out his hand. "You exceeded my expectations, Brock. I knew you had it in you, but I didn't know if you would come through. You put my doubts to rest. I'd gladly have you on any team of mine."

"Thanks, Coach. That means a lot to me."

"Any plans for the off-season?"

I grin. "A honeymoon. Never got to go on one."

"I'm guessing your wife had something to do with your performance these last few months."

"That she did." If it hadn't been for Ellie, I don't know if I would have kept to the straight and narrow. Any success I've had this year, I owe in large part to her.

I'd promised we'd travel to Fiji, but in the end, we choose Bora Bora in French Polynesia. Team commitments and Ellie's work responsibilities do not allow us to leave right away. But by early March, our schedules clear up and soon we're on our way. She'd never traveled out of the country, so the trip is one huge adventure for her. We snorkel with fishes, make love in secluded beach bungalows, swim naked in the Pacific blue waters, and eat several times our body weight. She can't get over the variety of fresh fruits. After ten days in paradise, we're reluctant to return home. But Ellie misses Kaylee, and to tell the truth, so do I.

We arrive home exhausted after the long flight but looking forward to whatever life will bring next. Still on Bora Bora time, I wake up the next morning groggy as hell. Ellie's side of the bed is downright cold. At some point, she'd rolled off the mattress to go on a grocery run. Not sure whether to go for breakfast or lunch, I grab a banana and slap meat on some bread. But I need something more to get through the day. Caffeine. As I'm pouring a fresh cup of java, my phone rings. Marty.

"How was the honeymoon?"

"Wonderful." I don't offer more than that. Most of it was x-rated, after all.

"Glad you had a good time. I have news."

"Oh?" I expect what's coming, just not the specific details.

"The South Carolina Wolves want you as their starting quarterback." NFL teams had to wait until mid-March to negotiate for an unrestricted free agent. So no surprise Marty didn't hear from them until now.

The Wolves are an up-and-coming team. Not good enough to make the playoffs. Yet. Although they have a pretty decent defense, they need to build their offensive line. That's where I would come in. "What's their offer?"

"Not high enough. But I can get them to where you want them to be."

"You sure?"

"Positive. I assume you want me to start negotiations."

"Yes." It would be nice to play in Charleston. I've missed the South's hospitality and easy spirit. But I can't put the cart before the horse. Not only might the deal fall through, but I need to discuss things with Ellie.

"I'll get the ball rolling then. I'll keep you posted."

"Thanks."

If I know Marty, and I do, the negotiations won't take long. The Wolves need me. If they don't make a high enough offer, some other team will. There were enough grumblings during the season about teams wanting me. So wherever I land, I'll win. The problem will be convincing Ellie to come with me. I had promised our marriage would be temporary. But I never intended it as such. I want her forever.

It's going to be difficult to pry her away from Chicago, though. She's planted deep roots here. This house, the first one she's owned. She won't give that up easily. Her job. And then there's Kaylee. Next year she'll attend the best public high school in the state. But that's not a factor. I can certainly afford private school tuition for her.

I grab the yellow pad Ellie keeps on the coffee table to jot down some ideas—warmer climate, friendlier neighbors. Educational options I'll need to research. Charleston's bound to have some great schools. The job issue can be easily resolved. After all, enough college teams in the South play ball. She could easily work from there recruiting players and such.

My stomach grumbles reminding me it still hasn't been fed. I drop the pad back on the coffee table, so I can chow down on my food. That's when I notice a small FedEx envelope from her agency addressed to Ellie with a check peeking out from the edge. Huh. Why would they be FedExing that to her? She normally gets her salary deposited into her bank account. Curious, I take it out. The check's for $20,000. In the memo portion it says "For extraordinary services rendered."

What services? As far as I know, Ellie spent the last few months doing background research on college players and working on endorsement deals. Nothing out of the ordinary. She'd done nothing special. Except for one thing.

Me.

My mind travels back to the night I found her in the condo. She'd explained things so glibly. The movers parading my bed posts through the lobby, dropping a box of my toys. All true since the turd knew about it. She never explained the extent of her discussion with Marty. What if he asked her to do more than unpack my things? I've seen Marty in action. He's a shark, about as cutthroat as they come. There's nothing he won't do for his clients.

And when he'd called about the trade, he'd warned me. No partying, no screwing around. I can only imagine what he thought when Ellie told him about the furniture fuck up. He probably saw his commission go up in smoke. He's not the kind to allow that to happen. No, he would have done something about it. And that something would have included Ellie, because he knows how eager she is to succeed. What if he'd asked her to keep me in line? And in return, she would get a big, fat, bonus check.

Acid churns in my stomach. Money means a great deal to her. Look at the way she'd snapped at me when I turned down my father's blood money. If Marty had asked her to go beyond the line of duty, she would have done everything he'd asked and more.

The sound of her car pulling into the driveway reaches me. Kaylee's still at school so we're alone for now. Good. We'll need privacy for what's about to go down.

Ellie rushes in, breathless from carrying totes filled with food. Sporting the gorgeous tan she got in Bora Bora, she's beautiful enough to make a grown man weep.

"You need any help?" I fight to keep my tone light.

"Do you mind? There are more bags in the car."

"Of course not."

Once the groceries are put away, she pulls out a baking pan and pours some pungent liquid over chicken. "I'm making that dish you like, the one with the spicy sauce."

Anything to keep me happy, right? "Can you stop that for a few minutes? We need to talk."

Some other person would ask 'What about?' Not her, though. "Sure. Let me put this in the fridge to marinate." After washing her hands, she walks toward me, wearing a happy grin. "What's up?"

I wait until she's seated next to me on the couch. "Marty called. The South Carolina Wolves want me as their starting quarterback."

"Oh." Her smile wobbles. "How wonderful. That's what you wanted."

"Their offer was too low. So he's going to work on them."

"Don't worry. He'll get it." Glancing down, she clasps her hands on her lap, as if she's struggling to contain some emotion.

"Yes, I expect he will." Even to my own ears, I sound downright miserable.

She lifts her head and spends time scrutinizing me. "You don't seem pleased. What's wrong?"

I hold out the paper I've been holding in my hand. "What's this all about?" I know damn well what it is and why she's getting it, but I want to hear it from her lips.

"My bonus check. I was going to drop it off at the bank, but I forgot it in my rush out the door." Her brow knits. "Did you open my mail, Brock?"

"It was right there on the coffee table." Not a lie. It's the truth. Just not the whole truth.

"Oh. I thought I'd put it back in the envelope." She brushes fingers across her creased brow. "My mind's all muddled. It's still on Bora Bora time. Guess I'll need to deposit it on the way to work."

She reaches out, but I don't give it to her. Instead, I point to the memo portion. "It says 'For extraordinary services rendered.' What does that mean?"

Her face heats up. That's when I know everything I fear is true.

She'd gladly spread her legs and fucked me. All for a few measly pieces of silver. God, I've been such a fool.

"You know why. I told you." Her words sound hollow to me.

Unable to be near her, I jump to my feet and round the table. Anything to put distance between us. "Tell me again." I grit out.

"After the furniture debacle, Marty asked me to move into the condo to provide cover for you. I argued against it, but he wouldn't give in. It was supposed to be temporary. Until you got a new place." She ends in a rush.

"Is that all you were required to do? Move in?"

She chews on her lip. "Yes." Even a blind man would know she's lying.

"Care to try that again?"

Her gaze bounces away from me. "No."

"What else did Marty ask you to do?" I'm furious, but I can't let her see. Not until I get to the truth.

"He asked me to babysit you." Her voice drops to a mere whisper.

"And how were you going to do that?"

"Make sure you didn't get into trouble. Parties, women. That kind of thing."

"Are you sure he didn't ask you to do more? Like screw me?"

Fire flashes in her eyes. "How dare you?"

"Oh, I dare plenty, Ellie." No longer able to control my temper, I stomp forward to tower over her. "Is that why you came back that night after you stormed out?"

"No. That's not why I did it." Tears mist her eyes as she trembles. So fucking beautiful. So damn deceitful.

"Liar."

"I never would have done such a thing." A lone tear rolls down her cheek. Gotta give it to her. She's good.

"Then why?"

"Because"—her voice quivers—"I couldn't stay away."

Disgusted, I spit out. "You're damn right you couldn't. After all, your precious bonus depended on keeping me in line. And what better way to do that than to spread your legs and fuck me."

She jumps to her feet. "You're wrong."

"Prove it, then. Give back the check."

"No. I worked hard for that money."

What a devious bitch she is. "You sure did, honey." I drop the check on the table. "And I must say, you earned every penny."

She slaps me. "You fucking bastard."

That's when Kaylee walks in the door.

CHAPTER 24

Eleanor

$\mathcal{E}$ VERYTHING CRASHED AND BURNED that day. When Kaylee walked in, Brock stormed out, and he didn't return for two days. Didn't take a genius to know where he'd gone—the condo. He'd kept the lease so we could go there when we needed privacy. All of his furniture is still in the apartment, and many of his clothes.

When Kaylee asks where Brock has gone, I answer her questions as truthfully as I can. "He's a free agent now, and he's had offers." Not a lie. Besides the South Carolina Wolves, two other teams want him. "So he's feeling them out."

That's when she realizes he won't be sticking around. "He's not staying in Chicago?" Her eyes fill with tears.

"No, honey. Ty Mathews is getting back his starting job. Your dad's too good to play backup."

She bites down on her lip to keep from crying.

When had they grown so close? All I ever saw was them sniping at each other. But maybe that was their way of showing affection.

Two days later, I walk into the kitchen to find Brock on the couch, the remote in his hand, clicking at the TV. Kaylee and Butch stare at us with worried eyes before disappearing into her room.

I drop the grocery bags filled with chocolate and junk food on the kitchen island. "Are you eating with us?"

"Yes."

"I'll make dinner then."

"Whatever." His gaze doesn't veer away from the TV.

The monosyllabic treatment lasts through the night. Kaylee takes her food into her room, something I don't normally allow. But tonight, I don't have the heart to forbid her. Not with the frozen treatment going on in the living room.

After dinner, when I'm rinsing the dishes, he says what he has to say. "I'm going to Charleston. The Wolves want to talk to me."

Makes sense. "Okay." I'm vibrating like a tuning fork from his nearness, from his heat, from his scent. I want to reach out, go back to the way things were, but I can't do that. Not after the hurtful words he hurled at me.

"When I return, I'll be moving to the condo."

My breath hitches. I don't want him to go. Maybe if I give a little, he'll meet me halfway. "It doesn't have to be like this, Brock."

He crushes me to him, grinds his mouth against mine, grinds something else as well. The part of him that's hard as stone. Coming up for air, he looks at me. There's no tenderness in his gaze. Anger blazes there instead. Anger and lust. "Damn you, Ellie." He lifts me by my ass, and I straddle his hips.

He carries me to our room and tears off my clothes.

Standing in front of him, naked and trembling, I whisper, "Brock."

He strips off his shirt, kicks out of his jeans, hauls me to him once more. "Don't talk. That's not what I need from you."

Sex. That's that he wants.

Fine. I want that too.

He picks me up and drops me on the bed. Eager for what's coming, I spread my legs.

He grabs my ass and pulls me toward him. In a lust-fueled frenzy, his mouth ravishes my pussy—licking me, biting me. He thrusts his fingers into my core, one, two, more. I don't stop him. He can do whatever he wants to me. Because I know this is the last time for us. He continues to torture me, bringing me to the brink and then receding, teasing me, not in a good way. I want to cum, but he won't let me.

When he rises over me, I protest, "Wait, I want—"

"I don't give a fuck what you want." He strokes the head of his penis against my opening. He doesn't have to. I'm more than ready for what he wants. Satisfied I'm wet and aching for him, he thrusts into me. So hard. So goddamn big, I bite down on my lip to keep from crying out. The bed squeaks violently beneath us as he pounds into me, taking everything he wants, everything I ache to give. I clamp my hands on his arms, wrap my legs around his while sweat pours off him. He works his cock in and out of me while, mindless with passion, I thrash on the bed. When the crisis hits, I come screaming his name. He's not far behind. Once he reaches his climax, he tucks me into his side. The one bit of tenderness this night.

When I wake the next day he's gone. But then I didn't expect any different.

Over the next few days, I don't wonder what's going on. I know. Marty's negotiating with the South Carolina Wolves, and Brock's in Charleston. The few days turn into a week. At the end of the second, the big announcement comes. The Wolves have signed Brock to their team. Of course, he didn't come cheap. Not that I had any doubts. Marty's a great negotiator. He got Brock a $140 million five-year contract and a $20 million signing bonus, making him one of the highest paid quarterbacks in the league.

The day the news hit, I walk into the house to find Brock there, big as life, waiting for me.

"Brock's here," Kaylee announces as if I've suddenly gone blind. "I'll go, err, finish my homework in my room." As sensitive as she is, she's always given us the privacy we need.

God knows we need it today. Once she's no longer within hearing distance, I ask, "How are you?"

"Fine."

He doesn't look fine. Just the opposite, he appears exhausted. He's got dark circles under his eyes, and his lids are rimmed in red. But then he's got cause to be tired. Contract negotiations are beyond nerve-wracking.

"You heard about the Wolves signing me?"

I dig my nails into my palm, so hard they're bound to mark me. "Yes, of course. It's all over the agency." Never mind the sports news. "Congratulations."

"Thanks." He should be happy. Ecstatic even. After all, this is everything he wants. The starting quarterback position and a lucrative paycheck. And yet. He's not. "While I was down there, I found a house near the Wolves' training facility. It's in a gated community to keep the gawkers out."

"That's good." I knew this was coming. And yet, it hurts so much.

"I also arranged to have my things packed and moved out of the condo."

"All right." Nothing more I can say, especially when my heart's breaking.

"So basically." He avoids looking at me. "I just came back for Butch. I'll just grab him and be out of your lives."

That statement burns right through me. More than I thought it would. But what did I expect? We'd agreed to a temporary marriage. With him moving to a new city, this is as good a time as any to end things. The problem is, I thought we could make a go of it. That our marriage could grow into something permanent. But I was just fooling myself. He's not interested in anything serious. If he were, he would not have jumped to the wrong conclusion when he saw my bonus check. If he loved me. If he cared about me, he would have allowed me to explain. But that's never going to happen. "So this is goodbye then."

"Yeah, I guess." His hard stare drills into me, tearing into my heart, making me bleed.

"I didn't want things to end this way. I thought we'd at least stay friends."

He jams his hands into his front pockets. "We've never been friends, Ellie. Isn't that what you said?"

Yeah. I did. Okay. He's made it clear where we stand, but he must deal with one thing. "What about Kaylee? She'll miss you."

"I'll be in touch. Or rather my attorney will. We'll need to arrange something."

Something? How dare he be this cavalier about our daughter? Especially after she's come to care for him. But I can't discuss this right now. Not when my heart's breaking. "Fine."

Kaylee flies around the corner. So much for thinking she wasn't eavesdropping. "You can't go," she screams at Brock while tears stream down her face. "You can't leave us."

"Kaylee, please." Don't know how much of her grief I can take without breaking down and doing the same.

"It's not right," she confronts Brock. "You're supposed to stay. You're supposed to be my dad."

"I'm sorry. I can't." His voice is raw with emotion. Saying goodbye to me was easy, but his daughter? This is hard for him. As well it should be.

"Why, Mom?" she cries out to me.

"I'll explain it to you later, honey."

Her gaze ping-pongs between Brock and me as her face crumbles. "It's not fair. I didn't know who you were. I didn't know you were my dad. You made me like you. How can you walk away?"

I give up the struggle to keep from crying. Somehow I have to make this stop. Toughening up my voice. I say, "Don't make this harder than it already is, Kaylee." I turn to Brock. "You better go."

"Right." There are tears in his eyes. "Come here, Butch."

But Butch, bless his heart, plops down next to Kaylee. She drops to the floor and wraps her arms around him.

"Butch," Brock says once more but his heart's not in it. Not when his daughter is crying her eyes out. He gives Butch one last pained glance, walks over and pats his head, pats Kaylee's as well. "Take care of each other." And then he turns and, without once glancing back, walks out of our lives.

CHAPTER 25

Brock

I CAN'T LOOK BACK. Much as I want to, it would hurt
too much.

I climb into the SUV and start the car before pulling away from
the one true home I've known. It was mine for a little while. Should
have known it wouldn't last. Nothing ever has.

With Charleston a half day's ride away, I could make it in one go.
But after six hours of driving, exhaustion sets in. I need to bunk down
for the night before I fall asleep at the wheel. The no-frills motel in
Lexington has a surprisingly comfortable bed. As a football player, I'm
used to sleeping in strange rooms. It should be easy enough to nod
off. Except I don't.

Instead, I spend the night fighting against the urge to go back to
Chicago and begging Ellie to move to the South with me. When dawn
comes, I climb bleary-eyed into the SUV and point the car toward
Charleston. I do have some pride after all.

When I find myself drifting off, I know I need coffee, so I stop at a
diner to grab some grub and caffeine. All fueled up, I get on the road
again. The heat's brutal. The further south I drive, the hotter it

becomes. So I crank up the AC sky high. As the miles pile up, my mind wanders to the might have beens. What if Ellie was riding shotgun with me? What if Kaylee and Butch were in the back and we were singing 'Who Let the Dogs Out'? Fuck it. I can't do that. I've never played make-believe. Crappy as my life is, I have to deal with it.

I fire up the radio to silence my mind. Some loser comes on, wailing in his beer about the gal who got away. Can't have that. I tune to another station. Same thing, except this time the schmuck lost not only his woman, but his truck and his dog. What the fuck is it with country songs? Don't they have anything else to sing about? Giving up, I shut off the damn radio and turn to say something to Butch, only to realize he's not there.

Hours later, I pull into my new driveway, drained of emotion, exhausted to boot. With no furniture and no food in the house, it's a lousy homecoming. But as it turns out, I'm wrong. At least about the food. A fruit basket sits on the front porch. As I reach for it, my phone rings. My realtor's number pops up.

"Mr. Parker?"

"Yeah." I grumble out.

"You home yet, Sugar?" That's not just for me. She calls everybody Sugar.

I could correct her. Tell her this isn't home. Not without Ellie, Kaylee and Butch. But what good would that do? "Just got here," I say, jamming the key in the lock.

"Great. How's everything?"

Everything looks peachy keen, I'm tempted to say. But I don't. Too snarky. "So far, so good."

"Wonderful. Did you get the fruit basket I sent?" She must have been born with that chirpiness in her voice.

Be nice, for fuck's sake. It's not her fault, your life is messed up. "Yes. Thank you." She'd timed the delivery perfectly, but then I'd told her when I meant to arrive.

"Super. Do you need help finding a place to stay until your furniture gets here?"

"No. I'm fine for tonight. A new bed should be here tomorrow. The rest should arrive in a week or so."

"Okay, Sugar. Let me know if you run into any problems, you hear? Remember our motto, 'We're not satisfied unless you're satisfied.'"

How could I forget? It's on the damn card attached to the gift basket. "I will. Thanks again."

I barely have a chance to drop the fruit basket on the kitchen counter when the front door rings. No clue who it could be. Except for Marty and the Wolves, nobody knows I'm here. I hope it's not another basket. There's only so much fruit I can eat. The stained-glass window on the door reveals a curvy blonde, holding a casserole dish, on my porch.

When I swing open the door, her smile's so bright it almost blinds me. "Hi."

"Hello." No fucking idea who she is.

"Thought I'd welcome you to the neighborhood, Brock." Flawless hair, impeccable makeup, scantily dressed.

I don't wonder what she wants. I know. "That's very kind of you."

"I heard you love Mexican food, so I made you my famous chicken enchiladas." Clutched as the dish is beneath her boobs, I can't help but notice her 36Ds.

"Thank you." I grab it from her. "Wish I could invite you in, but as you can see"—I gesture toward the empty space behind me—"my furniture hasn't arrived yet."

Her face crumbles, but she recovers quickly. "Oh, I don't mind sitting on the floor."

"But I do. Can't have a pretty little lady like yourself ruining your clothes. Thanks again." I give her my most charming grin and slam shut the door.

I'm starving and the dish really does smell delicious, but I have no plates, no forks and no knives. So I drop the casserole on the bottom shelf of the fridge and head out to eat. When I get back, I fetch the air mattress from the car and inflate it. Not the most comfortable accommodation, but it will do for the night. Somehow, I manage to get eight hours of sleep.

The next couple of days bring the king-sized bed I ordered and more women dropping by. Pretty soon my fridge's stocked with mac and cheese, beef stroganoff, and a really tasty chicken and rice. I'd bought some plastic knives and forks and a set of paper plates. So one thing for sure, I won't be starving any time soon. After heating the chicken dish in the built-in microwave, I serve a sizable portion. But the fragrant food reminds me of Ellie's, and two bites in, I lose my appetite. Damn it, I can't go through life being this miserable. I'm going to have to let go. Yeah. Like that's happening anytime soon.

For the umpteenth time since I arrived, I dial her number. But just like the last hundred times, she doesn't pick up.

I bow my head in misery. I should be fucking happy. After all, I'm the starting quarterback for an up-and-coming team. My contract's one of the best in the league, and this house is everything I've ever wanted. Six bedrooms with plenty of room and a huge backyard. I'd bought it thinking of Ellie. And Kaylee. And Butch. I'd pictured Ellie and me on matching rocking chairs, eating slices of apple pie, watching our children play. Yeah, children. I'd imagined more than one. Kaylee, of course. A tow-headed boy who looked just like me. Another boy and girl. But none of that's gonna happen. Not after I fucked things up.

When I saw that bonus check and the 'For extraordinary services rendered,' I saw red. She was getting that money not only because she'd moved in but agreed to 'babysit' me. She could have said no. I certainly would have. I certainly wouldn't have allowed Marty to browbeat me.

Except.

She's not me, is she? She's a single mother who held a mortgage and owed thousands of dollars for school loans. For years, she'd endured so much hardship, tried so hard to make ends meet. Ellie's scholarship had covered tuition, but not room and board. So she'd borrowed to keep the wolf from the door. But from something Ruth said, it hadn't been enough. Sometimes the cupboard went bare. So

Ruth and her husband made regular trips to bring Ellie and Kaylee food. It must have been hard for Ellie to accept that charity, even if it came from her own mother. But she would have swallowed her pride for Kaylee's sake.

God knows I didn't endure those hardships. My parents may have ignored me, but I never had to worry about food or having a roof over my head. So who the fuck am I to judge what she did? She gave in to Marty's demands because her job depended on it and the extra money would have paid off some bills.

But the thing that set me off wasn't her moving in, or even babysitting me. It was the thought that she'd gone beyond what Marty had asked. That she'd spread her legs to get that money.

But would she have done such a thing? That's the real question, isn't it? I refused to believe her when she tried to explain. How could I? My whole life people have wanted me for what I could bring them —fame for my teammates, sex for the groupies, money for everyone else. Nobody has ever loved me for me.

But Ellie never demanded a thing from me, even when she had the best reason in the world—child support for Kaylee. No, she never asked for a dime. So why would she all of a sudden do something for money? The truth is blindingly obvious. She wouldn't have.

God, what an idiot I've been.

She'd tried to explain, hadn't she? But I hadn't listened. Instead, I'd denied her, insulted her. And I'd hurt so much the last time we made love I'd stopped her from saying a word. Because I'm a selfish bastard, and all I can think about is my needs, my hunger, my pain. So if I'm fucking alone, it's my own damn fault. I have no one to blame but myself.

The days crawl by, slowly, painfully. Every day, once a day, I dial her number, even though I know she won't pick up. But it makes me happy to hear her recorded voice. When the loneliness gets to be too much, I watch that baking show she likes so much on my phone and make-believe she's right by my side.

A week later, my stuff arrives along with a raging thunderstorm. Somehow, the thunder and lightning suit my dark mood. These movers, unlike the clowns in Chicago, are true professionals, carefully handling the boxes and the furniture, including the bed of sin. Minus the restraints, of course. I had enough smarts to remove them before I arranged the move. After they leave, I unpack the bare necessities— the coffeemaker and toaster in the kitchen. My everyday clothes. The rest I leave tucked away until I have the heart to empty them out.

During the long spring days, I meet with the coaches, train at the facility, make the media rounds. Everyone wants to know when my family will join me. I tell them Kaylee's not finished with school yet. Which is the truth. But by June, I no longer have that excuse, and the media smells blood in the water. Rumors spread about the collapse of my marriage, although no one has the balls to ask me right out. Soon headlines pop up all over the place. One rag writes a particularly nasty article about the women who show up at my door. How on earth they found out, I have no idea. The vicious headline reads, 'Is Brock Parker cheating on his bride?' Bastards.

A week after the rag hits the stands, my phone rings. Ellie. My heart soars before crashing right back to earth. She never called before. Has something happened?

"Is everything okay? How's Kaylee? And Butch?" I ask, panic in my voice.

"She's fine. Everyone's fine, including Butch."

Thank the fuck.

"So you're all settled in now?"

"Yes." She called for a reason, but I don't want to rush her. I'm happy just to hear her voice.

"Kaylee wants to come down for a visit."

"She does?" Joy spears through me. I'd hoped this would happen. So much so, that I'd hired a Charleston family law attorney to establish visitation rights. She'd drawn up the papers and sent them to me. I never returned them. Because it would make my separation from Ellie more real than I could stand. But this phone call means Ellie trusts me with our daughter. And that means everything to me.

"Yes. She saw some interview on one of the sports channels. When they asked about your family, she got upset. Apparently, they hinted at our separation. So, she thought she'd come down and spend some time with you to squelch the gossip. Would it be okay for her to come down?"

"Absolutely." I'm grinning like a kid at Christmas time.

"You sure? I mean I wouldn't want her to cramp your style."

"Cramp my what?" I yell. Idiot. If I want any chance of winning her back, I can't be screaming at her. I take a deep breath and, in a more reasonable tone, I ask, "What do you mean?"

"I've heard rumors of women dropping by your house at all hours, day and night."

"Fuck the rumors." So much for staying calm. "I'm married to you. I'm not screwing anyone else."

"You sure? Because I don't want her walking into an—"

"Orgy?" I cut her off.

"Yes."

"I wouldn't do that. When are you going to believe I've changed?"

"Sorry. I had to make sure."

She doesn't sound the least bit sorry, the witch. God, I miss her. "Well, believe it." I tangle a hand through my hair. "When does she want to come down?"

"Sunday, if that's okay. You'll be in training camp soon, right?"

"In about a month or so."

"Good. Maybe you can take her sightseeing? That should help pass the time."

"Yeah, I can do that." I'd love to show Charleston to Kaylee. She'll love the cobblestone streets and horse-drawn carriages. And maybe we could book one of the boat tours and spot some dolphins.

"I'll send you the flight details."

"Okay." What if I could get not only Kaylee down here, but Ellie too? We'd sit down and talk. I would say I'm sorry. She won't accept my apology at first, but eventually, I'd sweet talk her into it. "Ellie, what if you—" But she's already hung up.

CHAPTER 26

Eleanor

"*M*OM?" Kaylee.

It's so good to hear her voice. She's only been gone a few days, but I miss her more than I can say. So does Butch. He and I spend our evenings moping around the house and our nights curled up in bed. Not even baking or treats can put us in a good mood. "How are you, honey? Is everything okay?"

"I'm fine."

"Are you having a good time?"

"I am. But I don't know about Brock."

My hackles rise. He said it was okay for her to fly down there. Did he change his mind? Before I jump to the wrong conclusion, though, I need to hear what she has to say. "What do you mean?"

"It's pitiful, mom. Except for the absolute essentials, he hasn't unpacked a thing. And he's been here for months."

That's what she's worried about? "Honey, he's probably busy with meetings and interviews." Never mind dealing with all the women popping up at his front door. "Maybe he just hasn't had the time."

"No. That's not it. He's here a lot. He just doesn't want to empty the boxes. I offered to help, but he said to leave them. And they're a pain because those boxes are everywhere."

My heart climbs to my throat. Oh, God. Has she seen his sex toys? When I called him with her flight details, I made him promise to hide those things. If he hasn't kept his word, I will fly down there and strangle him. "You didn't go into his, err—"

"Oh, please. I know all about that room. Meghan told me."

That little busybody is too inquisitive for words.

"Don't worry. It's locked up tight. I couldn't get in even if I wanted to. Which I don't. Because, ugh. But if it's like every other room in this place, everything in there is boxed up too."

And hopefully padlocked as well. What sounds like a doorbell rings in the distance.

"Not again!" Kaylee huffs out.

"What is it, honey?"

"Hold on, Mom."

She takes her cell with her because I hear the entire conversation.

"Hi, is Brock home?" some chirpy female voice asks.

"No. He's not here. Can I help you?"

"You must be his daughter. Kaylee, isn't it?"

Who the hell is this woman and how does she know my daughter's name?

"Yes."

I know that tone. It's Kaylee's hurry-up-and-get-this-over-with-because-I-don't-have-time-for-you voice.

"Well, aren't you adorable?"

Dead silence on Kaylee's part. I don't blame her. Since when do you call a twelve-year-old adorable?

"I'm a neighbor. I thought I'd come over and introduce myself. I brought a casserole."

You and everyone else, apparently.

"Thanks," Kaylee says. And then something thuds.

"Kaylee! Did you just slam the door in that lady's face?"

"Sure did." She doesn't sound the least repentant.

"That's rude, sweetheart."

"You'd do the same thing if you were here, Mom."

"Now why would I do such a thing?"

"Because they're pests, locusts. The whole lot of them. You'd think those women would have something better to do than drop by day and night, always with a casserole, or a dish, or a pizza box. One even brought a bucket from the colonel. The fridge's groaning from the food in there."

"They're neighbors, honey." I try to put the best spin on it. She shouldn't be this cynical at her age. "Maybe they're just trying to be friendly."

"Three cars had out-of-state tags."

"Really?" How's that even possible? Brock lives in a gated community with only private access. How on earth are they getting in? Are they bribing somebody at the front gate? "Just how many have shown up?"

"Since I arrived . . . about ten."

She's been there only a few days. "Good lord."

"Yeah. The ones that don't bring food ask if they can borrow a cup of sugar." She snorts. "Like he'd have any. They're vultures, that's what they are. Mom, you have to get down here."

"Honey, we talked about this. I can't." After Brock walked out, she'd refused to accept that he'd left for good. She'd sulked, she'd cried, she'd hidden in her room for hours on end with Butch by her side. When a week had gone by with no more arguments from her, I'd thought she'd finally come to terms with it. Turned out she'd been making plans. When she'd politely asked if she could fly to Charleston to spend time with her father, I didn't have the heart to say no. It wouldn't do her any harm, and I could certainly use the break from her teen angst.

Before she flew down, I'd told Brock what I'd do to his package if he did anything inappropriate. Rather than get insulted, he'd laughed and promised he'd take good care of her. Still, I couldn't help but imagine the worst. But now it seems I have nothing to worry about. At least not until she says the next words.

"I met a boy, Mom."

"A boy?" I hadn't cautioned Brock about Kaylee and boys. I didn't think I had to. Since her puppy crush on Meghan's brother fizzled, she'd shown no interest in other teens. But she's about to turn thirteen, so her hormones could be kicking in.

"Yeah. He lives right next door. And guess what? He loves computers, just like I do. He invited me to his house to check out his setup."

"What?" My stomach flip-flops. Is that what teenage boys do these days? Ask innocent girls to their houses to check out computer setups? What if he's tried something? Even worse, what if she's let him? I frantically do a search on my phone to find the next flight to Charleston. I'm flying down there and bringing Kaylee home.

"You got nothing to worry about. His mom was there the whole time. She made us chocolate chip cookies."

Okay. That makes me feel a little better. A very little. I can't help but worry, though. I don't know the boy's mom. I don't know the boy. I don't know the neighborhood which seems dicey at best. After all, their 'security' is letting in all kinds of friendly 'neighbors.' "What grade is he in?"

"He's a freshman."

"In high school?" Please don't let it be college.

"Yes, he's only a year ahead of me. Anyway, you should see his equipment."

My heart jumps to my throat. Get a grip, Ellie. She's not talking about his junk.

Blissfully unaware of the track my mind has taken, Kaylee runs on. "It's the bomb. He attends the number one high school in South Carolina. Number 29 in STEM education in the entire country. When he saw how good I'm at programming, he said I could probably get into his school next year. But I'd have to be enrolled here this fall. They don't admit kids from out of state."

Alarm bells go off. She can't be talking about moving to South Carolina, can she? Because if she is, that's definitely not happening. It's one thing to spend part of her summer with her father, it's another to move permanently to Charleston. But I can't come at her heavy-handed. If I do, she'll definitely dig in her heels. "Honey, they have STEM schools in Chicago as well."

"Not rated as highly as this one, they don't. Did you know Advance Tech has a hub here?"

Advance Tech is one of the top technology companies in the United States. They're involved in everything from robotics to self-driving cars.

"No. I didn't know that."

"Kids from his high school intern there during the summer. It would be a great opportunity for me. Lots of their graduates go on to MIT." Her dream school. No wonder she's beyond excited about the prospect of attending that STEM school.

But no way is she going to school in Charleston. "Honey, we can talk about it when you come home for your birthday."

"Uh, about that, Mom. I think I'll stay down here for the rest of the summer."

I'm breathing in and out so fast I'm going to need a paper bag. "Sweetheart—"

She doesn't wait to hear what I'm about to say. "You can fly down so we can celebrate. All three of us. It's not like Charleston is on the dark side of the moon."

The three of us. What's going on? Is this a ruse? "Kaylee, is this your way of getting your father and me back together?"

"No." A pause. "Maybe. But I really do want to go to school here. I'm not lying about that."

I take a deep breath, let it out. "Kaylee."

"You like him, Mom," she rushes on. "I know you do. And he's totally miserable. When he's home, he mopes around the house, watching that cooking show you like."

"The Great Bake Off?"

"Yeah. He blabbed about it on one of those interview shows. Like he knows anything about baking. Come to think of it, maybe that's why some of those women drop by to borrow some sugar."

That's not the kind of sugar those women want.

"Mom, I really want you to come down."

Her pleading breaks my heart. She thinks all she has to do is get Brock and me in the same house. And then magically, things will go back to the way they were. But that's not going to happen. I can't go back to Brock, not when he believes I sold my body for money. And she can't attend that tech school, not when it would require me to move to Charleston. And living with her father is out of the question. Sooner or later, he'd go back to his old ways, and his daughter would be in the way. So her heart's bound to be broken. Although hers would mend, I have doubts about mine.

But she's right about one thing. I need to fly to Charleston so I can handle what's happening down there. And to bring her back. No way am I leaving that city without my daughter. "Okay, honey, I will."

"Yeahhhh! I love you, Mom."

"Love you too, honey. Where's your father?" He can't possibly be there; he would have answered the door.

"He's at the Wolves' stadium doing some kind of training." A tinge of worry creeps into her voice. "Are you calling him?"

"Sweetheart, I can't drop in on him out of the blue. He has to okay my visit before I head down." Although I suppose, I could always stay in a motel.

"Okay, but don't tell him about my wanting to stay here. I haven't talked about that with him yet."

"I won't." My conversation with Brock's going to take a different tack.

It takes eight rings before he picks up.

"Ellie?" He sounds out of breath. Probably doing weight training or running on a treadmill.

"Yes." My imagination runs wild as I picture Brock's hard body, glistening with sweat, muscles bulging out. I can almost see him. I can almost smell him. God, Ellie. Get a grip.

"Anything wrong?"

"No. Everything's fine. Have you checked in on your daughter?"

"Yep. Called her about an hour ago." He sounds so proud of himself. Too bad I'm about to burst his bubble.

"Did you know she's been going next door to your neighbor's house?"

"Sure do. She asked my permission."

"And you let her?" Is he insane? "That boy is in high school."

"He's a ninth grader, Ellie."

"And what were you doing in ninth grade?"

"Not what you think I was doing. I was a late bloomer."

I snort. "Right. This is me you're talking to. You were legendary even in ninth grade." He can't get away with lying to me. Not when I know all his past sins. Well, most of them anyway.

"What's this about, Ellie?"

"I don't want her going to your neighbor's house."

"Why the hell not?"

"She can get into trouble."

A pregnant pause. And then he explodes. "She's twelve, for fuck's sake."

"And a month shy of thirteen."

A low growl followed by a deep breath. "Look, the Johnsons are good people. And Sandra is the best. You have nothing to worry about."

I snort. "Oh, so you're on a first name basis with Sandra." Figures. It probably took all of five minutes for that woman to show up at his house.

"She lives next door, Ellie. Of course, I am. You do remember how southern hospitality works."

"I suppose she came by with a casserole."

"Sure did. Lasagna. It was damn good too. Wait a minute. Are you jealous of her?"

Damn right I am. But he doesn't need to know the green monster has parked itself on my shoulder and is whispering things in my ear. "Of course not."

"She's in her mid-forties, Ellie."

"Like that would stop you."

"She has two kids."

"Uh-huh."

"And she's married to Tom Johnson who throws a mean barbecue. As a matter of fact, Kaylee and I have been invited to one this Saturday. If you were here, I'd ask you to bring that potato salad of yours."

"Well, you got your wish, cowboy."

"What do you mean?"

"I'm flying down. On Friday." I'll be damned if I ask his permission.

"You are?" He sounds happy, but he won't be. Once I get down there, I mean to take a piece out of him. And I'll make sure it hurts.

"Yep. And when I fly back I'm bringing Kaylee with me."

"But she just got here." He sounds disappointed.

But I don't care. I have to do the right thing for Kaylee. "And look how much trouble she's gotten into."

"You're insane, woman."

"Wait until I get down there, buster. You haven't seen insane."

CHAPTER 27

Brock

"WHAT FLIGHT IS YOUR MOM ON?" I ask Kaylee. Again. She'd mentioned it a time or two, but I'd been so preoccupied with my thoughts on the drive to the airport I'd missed what she said.

She gazes at me like I've suddenly become the prize idiot at the county fair. "United 1510."

Inside the terminal, I scan the arrival board. "We better hustle. Looks like the plane's pulling up to the gate."

Charleston International Airport is nowhere as huge as O'Hare, so it takes us no time to get to Concourse A. Unable to proceed beyond security, we stand outside the restricted area waiting for her. To say I'm nervous is an understatement. She's not coming to reunite or patch things up. She's only here to fetch Kaylee and take her back with her. Still, I can't help but be happy. I haven't seen her for three long months and that has seemed like an eternity. Fifteen minutes later, I spot her heading our way.

"There she is!" Kaylee points out.

"I see her," I whisper, as my heart skips a beat.

Kaylee barely waits for Ellie to clear the concourse before she runs up to her. "Mom."

"Sweetheart." For a few seconds they hug and kiss. It's been only a week, but to them apparently, it's been forever. When they turn toward me, they both have tears in their eyes. But then, so do I. Nothing more beautiful than the sight of Ellie and our daughter smiling. They wear happiness well.

I walk up to the love of my life, drop a kiss on her lips. The sweet taste of her mouth is not nearly enough, but I can't very well do much more. Not when we're out in public.

After the all-too-brief greeting, she steps back. "Brock."

It's my first chance to get a good look at her. She's gained a few pounds, and they look great on her.

"I got these for you." I hand her the bouquet I'd been holding behind my back, the one I spent half an hour picking out. After going back and forth between roses and a mixed bouquet, I'd gone for the classic choice figuring you can't go wrong with that. "How was your flight?"

"Uneventful," she clips out.

Okayyy. Not terribly friendly, but not unfriendly either. "Did you check any bags?"

"No. Brought only the overnight." She points to the suitcase by her side.

I'm reaching for it, when something clicks close to us. I've heard that sound enough times to know what it means. Somebody's taking our picture.

Looking around for the culprit, I spot him not too far from us. Can't miss him, busy as he is snapping away.

When he realizes he has my attention, he flashes a press card. "Rod Howard. *The Charleston Times*." I've met the Times' sports reporter. This guy is not him. He's probably some flunkie charged with taking a few pictures and asking some questions. But how the hell did he know I'd be here to meet Ellie?

I straighten up. Between my bulk and my height, I tower over him. Much as I want to pummel this slime for intruding into our privacy, I can't make a scene. "Okay."

"Can I take a picture of the happy family? Ask a couple of questions?"

Before I can say 'Hell, no', Kaylee jumps in with "Sure thing." She scoots up to her mother. Hugging Kaylee to her, Ellie pins on a smile. The fake kind. I throw my arm around both and force out a grin. There, a picture-perfect happy family.

"Great." Rod Johnson clicks away. Done with the camera, he points a recorder at Ellie, "So, Mrs. Parker, are you visiting or coming down for good?"

"Errr," Ellie says. Can't help her. I don't have an answer for that either.

But Kaylee does. "She's here for the weekend."

"Only the weekend?" Rod Howard asks.

Okay. That's enough. This turd's not from the sports desk. He's probably part of their 'style' section. The one that takes pleasure in printing dirt. I'll be damned if we get dragged through the mud. But I can't fly off the handle, not with the growing crowd around us. As politely as I can, I say, "Mr. Howard. My wife just arrived. She hasn't had a chance to catch her breath. If there's anything else you'd like to know, please contact the Wolves' PR office. They'll arrange for me to have a sit-down with you." Not that he'll have a chance in hell of getting that interview. I'll make damn sure of that.

I grab Ellie's hand and head toward the exit, dragging her overnight along. I don't say a word until we're inside the SUV. But then I explode. "What the hell was that all about? How did he know we'd be at the airport?"

From the back seat, Kaylee pipes up, "I *may* have called *The Charleston Times*."

"Kaylee." Frowning, Ellie twists to face our daughter, who's looking pretty satisfied in the back seat.

"Why would you do such a thing?" I bark out.

With both parents pissed off at her, she should be sorry. But she's not. In a show of teen defiance, she crosses her arms against her chest and sticks out her chin. "Because they kept insinuating you guys are splitting up, and I'm sick of hearing it. Now they have proof you're together. So they can stop talking about us." Puffing out her lower lip, she stares out the window. And that's that as far as she's concerned.

Unfortunately, she's wrong. If anything, those photos will start up the rumor mill again. Damn it. Just when they were winding down too. But what's done is done. Except. "You didn't contact anybody else, did you?"

"No. *The Charleston Times* was it."

"Good." I put the car in gear and point the car toward the exit.

Everyone remains deep in their own thoughts until I merge unto the highway.

"How far is your house?" Ellie asks. Not our home, or even your home, but your house.

"About twenty minutes away."

"Do you like it?"

I should be grateful she has questions. But I'm not. She's only asking to be polite.

"It's the home I've always wanted. Six bedrooms, a wraparound porch, huge kitchen." You would love it, if you would just give us a chance.

She swipes moisture from her upper lip. "Can you turn up the AC? It's quite warm."

"Sure." I gaze at her. "You gained some weight, I see. Looks good on you."

She tenses. "Thanks."

Fuck. Shouldn't have said anything. Women hate any mention of their weight, even when it's a compliment.

Evening traffic's a breeze so it takes us no time to get home. When we step into the kitchen from the garage, Ellie takes some time to glance around, "The house looks great."

"Thanks." With all the boxes gone, you can actually see the beauty of the place. "Kaylee has been working hard on setting things up."

"Yeah, Mom. Dad finally let me help him unpack."

Ellie swivels toward Kaylee. "Dad?"

"Yeah. Seemed stupid to keep calling him Brock. He's my father after all." Her words light a warm glow within me. I'm glad Kaylee came to Charleston if only because it got her to call me Dad.

Ellie strolls up to Kaylee and hugs her. "So what have you been doing, sweetheart?" Her casual question doesn't set off Kaylee's radar. Little does she realize what Ellie really wants to know. Has Kaylee been fooling around?

"Helping Dad with the unpacking, messing around with—"

"What?" Ellie steps back and hard stares at Kaylee.

"—computers."

"Is that all you were messing around with?"

Now she's gone and done it. Kaylee is not going to miss that. Not as bright as she is.

For a second, Kaylee's brows knit as if she's trying to work out a puzzle, and then it clears up. "You're worried about Mitch, aren't you?"

"Well, he is a boy, and you are growing up."

Kaylee throws her arms around her mom and kisses her cheek. "Mom, that's so sweet of you. But you got nothing to worry about. Mitch's not boyfriend material. He's more interested in computers than girls."

Thank God for that.

"Besides, I never go over there unless Mrs. Johnson's home. And, Mom, she bakes the best cookies. The two of you would get along like peas in a pod."

Ellie's shoulders droop. "That's . . . great." Seemingly, Kaylee's words took the wind out of her sails.

I told her she had nothing to worry about, but did she believe me? No.

"Have you done any sightseeing?"

What is Ellie up to now? She knows I hadn't taken Kaylee out on the town. "No. Dad was going to take me tomorrow. But then we got invited to the Johnsons' barbecue. Maybe next weekend we'll do that. Right, Dad?"

"If that's what you want." I exchange glances with Ellie. If she has her way, Kaylee will be back in Chicago by then. I'd love to keep my daughter for at least another week, but Ellie has a bug up her ass about my neighbors. I'm just hoping once she meets them, she'll be okay with them, and Kaylee will be allowed to stay. But I refuse to worry about that right now. "Do you need to freshen up? I thought I'd take you and Kaylee to one of the best restaurants in Charleston for dinner. Nothing fancy. Just great seafood."

She tilts her head to the side. "Or we can eat in. I hear you have quite a number of casseroles in your fridge."

My gaze cuts to Kaylee.

"Sorry. I blabbed." She doesn't look the least bit sorry. Just the opposite. She's smiling.

Did she tell her mom about the welcome wagons to get her mother down here? Is that why she mentioned the boy next door? Maybe. I'm beginning to think my daughter has quite a devious mind.

Kaylee's phone rings. Glancing at it, she smiles. "It's Mitch. I'm helping him write an app." Talking a mile a minute, she disappears into her room, leaving Ellie and me alone.

"I'd rather take both my girls out to eat."

She snaps out. "I'm not your girl."

"You're right. You're my wife." I refuse to let things go ugly.

She takes a deep breath, lets it out, and lets her defenses down. "I'm exhausted, Brock. It's been a long day. I'd just as soon eat here."

Knowing her, she probably worked most of the day before heading off to the airport. "Okay. I guess we can order in." No way am I feeding her one of those casseroles, though. "Want to bathe before dinner? I can join you." As soon as those words leave my lips, I regret them.

Especially when she steps away, putting the kitchen island between us. "I don't think that would be a good idea. We're supposed to be separating."

"That was your decision. Not mine."

Anger flashes in her eyes. "You walked out on me. Remember?"

How could I ever forget? Biggest mistake of my life.

"So don't you dare blame this separation on me."

"I called to apologize. You never picked up." I'd left message after message on her voice mail, telling her I was sorry, to please call me back. She never did.

"We're over and done with, Brock."

"Why?"

"Because I can't live with a man who doesn't trust me."

"I apologized. I'm apologizing now."

"It's too late."

No, it's not. And I'm going to prove it to her.

"We can't sleep in different beds. It will upset Kaylee too much. But everything else stays separate."

"Fine." I retrieve my cell. "What do you want for dinner? Pizza, Chinese. Or something else?"

"Doesn't matter. Order whatever you like."

I one-button dial the Italian place. "Pizza it is."

We eat the food in silence while Kaylee gazes at us out of worried eyes. Once the meal's over, Ellie heads to the bedroom. Kaylee goes back to her cave. Seems like old times. Except it isn't. Turning on the TV, I watch some show with unseeing eyes.

An hour later, I walk into the bedroom to find her sound asleep, wearing a granny gown that covers her down to her feet. Doesn't matter how much skin she's hiding from me, I still get hard.

After changing into pajama bottoms, I slide into bed and pull her into me. An intoxicating fragrance of cinnamon and paradise greets me. God. I want to ravish her, sink into her, pleasure her until she screams my name. But I can't do any of those things. I can only hold her, breathe in her scent and torture myself.

In the morning, I wake up to the smell of pancakes and bacon and the sound of Ellie and Kaylee's happy chatter. From their convo, they're setting the table, pouring orange juice. A sense of peace rolls over me while I wish it could always be this way. When I walk into the kitchen, the scent of freshly brewed coffee fills the air.

"Want a cup?" Ellie holds up the carafe. Seemingly, she's declared a peace truce, probably for Kaylee's sake.

"Sure." I park my ass on a kitchen stool and enjoy the best breakfast I've had in a long time.

Once the dishes are cleared away, Ellie grabs her purse. "I have to go to the grocery store."

"What for?"

"To get the fixings for the potato salad." And then she gets this light in her eyes. "Unless I can ask one of your drop-bys to make one for me."

Happy to see her sassy side again, I grin. "I would if I had a way to reach them."

"Oh, come on! What self-respecting woman forgets to leave her phone number with a casserole?"

"They did. But I tossed them away."

She arches a brow. "Too bad. They could have fed you until the start of the season."

"Very funny." I sling my arm around her shoulders and drop a kiss on her lips. She tenses, but doesn't push me away.

Baby steps.

CHAPTER 28

Eleanor

WE ARRIVE AT THE BARBECUE AS A FAMILY with me tucked in between Kaylee and Brock as if I needed protection from the crowd gathered in our neighbor's yard.

But they have nothing to worry about. As soon as we step inside the fenced gate, a forty-something woman, flashing a broad smile walks up to greet us. "Hi. I'm Sandra. You must be Ellie."

"Guilty as charged. I brought potato salad." Nothing like stating the obvious. A blind man could see what I'm carrying.

"Well, aren't you sweet?" Sandra takes it from me and lays it on a table chock full of side dishes—baked beans, corn fritters, hush puppies. And four bowls of potato salad.

Oh, geez. "I should have asked what I should bring," I say, chagrined.

"Nonsense. You can never have too many potato salads with this bunch. They practically inhale it."

She's being kind. I can tell. Well, too late to do anything about it.

Sandra wipes her palms on her apron. "It's so nice to finally meet you."

Before I can say 'me too', a tall man wearing a 'King of the Grill' apron pops up next to her and wraps an arm around Sandra's shoulders. "Hi, I'm Joe. Excuse me for not shaking your hand."

No wonder. He's holding a barbecue spatula that's been put to good use.

A smiling Sandra bops him on the chest. "My better half. As you can see, he's in charge of the grill."

He has stains upon stains on his apron, proof positive he's most definitely a master of the barbecue. "Nice to meet you, Joe."

"Likewise." Something flares on the grill, catching our attention. "Oops, gotta go before those hamburgers get done a little too well." But before he takes off, he points the spatula at Brock "Wanna a beer?"

"Sure thing," Brock says, before turning to me. "You gonna be okay?"

"Of course." Last thing I need is a babysitter.

"If you need me, I'll be over there." He points toward the grill where a bunch of men are hanging out. When he joins them, he's welcomed with hearty backslapping and handshaking. Not a surprise. He's their home team's quarterback star, after all.

Sandra nods in Brock's direction. "He's the best."

"Yes, he is." I struggle to smile as I wipe off a trickle of sweat. Darn it. The heat's getting to me.

"You okay, Mom?" Kudos to Kaylee for noticing how hot I am. My cheeks must be blazing red.

"Yes, honey. I am." A total lie. I may have lived most of my life in the South, but my body has acclimated to the Chicago weather where it rarely reaches ninety degrees. And that's exactly what it feels like right now because I'm burning up. The way I'm dressed isn't helping. I'd chosen long sleeves and slacks. Even worse, I can't run to Brock's house and change. I didn't bring any summer clothes.

"Want something cold to drink, Ellie?" Sandra asks, a look of concern on her face.

"Yes, please. Iced tea if you have it. With lots of ice."

"Coming right up, honey."

When she returns with the glass, she brings a young man with her.

"Wanted you to meet my son, Mitch. I expect you've heard a lot about him. He and Ms. Kaylee here"—she nods toward my daughter—"have been inseparable all this week."

Mitch has a mouthful of hardware, coke-bottom glasses, and appears just as geeky as they come. Brock was right. I have nothing to worry about.

"How do you do, Mrs. Parker?" And very polite too.

"Hello, Mitch." I take the glass from Sandra while fighting the urge to guzzle the tea. Barely winning the struggle, I take a healthy gulp that feels great going down.

"Kaylee, I hit a snag with that app we're working on. Can you take a look at the code?"

"Can I, Mom?" Kaylee pleads.

"Sure, honey. Don't forget to eat."

"Oh, don't worry, Mrs. Parker," Mitch says. "There's a ton of food in the basement." Talking a mile a minute, he and Kaylee disappear into the house.

Sandra shakes her head. "Can't get them away from computers. Those two are going to change the world."

"I bet." What more can I say? They're not going to be together, or even neighbors. Tomorrow, she'll be flying home with me.

"So are you here for good?" Her question doesn't seem nosy, but simple curiosity.

"No." I shake my head. "Just visiting. I'm a sports agent and things are kind of hectic at work. What with trading season and all." Not really a lie. Things are busy. But then they always are.

"Oh?" She glances toward Brock who's moved on to coaching ball-tossing skills to some of the youth at the barbecue. Needless to say, they're hanging on to his every word.

"He's so good with them. We've had several get-togethers, and it always ends the same way. It won't last past his training camp, of course. He'll be too busy then. But in the meantime, they sure are making the most out of him." She flicks her gaze back to me. "He's wonderful with Kaylee. So he's bound to be a great dad to a son."

I choke on the tea.

"You okay?"

"Sorry." I wheeze out. "Some ice went down the wrong way."

While I regain my ability to breathe, a woman slithers up out of nowhere. She's wearing a ton of makeup and a skimpy top that barely corrals her triple Ds. "You Brock's wife?"

I cough and take a deep breath. "Yes, I am."

"He's such a good neighbor."

Good neighbor? What the hell does that mean? Rather than pull her over-processed, bleached-blonde hair out by the roots, I smile sweetly. "I know."

"The other day I was plumb out of coffee, and I stopped over to borrow some."

Coffee. The one thing Brock has in abundance. "Did you now?"

"Yeah." She twirls a curl around one of her talons as she ogles Brock.

Coveting is a sin, honey.

"And he sure gave it to me." She cackles before wandering off.

The double entendre gets on my nerves. But I'm not getting down in the dirt with her. My mama taught me better.

"Don't pay her any attention," Sandra says. "She's desperate."

"Oh?"

"Her husband's business went belly up, and he took off for parts unknown. Rumor has it her house is being auctioned to pay off his debts."

"Oh, that's awful." Almost makes me feel sorry for her. But what is she doing about it? If I were in danger of losing my home, I'd take a second and third job. Anything to keep a roof over our heads. "She's not employed?"

"No. She doesn't have any marketable assets. Except for the obvious." Sandra cups her boobs.

Ooooh. Go Sandra. Who knew this sweet, mild-mannered woman had such sharp claws? I like her. A lot. Too bad I'll never get to know her. We could have been friends.

"Want more iced tea? Looks like you're done with that one."

For the first time since I arrived, I smile honestly. "Yes, thank you, Sandra."

"Sure thing, honey." After she brings me more tea, I mingle with some of the guests. Except for the occasional catty remark, most seem quite nice. To my surprise, I actually enjoy myself. Something I hadn't expected. But as the afternoon progresses, I lose the fight with the heat. Pretty soon I'm looking for a place to lay down.

Sandra's been busy with hostess duties, but somehow she notices my distress. "You looking a little peaked there, Ellie."

I fan my face with a paper plate, but the slight breeze is nothing but hot air. "I'm afraid the sun's getting to me."

"Ellie?" Brock pops up by my side. "What's wrong, sweetheart?"

Rather than hang over me, he'd given me space, which is what I'd asked him to do. But now I desperately need his help. "I think"—I swallow hard—"I think I better go home."

"The sun's too much for her," Sandra offers by way of explanation.

Feeling like I'm going to pass out, I droop against Brock's broad chest and stumble a couple of steps. Without bothering to ask any questions, he picks me up and rushes past all the gawkers who whisper as we pass by.

"Feel better."

"Take care."

"Oooohhh, wish it were me."

No, honey, you don't. I'm about to barf.

Back home, he lays me on the couch. "Tell me what you need." His eyes are full of worry.

"A glass of cold water would be nice. Not too cold," I say as he heads to the kitchen. In a flash, he's back holding a frosted mug.

"Sip it slowly. You don't want to upset your stomach."

"I know." Taking small sips with rests in between, I drain the glass.

While I'm doing that, he retrieves two bed pillows and tucks them behind me. "Feeling better?"

Exhaustion's setting in. Before I can say 'yes,' I drift off into a dreamless sleep where nothing can touch me. Not the sun, not Brock, not even Kaylee. Sometime later, I come awake with a jerk. No idea what woke me up. A little disoriented, I glance around to find him in the reclining chair next to me, his head leaned back, his eyes closed. He's not sleeping. Only keeping me company.

I breathe a sigh of content. If only it could be always like this. If only we could be together. But that just can't be. I can't live with a man who doesn't trust me. Who's willing to believe the worst of me.

"What time is it?" I ask. Sunlight's no longer streaming through the front window, so it's got to be night.

Sitting up, he glances at his watch. "Nine-fifteen."

I've slept for three hours. "Where's Kaylee?"

"In her room. She rushed over when she heard. But when she saw you were sleeping, she headed to her room to work on some computer stuff. Want something to eat? Sandra dropped off some food."

"Nooooo." The mention of food turns my stomach, and I'm running for the bathroom.

A while later I emerge, weak and shaking.

He stands in the living room, fists propped on his hips. "That's it. I'm taking you to the ER."

"Don't be silly. It's just a touch of sun poisoning." Actually, it's a lot more than that, but I'm not sharing the real reason with him.

"You sure, Ellie?"

His concern touches me. "Yes."

Trying hard not to jostle my innards, I creep toward the couch. Right now, that's the best place for me.

"Wouldn't the bed be more comfortable?"

"No. This is fine. Just don't say the 'F' word. If you have to e-a-t, don't do it in front of me."

He smiles that grin that rocks my world. "I can do that. You want to watch some TV?"

"Yes, please." It'll take my mind off my stomach, which is still pissed off at me.

"What would you like to watch?"

"Doesn't matter."

"What about your baking show?"

I shoot him a death glare. Or try to anyway. Too weak to really achieve it. "You're a cruel, cruel man, Brock Parker."

"Sorry." Going by that grin, he's not the least bit sorry.

He pulls up one of the premium channels. "Sleepless in Seattle" or "Notting Hill?""

Two romantic comedies. He knows how much I love them. But both those movies have dinner scenes. "Nope. Isn't there some nice musical where people don't eat?"

"Ooh, tough one. How about "West Side Story?" "The Sound of Music?" "My Fair Lady?"" I drift off again while he runs through the list. Hours later, I wake up in his bed. How I got there I have no idea. But one thing's for sure, I'm starving.

He's curled around me which is going to make it tough to slip out of bed. At a snail's pace, I inch away from him, until I'm finally free. Grabbing my cell so I can check for messages, I head toward the repository of all food—the kitchen. Hopefully something there will spark my appetite. Sure enough, the fridge is chock full of food, from the barbecue, from his drop-bys. But only one thing grabs my attention.

He's got to have peanut butter to go with it. He loves that stuff. I go searching in the cupboards for a jar. On my third try, I find it. And it's the crunchy kind too. My favorite.

Parking my fanny on a kitchen stool, I open both jars. Pretty soon I'm spearing the peanut butter with the tasty treat, sucking the salt off my fingers, licking them too.

When steps approach, I realize it's much too late to hide what I'm eating. I'll have to brazen it out.

"You're eating?" Brock asks, semi-awake. Semi-hard too. But then why wouldn't he be? It's already morning.

"Yep. Got hungry." I swipe the brine off my lips.

"That's good." His sleepy gaze drifts to the jars. He blinks a couple of times before his eyes flare. "Peanut butter *and* pickles?"

"My favorite." I grin.

His brows knit. "Since when?"

I play it off like it's no big deal. "Since always."

"I don't think so. You've never eaten that combo before." Wide awake now, he crosses his arms against that broad, bare, lickable chest of his.

God. I can't get horny right now. Not when I need all my working brain cells. "Yeah, I have. You just weren't around."

His gaze narrows. "When Sandra dropped off the food, she asked me something."

"Oh?"

"She wanted to know when the baby was due."

CHAPTER 29

Brock

"WHEN WERE YOU GOING TO TELL ME, ELLIE?" How could she have hidden this from me?

"Tell you what?"

Can't believe she's doing this. "Don't fucking play with me. When?"

Unable to look at me, she gazes down at her feet. "September, maybe October."

"When's the baby due?"

"Christmas time."

I do a quick math. "So you're four months along?"

"Yes."

Four months ago we were in Bora Bora. Shortly before our trip, she'd developed a reaction to her birth control pills. Rather than chance a new prescription while we were out of the country, we'd opted for condoms. But there had been times—in the beach bungalow, in the ocean, on a freaking sailboat—when we'd made love without protection. I hadn't given a damn because more than anything else I want more children with her. And now that wish is a reality.

Except.

216

She doesn't want me to be part of it. Once again she's hidden her pregnancy from me. Something easily done since we live hundreds of miles apart. She probably thought if she waited until October to tell me, I wouldn't do anything about it. But she's wrong. Dead wrong. That's my child she's carrying, and I'm not about to let her go at it alone. Not this time. Not ever again. "I may have missed out on Kaylee, but I'll be damned if I miss out on this one." I point to the floor. "You're moving down here."

She clambers off the stool to confront me. "No. I'm not."

I want to shake sense into her, kiss her into submission, but neither is going to get me what I want. "For God's sakes, Ellie, how many roadblocks are you going to put in my way?"

She hitches up her chin. "As many as it takes."

Breathing hard, I fist my hands. "I want you here. With me."

"Why? So I can watch you play hide the salami with those single neighbors of yours?"

Idiot woman. "I haven't done it so far, and I've had every opportunity to do so. What makes you think I will?"

Jutting out her jaw, she slaps her fist on her hip. "One of them came up to me at the picnic."

"Who?"

"I don't know. She borrowed some coffee."

"Ahh. Suzi."

"You know her name?"

"Of course, I do. She told me. You got nothing to worry about. I don't have the least interest in her, or any of the other women who've dropped by." As gently as I can, I cup her shoulders. "I only want you."

She shrugs me off as her lip curls. "You're only saying that because for some weird reason you want a family. And Kaylee, and this baby and I"—she hugs her stomach—"fit the bill."

"I do want a family with you and Kaylee, and God willing, this baby. But I've always wanted you."

"Really?" She folds her arms across her chest. It's only now I notice her growing belly. How could I have been so fucking blind?

"Yes."

"Then why did you decide our marriage would be temporary?"

"Because that was the only way to get you to marry me."

She drops her arms as doubt rolls over her face. "What?"

"I knew if I offered anything permanent, you would have said no. And I couldn't have that. Not when I've wanted you for so long."

Her breath hitches. "Since when?"

"Since always." I cup her cheek, stroke a thumb across her velvety skin. I love her so much, but I can't say the words. She'll never believe me.

"If you wanted me so much, why didn't you come looking for me?"

She's right. I should have. But nobody knew where she'd gone. I'd been so devastated when she left, I'd barely eaten, hardly slept. It'd taken my high school football coach to pull me out of my funk. After I'd missed several practices, he'd told me I was in danger of not being recruited by Clemson, Mississippi State or anyone else. And then he'd ordered me to pull my head out of my ass. The tough talk worked so well I pretty much mowed down defenses after that. By the time I'd arrived at college, I'd learned to focus on football in order to live with the pain. But I never forgot her. "You left without saying goodbye. I thought you didn't want me, Ellie."

"I couldn't. I didn't know what to say."

"How about I'm having your baby. Please help."

"You were seventeen, Brock. Last thing you wanted was a baby. You said so yourself."

I don't recall that conversation. "When?"

"After the Outlaws' banquet. You said it'd been for the best you hadn't knocked me up."

"I didn't know, Ellie. But if you'd given me half a chance, I would have fucking learned."

"You were the biggest stud in high school, Brock. What kind of a father would you have made? I had to think about the baby. I had to think about me."

"From the day we made love, I never looked at another girl, much less hooked up with one. I would have done right by you."

"And what would you have done, Brock? Told me you'd take care of us until the end of time?"

"Yes."

"I don't believe you."

"No. Of course, you don't. It's easier to believe what you want to believe. Life is a whole lot easier when you push people away. That way you'll never get hurt."

Tears rain down her cheeks as she puts both hands over her ears. "Stop this. Stop this."

I pull down her hands because I want her to hear every word I have to say. "But understand this. You're throwing us away when we could be wonderful."

"You'd say anything, do anything to keep us by your side." She spits out.

"Not anything, Ellie. I would never lie about this. I want you in my life. You and Kaylee and Butch. And that's the God's honest truth."

We're standing inches from each other, and yet a whole world apart.

Kaylee rushes into the kitchen, a concerned look on her face, and we grow silent.

"What are you arguing about?" she asks.

I take a deep breath, let it out. "Your mother forgot to tell me she was pregnant."

Kaylee's cheeks turn pink.

"You knew? And you didn't tell me?" Betrayed by both my wife and my daughter.

"I couldn't." She stares at the floor. "It wasn't for me to tell."

Ravaged by emotion, Ellie swipes the tears from her face. "Kaylee, pack your bags. We're leaving."

"No, I'm not." Our daughter backs away from her mom and anchors herself to me. "I'm staying. I want to go to Mitch's school, learn advanced programming and intern at Advanced Tech."

When did she decide all this? Is that the real reason Ellie flew down? Not because of the welcome wagons or because Kaylee mentioned Mitch, but because Kaylee wants to stay? Seems Kaylee is not the only devious one.

"No. You're not, young lady."

Still latched on to me, Kaylee glances up. "You guys have joint custody. I can stay with either parent, can't I?"

Rather than wait for me to answer, Ellie jumps in. "No, you can't. The agreement specifically calls for you to live with me during the school year."

She'd made sure to include that in the joint custody papers we drew up before our wedding. At the time, I'd wondered why. Now I know. She wanted to make sure Kaylee stayed with her.

Kaylee turns toward her mother. "So move down here, and we can live together, Mom."

"I can't."

"Why not?"

"My job's in Chicago."

"Can't you be an agent anywhere? There are a lot of college football teams down here. You can find players to represent."

I hate to hear the hope in her voice. Her mother's already made up her mind and nothing is going to change it.

"It's not that easy, Kaylee."

"If you establish an office here, word will get around. You're good, Mom. You know how to negotiate a deal."

Ellie pleads with me. "Brock, say something."

"Dad?" Kaylee's eyes are swimming with tears. She's miserable. But then so are Ellie and me.

Regardless, I have to be an adult about this. I have to do what's best for Kaylee. And that's not staying with me. "I don't want you to go," I say, my voice crushed.

A tiny smile trembles on her lips as she turns to her mother. "See?"

Ellie doesn't say a thing, leaving it up to me to crush my daughter's spirit. "I appreciate your wanting to live with me, but you have to do as your Mom says." It hurts to say that, more than Kaylee will ever know.

"You don't want me?"

How could she believe that? "Of course, I do. I'd love to have you here, year-round." I jam my hands in my pockets to stop them from trembling and toughen my voice. "But you have to live with your mom."

"Why?" She lets go of my arm. Her heart's breaking too.

"Because she's your mom. Right now it seems all fun and games because it's summertime, but once school starts, you'll miss her. You know you will."

Her gaze swivels from Ellie to me and back again. "But I don't understand. We could be a family. You, her, Butch and me. And the baby."

"You're right, we could, except it's not going to work." Please don't ask me to explain. I don't understand it myself.

"But you love her and she loves you."

Something in me shatters. I do love Ellie. More than she'll ever know. But she doesn't love me. But I can't let my pain affect Kaylee. I have to do what's best for her. And that means giving her something to anticipate. "You can come and visit during Christmas." As a consolation prize, it pretty much sucks. But I don't have anything else. I'm hurting too much.

"How are you going to work things out? I might be all grown up, but what about the baby? Is he going to come down for Christmas too?"

I rub my hand across my brow. God knows I don't have an answer for that. I'm all tapped out. "Ellie. You want to take that one?"

But before she can do so, her cell rings. Glancing at it, she says, "It's Grandma."

I nod.

She takes a deep breath, swipes the phone. "Hi, Mama." As she listens, her face turns white as a sheet.

What the fuck happened? "What's wrong?" I ask.

Trembling, she holds the cell to her chest. "It's Butch. He was hit by a car."

CHAPTER 30

Brock

FOUR HOURS LATER, we're landing at O'Hare. The jet got us to Chicago as quickly as it could.

The flight north wasn't easy. Kaylee cried the whole way. "It's all my fault. I should have brought him with me."

Ellie folds Kaylee into her embrace. "Honey, that wouldn't have worked. Dogs have a hard time in a plane's cargo hold."

Turning into her mother's shoulder, Kaylee breaks down into sobs.

Not that I have anything to comment about. I'm barely holding on. If anybody's to blame, it's me. I should have brought him to Charleston. Except, I couldn't. As close as he'd grown to Kaylee, separating them would have been cruel.

There's no luggage to retrieve at O'Hare. We hadn't packed a thing. As soon as Ellie had hung up with Ruth, I'd contacted the South Carolina Wolves. If anybody would know how to lease a jet, it would be them. But they did one better. The owner of the team lent me his.

Outside the airport, the Lincoln car the team reserved waits for us. Much as I want the driver to tear through traffic, he can't. It takes a full hour to arrive where Butch is. The Windy City Emergency

Animal Hospital is one of the best in Chicago with a sterling reputation so Butch's in good hands. But knowing there's only so much a vet can do, I brace myself for the worst sort of news. As soon as we walk in the door, we're met by Ellie's mom.

"I'm so sorry, honey," Ruth embraces Kaylee which, of course, sets off a rush of fresh tears from her. "I should have done a better job of watching over him."

"Nobody blames you," I say. Ruth had stopped at the house to check in on Butch and feed him. But when she'd opened the door, he'd taken off like a shot into the middle of the street. A driver hadn't seen him in time and struck him head-on.

"Thank you, Brock, for saying that. I know how much he means to you." With a free hand, she reaches out to Ellie. "How are you holding up, honey?"

Ellie grasps her mother's hand and swallows hard. "I'm fine. The baby's fine. How's Butch?"

"He hasn't—" Kaylee interrupts, her lips trembling, a world of hurt in her eyes.

"He's hanging in there, sweetheart." She disentangles herself from Kaylee and points to the receptionist. "This is Carmen. She'll take you to where he is."

As I walk past her, she hugs me as well. "I'm so sorry, Brock."

I nod. Can't say a thing past the lump in my throat.

The surgery suite where Butch's recuperating is pristine, but the chemical smells sicken me. It's not anything new. I've been around hospitals before, but because it's associated with my best bud, I want to upchuck, especially after I spot my big, beautiful boy. He's lying on a table, his chest barely moving, bandaged around his middle, and a mask covering his snout. If all that wasn't enough, two legs are wrapped in white, and an intravenous infusion flows into him through a needle stuck into an un-bandaged leg.

As soon as we come into the room, the vet listening to his heart glances up. "Are you Butch's family?"

"Yes. Yes, we are. I'm Brock Parker. This is my wife, Ellie, and our daughter Kaylee."

He hangs the instrument around his neck and walks toward us. "I'm Dr. Burns. Ms. Tate"—he nods toward the woman monitoring the infusion—"is one of our veterinary technicians."

Their names barely register. "How is he?" I ask.

"He has very serious internal injuries. And, as you can see, two broken legs. We've performed surgery. Given him a blood transfusion."

"He's not suffering, is he?" God, please let him say no.

"No. He's getting an intravenous drip of morphine and ketamine to deal with the pain."

"Is he going to make it?" Kaylee asks, her face ravaged with grief.

The vet's gaze bounces to me, a question in his eyes. I nod. Might as well get the bad news out of the way.

"I don't know," he says to Kaylee in the kind tone he must have used a thousand times. "He's strong, well-fed. We're doing as much as we can. The rest will be up to him."

"When will we find out if he . . ." She can't say it out loud. Doubt any of us could.

"Within twenty-four hours, we'll know."

Kaylee carefully wraps a hand around one of Butch's good legs. "I love you, Butch. Please don't die. Please." Her voice turns upbeat, as if she's trying to cheer him up. "I'll get you those treats you wanted. I'll buy you oodles of them." But Butch doesn't respond. He just lies there unconscious.

Ellie bends over him and whispers into his ear. "Butch, I'll make you a deal. You don't die, and we'll all live together as a family. Plus, you'll have a new baby to love. You'd like that. Wouldn't you, boy?"

I don't say anything. Caught between the joy from hearing her words and the agony from seeing my injured best bud, doubt I could speak.

After a technician brings us chairs so we can sit down, we remain by Butch's side, whispering words of encouragement, hoping he'll make it through. He doesn't get worse, but he doesn't get better, either. Finally after two hours, I call it. "Go home. I'll stay behind."

"But," Ellie says.

"I don't want to leave," Kaylee protests.

I hug her to me, drop my chin on her head while glancing at Ellie. "Think of the baby, Kaylee. Your mother needs her rest."

With her breath hitching, Kaylee nods through her tears.

Coming to her feet, Ellie turns sad eyes to me. "Call us if there's any change."

"I will."

After they whisper some last words of encouragement to our boy, I walk them out front where Ruth waits for them. "How is he?"

"Hanging in there." My words come out rusty as if I forgot how to talk. "Can you take them home? I'm staying behind." Ruth is wise enough to read between the lines. I don't want them here if Butch passes away.

"Of course." She squeezes my hand. "It's in God's hands now, Brock."

I return to the post-surgery room and drop into the chair. With no one around to witness my grief, I allow the tears to flow. I'm not a religious man. Never bothered with church and such. But today, I pray with all my heart that God will heal my beautiful boy. And then I rest my head next to his body to feel the rise and fall of his chest. If he loses his battle, his loving heart will cease to beat.

As time passes, I whisper to him. "How you doing, boy? How you doing, champ?" The vet drops in to check his vitals. The technician drifts by to adjust his drip.

An hour passes and another. Close to three in the morning, his heart speeds up. Is that a good sign or bad?

God, don't let it be bad. Needing to do something, anything, I break out into a chorus of "Who Let the Dogs Out?" And miracle of miracles, his tail moves a little. Encouraged by his response, I keep it up, at first softly and then more loudly. By four o'clock, I'm hoarse and so, so tired, I rest my head against him.

"Woof."

I come awake in a rush. Was that? Did he?

"Woof."

My heart soars. That's the sound he makes when he's dreaming. "Doc. Doc!"

The vet comes running. "What's wrong?"

"He woofed. That's a good sign, right?"

The vet listens to Butch's heart, checks his vital signs, and stands up, a look of wonder on his face. "Well, I'll be damned."

"Is he"—I swallow hard—"Is he better?"

"Yes. He is."

"Thank you, God."

I pick up the phone to call Ellie, but before I do, my cell rings. It's her. "How is he?" Going by the trembling in her voice, she expects the worst.

"He woofed at me."

"He did?" Her tone's perked up.

"Yeah. The vet thinks he's going to make it."

The vet arches a brow. He never said such a thing. But I don't care. I know. Butch's going to be okay.

"We'll be right over," Ellie says.

By the time she and Kaylee arrive, Butch's semi-awake. So naturally, Kaylee bursts into tears. And he, of course, wags his tail for her. Especially, when she strokes his beautiful head. "I'll never leave you again, Butch."

"Now, honey," Ellie says, "he's going to have to spend some time in the hospital to recuperate."

"How long, Doc?" I ask the vet who's stopped by to check on Butch again.

"Three days. Give or take."

I can live with that as long as he does come home.

Somehow, we pry ourselves from Butch's side. He needs his rest and, frankly after having gone without shuteye for a day and a half, so do I.

I crash as soon as I get home. But when the scent of apple pie drifts into the bedroom, I'm up like a shot.

Ellie's in the kitchen, apron over the small bump in her belly.

How did I not know she was pregnant? I ask myself for the umpteenth time, scrubbing the sleep from my eyes. "Where's Kaylee?"

"Meghan's house. I think she wanted to give us some privacy."

Smart girl. "And Butch?"

"I called the vet. He's eating."

"A good sign."

"Yeah."

She takes the pie from the oven and drops it on a cooling rack. As long as I live, the scent of cinnamon and apples will always remind me of her. She hangs her apron on a peg before glancing around the kitchen. "I'm going to miss this place. So many memories."

I hadn't imagined her words. She intends for us to live together as a family. "We'll make better ones in Charleston." But first, there's something I need to hear. "The thing is"—I clear my throat—"The thing is . . ."

She leans back against the kitchen counter and folds her arms across her front. "What is the thing?"

"I love you."

She grins. "I know."

She freaking knows? How could she? I hadn't said it to her.

"Okay. But the thing is . . ."

She arches a brow.

"You haven't said it to me." I rush it out at warp speed.

"No. I haven't." She laces her hands in front of her.

No, I haven't? What the fuck? "As much as I love you. And I do."

Her serene smile resembles a Madonna's. I really should have her painted that way.

"I need to hear you say you love me back."

She tilts her head to the side. "And if I don't?"

I jam my hands in my jeans pockets. "I don't think we can stay together."

"Really?"

"Yes. Really."

"Okay."

Okay? What's that supposed to mean? I rack my brains trying to figure it out while we pack up the house, make arrangements to sell it, hire workers to move our stuff. At night, we make sweet love in the bedroom. Days, we listen to Kaylee chat with Mitch. When her transfer to her new school is confirmed, Kaylee dances around the house like it's Christmas, the Fourth of July, and her birthday all rolled into one.

After five days in the hospital, Butch comes home. Moving a little slower than before, but still moving. Pretty much ignoring Ellie and me, he spends his days in Kaylee's bedroom, only coming out to eat and do his business in the yard. The way she continuously blabs at him would make my ears bleed, but he just gazes at her with this adoring look on his face. And that's exactly the way it should be.

To my surprise, Ellie decides to call it quits at her sports agency. After years of college and full-time jobs, she's more than ready for a break. Sometime after the baby is born, she figures she'll go back to work. Given her credentials, something's bound to turn up.

Two weeks later, it's time for me to fly back to Charleston. Training camp is starting in a couple of days. Ellie is staying to deal with the last of the packing, but she and Kaylee and Butch will drive down in two weeks. Ruth will remain behind to handle the sale of the house, hers as well. Once that's all taken care of, she and Steve will move down to Charleston. I've offered them a place in our home since it has plenty of room. But Ruth has her eye on a cottage by the water where she won't be far from us.

When it's time for me to leave, Ellie and I head off to O'Hare. She still hasn't said the 'L' word. So being the bigger person, I say it. Again. "I love you."

She smiles back.

Fuck it. I'm not going to beg. I jump out of the car, grab my bag and huff it into the airport without looking back.

Training camp with the Wolves is just as brutal as the Outlaws'. Except it's worse because it's ninety degrees in the field. We get longer breaks, but by the end of it, all I want to do is go home and chill with Ellie and Kaylee and Butch. As many times as we've talked since I left Chicago, she's never once said she loves me. But I've finally come to terms with it. She doesn't have to say it. I have enough love for the both of us.

I pull up to the housing development's front entrance, expecting the gate to go up. But to my surprise, the guard flags me down.

"What's up?" This guy knows who I am. Been in and out a zillion times.

"Hello, Mr. Parker. Just wanted to let you know. We got word from the front office. You won't have to worry about those, err, ladies dropping by anymore."

"Good to know." Suspecting a guard at the front gate had been taking bribes, I'd filed a complaint with the management company. It appears they've finally worked it out. "That would be a problem since my wife's here now."

He grins. "I know. Go on through." He lifts the gate and I ride through.

What was that all about? That codger had not once smiled at me, but today I could see all his front teeth. I shrug. He's probably just trying to earn a big Christmas tip.

As I get closer to my house, a bunch of people crowd the sidewalks and the road, almost like it's a parade. Where are they going? As it turns out, the 'parade' ends at my house. My driveway's so crowded with people I can't even pull up into it, so I park on the only free spot on the street. Is Ellie having a garage sale? It is Saturday after all. Nah, she donated a lot of stuff to Goodwill before we left.

When I step on the sidewalk in front of my house, the crowd parts. They're all grinning ear-to-ear. What the hell's going on?

As I take the path to my front door, I notice a whole bunch, and I mean a whole bunch, of casserole dishes on the lawn. Empty dishes. In all shapes and sizes. And colors. Maybe she is having a garage sale. But that sure is an odd way to lay them out, scattered as they are all over the grass. That's when I realize they're spelling out words. Three words to be exact.

Ellie loves Brock.

She's telling not only me, but all of our neighbors. Probably the entire world too. Because as sure as I'm standing here, with a goofy grin on my face, somebody's already posted it on the internet.

Ellie's waiting for me at the top of the porch steps, holding a plate in her hands. I'm not close enough to smell it, but I know it's apple pie.

I walk up the path, struggling to remain cool. When I get there, I climb up one step so we're eye to eye. "Apple pie?"

"Yes." A light glows in her eyes.

I nod toward the lawn. "So you do love me?" Dying to kiss her, I content myself with cupping her face and brushing a thumb across her satiny cheek.

"I've always loved you, Brock." Her breathless voice is sexy as fuck.

"Since when?"

"Since high school. Why do you think I spent so much time at practice?"

"And here I thought you were just interested in football."

"I was watching you, you idiot." She makes 'idiot' sound like a caress.

"Yeah?"

"Uh-huh." She bites down on her lip.

I'm going to put that lip to good use first chance I get. But first, we have to do something else. Something I've been dreaming about for a long time. "How about we sit on the porch and eat our pie?"

She gestures to the mob out front which, if anything, has grown larger. "In front of God and everyone?"

"I don't care about them or anything else as long as you love me, Ellie." And that's the God's honest truth.

She cups my face with her free hand. "Well then, Brock Parker, you're bound to not care about anything for a good, long time because I will love you forever."

I kiss her, sweetly, deeply, because the most beautiful woman in the world loves me and always has.

EPILOGUE

Five Years Later
Brock

"PITCH ME THE BALL, DADDY!" My son, Brock, Jr., all of four years old. Pretty much like Kaylee, he's all me. Unlike Kaylee, though, he inherited my athletic ability. He wants to play ball which is fine with me. It won't be football, though. Too much punishment for your body to take. Baseball's much safer, so I'm teaching him to catch and pitch.

"Brock. It's time for you to go." Ellie yells from the porch. She's plopped on a rocking chair, looking about ten months pregnant, although she's only eight. With twins. Yeah. Her doctor put her on bed rest, but with Kaylee leaving for college, the best we could do was park her in a spot where she could watch the goings-on. If she so much as moves a muscle, I've threatened to hog tie her to that chair, though.

I'm driving our daughter to MIT. MIT! Who knew a kid of mine would be that smart? Harvard and Yale, along with every college she applied to, accepted her. But she chose MIT to study Bioengineering.

Someday she's going to design an entire body suit that people can wear to walk, talk, and move. So, so proud of her.

I lob the baseball one last time to Brock, Jr. He catches it in his mini-glove and beams me a smile. He might look just like me, but that grin is pure Ellie. Makes sense. He spends much more time with her than me.

I'm on the last year of my contract with the South Carolina Wolves. Last season, I took them all the way to the Super Bowl but lost. This year, I intend to win it all. But whatever happens, at the end of the season, I'm hanging up my cleats. I want to spend the rest of my life with my family—Brock, Jr., Kaylee, the babies, and Ellie. Always Ellie. God willing we'll grow old together rocking those chairs on the porch.

"Gotta go, Ace."

Brock, Jr. runs up and slings his little dude arms around my knees. "Do you have to, Daddy?"

I ruffle his honey blond hair. "Yeah, I do, Bud. Gotta drive Kaylee to school."

"When is she coming back?"

"Thanksgiving."

"That's"—he counts on his fingers—"that's three months away."

"Yeah, it is."

Hauling a suitcase behind her, Kaylee trips down the steps. Butch, ever her shadow, hobbles along next to her. His legs healed, just not 100%. Although he doesn't have the vibrant stride of before, he still has the heart of a champion.

Tongue lolling out, Sundance bounds down the steps. Butch side-eyes him, seemingly saying, "How rude."

Shortly after the whole family moved to South Carolina, we adopted Sundance, figuring Butch needed a buddy to play with. But Butch never warmed up to him. He'd already given his whole heart to Kaylee. Out of all of us, he's going to miss her the most.

Ruth, a little grayer, a little older, walks onto the porch, a brown bag in her hand. "Kaylee, I made you some sandwiches for the road. Your favorite, peanut butter and jelly."

Having stashed her suitcase in the car, Kaylee runs back to her grandmother and embraces her. "Grandma. You're the best."

And then it's time to say goodbye to her mother. Not an easy feat. Even from where I'm standing, I can see the droop of her shoulders. Bending down, she gently hugs Ellie. "Mom."

"Bye, honey," Ellie pats her daughter's cheek. "Call me and be careful."

"I will. Don't worry."

Easier said than done.

Shortly after Kaylee's 14th birthday, Ellie had 'the talk' with her. Something that was totally needed. Turns out Ellie had been right all along about Mitch. During his sophomore year, he'd grown six inches, replaced his coke-bottle glasses with contacts, and lost the dental hardware. And just like that, he'd turned into a stud. A nerdy stud, but a stud nonetheless.

When his friendship with Kaylee had blossomed into something more serious, I'd pulled Mitch aside and done a little talking of my own. I'd told him if he ever hurt my little girl, he wouldn't live to see his next birthday. He'd nodded and said he had nothing but respect for her. A year ago, he'd left for MIT. To my surprise, their friendship hadn't wavered. They Skype at least once a week.

Without parental supervision, these kids could get into a world of trouble. But they won't. Because they know better. But in the end, all I can do is pray. And tuck a box of condoms into Kaylee's suitcase.

At first, I attribute Ellie's facial contortions to her attempt to keep from crying, but Brock, Jr. alerts me to the true state of things.

"Mom, you pe-peed." He says pointing to the pool of liquid beneath Ellie's rocking chair.

"Honey," Ruth says, a note of alarm in her voice.

"Mom!" A wide-eyed Kaylee screams.

I bound up the stairs and kneel next to the love of my life. "Ellie?"

Ellie's quiet demeanor belies the intensity of the moment. "I've been having contractions since early this morning. I guess my water broke."

"Right." I could demand to know why she didn't say anything, but that's not important right now. Not when I have to get her to the hospital. "Kaylee, get your mother's go-bag."

Taking Ellie's hand, I help her to her feet. But when I guide her down the front porch steps, she stops. "Wait. I'm not going to the hospital like this. I need to change."

Ruth, ever the voice of reason, says, "Honey, you're just going to get another dress wet."

Brock, Jr. pats my leg. "Daddy."

I pay him no attention.

Which doesn't stop him from smacking me again. "Dad!"

"Yes, son."

"What did mom mean her water broke," he says, scratching his nose.

"It means your brother and sister are coming."

Kaylee runs out with Ellie's go bag and squeezes it into the back of the car. Somehow, she had the presence of mind to bring a towel as well which she lays over the SUV's passenger seat.

"I'm coming, too," she says.

"Okay." She'll have to drive her own car, since mine is packed to the gills with her college things.

"I'll stay and watch over Brock, Jr.," Ruth hollers from the porch.

"Thanks, Ruth," I yell over my shoulder.

Sundance is jumping around Ellie and me, making a nuisance of himself. Butch's plopped his butt on the porch, next to Ruth and Brock, Jr. As if to say, you go and take care of things. I'll watch over the kinfolk. As proof he's on the job, he barks at Sundance who promptly makes a beeline for the porch.

"You okay, sweetheart?" I ask, Ellie.

"Never better."

I lean over to kiss her lips. "I love you. Always and forever."

She cups my cheek. "Me too."

On a normal day, the drive to the hospital lasts thirty minutes. I intend to make it in twenty. If anybody stops me, I've got the best excuse in the world. On the way, I call the hospital, so when we arrive, they're at the entrance waiting for us. Once Ellie's tucked into the ugly hospital gown, they allow me to enter the labor and delivery room. I assure them this is not my first rodeo, that I was present for the birth of my son.

At first, everything proceeds smoothly, but two hours later, one of the babies goes into distress.

Her obstetrician says, "We're going to have to do a C-section."

My heart plummets. I can't lose this woman I love more than life. "Do what you have to, Doc."

They only allow me inside the surgery suite, so Kaylee has to wait outside in the family room.

"She'll be okay, Dad. She's strong."

"I know." I know no such thing. Inside I'm a quivering bowl of jelly. If something were to happen to Ellie . . . I can't finish that thought.

As it turns out, I have nothing to worry about. The procedure goes off smoothly, and before I know it, Ellie's putting our baby boy to her breast.

She smooths his honey wheat hair. "He looks just like you." She sounds wistful.

"You're right, he does." Down to his, ahem, willie which appears way out of proportion to the rest of him.

"I'm never going to have a child who resembles me."

"What can I say? My seed is potent."

She rolls her eyes. Doesn't matter, I lean down and kiss her anyway. When I do, the peanut in my arms squirms as if she wants some attention too. "Welcome to the world, Sunshine."

"That's not her name."

I nod toward Ellie. "She wants to call you Susan, but your real name is Sunshine."

"No. It won't be."

"What does she know? She's only your mother."

They say babies don't smile, but Susan Sunshine does. Because she already knows how bright her future will be.

EXCERPT FROM DIRTY FILTHY BOY

Chicago

Early October

Ty

THE SECOND I STEP ON THE PRACTICE FIELD, I'm besieged by fans. Young, old, women, men.

A gap-toothed, tow-headed boy wearing my number 10 jersey stands at the front of the line, Sharpie in hand. "Ty, sign my shirt. Pleeeease." Gotta give the kid credit, he came prepared.

"Sure." I write Ty Mathews with my trademark flourish at the end. Even though I've signed thousands of autographs, I still get a kick out of seeing the excitement in a child's eyes. Of course, some of them aren't kids. And some of them have asked me to sign something other than shirts. Tits, asses. I draw the line at pussies. Yeah, I've been asked. After I sign a few more shirts and photos, a staff member waves off the fans, promising I'll sign more after practice.

If my arm holds out.

My shoulder throbs from yesterday's grueling session. I've iced it, had it massaged, but it still hurts like hell. At twenty-eight years old, I shouldn't hurt so damned much. The smart thing would be to give it a rest, but we're facing San Francisco this week, and there are some mean sons of bitches on that team who'd just as soon tear my head off. So I better be ready to get rid of the ball. Besides, I'll be damned before I ask for a light workout from Coach 'No Pain, No Gain' Gronowski who played with a broken foot at a clutch match during his NFL days. I can't fault his attitude. Last year, we went all the way to the AFC playoffs, only to lose the championship game to our conference nemesis, the Texas Roughriders. I don't intend to fail my team. This year I'm taking the Chicago Outlaws all the way to the Super Bowl.

As I'm tying my shoulder pads, I notice three of my teammates gesturing at something, laughing hard enough to split a gut. I throw on my practice jersey, and, curious, I walk up. "What's so funny?"

One of the linebackers points toward the sideline where a redhead with hair down to one luscious ass is interviewing our number one wideout, Ron Moss. The breath whooshes out of me. She's wearing a micro skirt, short enough for me to almost see the promised land. Her blouse, unbuttoned down to there, displays a truly impressive cleavage.

My cock, which hasn't gotten any action for two days, swells painfully against my cup. I tug to give it room. Where has this reporter been hiding out? I haven't seen her before. And believe me, I would have noticed.

The woman keeps touching Ron, his arm, his hand. Problem is, the more she does it, the more stone-faced he becomes. No wonder the linebackers think it's funny. Ron doesn't drink, doesn't smoke and he certainly doesn't like aggressive females which the reporter appears to be. I, on the other hand, like all kinds of women, especially those built like brick houses.

When Ron twitches away from her, she glances toward the three amigos with a questioning look on her face. Before I have a chance to wonder what that's all about, one of the three makes a squeezing motion. Fuck. I know what she's going to do. Yep. Sure enough. One of her dainty hands slides over Ron's ass and squeezes it for all she's worth.

Predictably, Ron says, "Excuse me," and starts to walk away.

"Where are you going? We're not finished," Red protests.

The wideout turns back to her. "Ma'am. I don't want to be rude, but I don't care for women who grab my buttocks." That's Ron. Polite to the end.

"But they said . . ." She points to the three chuckleheads next to me who are laughing their heads off. But it's too late. Ron's already stalked off.

Lips tight, cheeks flushed pink, she stomps to where we stand. "You set me up." Smoke's practically streaming from her ears.

They're guffawing so hard they can't get a word out. But I can. "What's going on?"

"They told me that if I wanted to get a great interview with Mr. Moss, I should 'flaunt what my Mama gave me and grab his ass.' So I freed a couple of buttons, hitched up my skirt. And I . . . touched his heinie." As she talks, she wiggles her skirt down, rebuttons her blouse, slips into the jacket she'd been holding over one arm.

My cock doesn't know whether to toss confetti at the erotic dance or curse the covering up. I, on the other hand, know an explanation is in order. "Ron Moss's a born-again Christian. He doesn't care for, err, bold women."

"I'm not bold!" She shoots me a scathing glance, hot enough to leave a burn.

"Sorry. It certainly appeared that way."

Giving her skirt one last tug, she turns to the linesmen. "You guys are big fat jerks. I needed that interview for my job. Hope you all fry in hell."

"Sorry?" One of the three big fat jerks says without an ounce of remorse in his voice.

"Go stuff yourself." That's the best she can come up with? In the world of curses, that's about as mild as it gets. Obviously, the hard-core ones are not in her vocabulary. She storms past Larry, Moe and Curly toward the gate that opens to the parking lot. You have to get through security to get into the Chicago Outlaws' complex, but inside, everything is pretty accessible. Only a waist-high link fence separates the field from the parking lot.

"What did you guys do?" I ask.

"Man, you should have seen her," the outside linebacker says. "She showed up all buttoned tight in a skirt down to her knees. You know, the schoolmarm look. We told her Ron liked his women a bit more lively." He snickers again.

The sad thing is Ron would have gone for the schoolmarm look, but now . . . My gaze follows her as she reaches a junker. That thing's gotta be at least ten years old. She drops her notebook, wipes something off her face as she picks it up. Is she crying? I curse and go running after her. When I catch up, she's juggling her car keys, talking to herself. "Stupid, stupid, stupid." Her notebook hits the ground again.

"Hi."

She stabs me with a glance. No tears, though. "Don't you have some braying to do with those jackasses?"

Her eyes are the color of crushed bluebells. I should know bluebells. They grew all around the run-down shack I lived in back in east Texas. The only spot of color in a dreary landscape. "I'm not with them."

"Oh?" Her eyes scrunch as she gives me the once over. "You're wearing the same uniform."

"I'm on the same team, yes, but I didn't play this prank on you."

"Prank?" She kicks the notebook with her high heeled, open toe shoe. If she keeps that up, she's going to hurt herself. "You call that a prank? I got handed this assignment at the last minute, and this was my chance to impress my boss." Her face crumbles.

Is she about to turn on the waterworks? "Hey, hey." I pat her shoulder. "Don't cry."

She swats off my hand and hiccups. "I don't"—hiccup—"cry. I never cry." She takes a breath, holds it in. "Idiot." She mumbles out.

Smiling, I cross my arms against my chest. "Been called worse."

Her eyes flash blue fire. "What are you talking about?"

"You just called me an idiot."

"I wasn't talking about *you.*"

I jerk a thumb backward. "Them, then. You're absolutely right. They are low-class worms."

"I was talking about *me.* Idiot."

Is it me or her she's talking about now? Her expression hasn't changed. Gotta be her. "Why would you call yourself that?"

"I knew it was wrong. Knew it. But I did it anyway. First week on the job, and I wanted to impress my boss, so when they suggested I lose a few buttons, show some leg, I did it. Stupid, stupid, stupid." With each 'stupid', she nails the notebook. With its spine loose, guts spilling out, the damn thing's on life support.

Better change the subject. "Where do you work?"

"*The Windy City Chronicle.*"

Never heard of the rag. Poor kid. Probably her first job too. I scratch the back of my head. Maybe I had nothing to do with the nasty trick the three stooges back there played, but I feel bad for her. "Does it have to be him?"

"What do you mean?"

"Does it have to be Ron Moss or can you interview somebody else on the team?"

She shrugs. "Guess it could be anyone." She looks back toward the practice field. "What does it matter? No one else will give me an interview. Not after I allowed those jerks to make a fool out of me in front of everyone."

Don't have to turn around to know we're probably drawing attention from the players. You think women gossip? Got nothing on professional football players. Busybodies, every last one of them. "Well, there's one person who'd be glad to talk to you."

"Who?"

"Me. Ty Mathews." I stick out my hand.

"MacKenna Perkins." Her dainty hand disappears in my oversized one. What can I say? I'm big all over. And I mean *all* over. "Would our readers be interested in reading about you?" She gazes hopefully up at me.

"You might say so. I'm the quarterback." I lean forward, hoping to

impress upon her the importance of my position. "The starting quarterback."

"The starting one, huh? That sounds important. Is it? Important?"

I fight back the urge to laugh. Given her recent experience, I don't
think she would take it well. "You really don't know much about football, do you?"

"No. Sorry. I'm interested in social issues. Poverty, women's topics,
politics. The important matters of the day. Sports do not seem that . . .
important."

Did she just insult me and my profession? Man, she's got a lot to learn
about kissing up. Given that she's new at this, though, I decide to cut
her some slack. "Sports were all that mattered where I came from."

"Where are you from?"

"Texas." Before I can explain further, someone bellows my name.

"Hey, Mathews, you planning on joining us sometime today?"

"Umm, gotta go. Practice for that non-important job." I grin and
add a wink for good measure.

She gives me a sheepish smile. "Okay."

"I can meet you another day, and we can talk."

"Tomorrow?"

This time I can't hold back the laugh. "No, tomorrow is Sunday.
Game day? How about Monday?"

She pauses a second and then narrows her gaze. "You're not being
nice to me just to get in my pants are you?"

Good to see she has *some* protective instincts. "Would you believe
me if I said no?"

"Not really. You look like the type."

She's got a point. I do want to get in her pants. But then, what red-
blooded American male wouldn't? She has masses of auburn hair,
world-class tits, and legs that go *all* the way up. A man's dick would
rise from the grave to ride that rodeo. But the truth is she got the shaft
from the three amigos, and that doesn't sit right by me. "We can meet
in a public place if you like." Why am I almost begging here? I never
have to work this hard to get a woman.

"Not here?"

"No." For personal reasons, I never give out private interviews. So I don't want our press office to find out about this before the article appears in her paper. If somebody asks afterward, I'll say I did it to avert a public relations disaster. Not that any one's going to question my motives after I explain what those three did to her. "There's a diner down the street from where I live. We could meet there." I run into that place at least once a week and am pretty sure she can conduct her interview without us being interrupted.

"Okay." When she bends down to pick up the hapless notebook, I almost swallow my tongue. My cock twitches at the thought of clutching those hips, sinking into her hot pussy and pounding her all the way to—

"Where is it?"

Where is what? Oh, the diner. "The Honey Bee's on Beach Drive. Let's say ten Monday morning?" I fight the need to tug my damn cup which seems to have shrunk two sizes. Last thing I want is to make her uncomfortable.

"See you then." All smiles now, she gives me a little wave before she slides into her piece-of-shit car. She turns on the ignition, and the damn thing knocks for awhile before something grinds and the car lurches forward.

Like a prize idiot, I stand there and watch her drive off before giving my dick some breathing room. It's only when she's out of sight that I jog back to the practice field where the quarterback coach waits for me.

"Five more minutes and you would have been late for practice. An automatic $10,000 fine."

"Sorry coach. Won't happen again." $10,000 is a lot of money, but honestly, if I had to pay? MacKenna Perkins would be worth it.

Available from Amazon Dirty Filthy Boy